The Devil's Utopia

A Novel by

J. Schimschal

The Devil's Utopia is the first novel in the Darken Realm series of books.

The Devil's Utopia

Published by Fossil Ridge Books Inc.
P.O. Box 33218
Northglenn, CO. 80233

ISBN 0-9777327-0-3

Published in the United States of America

Acknowledgements
This book is dedicated to my loving wife who encourages me to do
the impossible.

About the Author

J. Schimschal is the author of the Darken Realm series of books. He lives in the western United States with his family. Additional information can be obtained by visiting www.darkenrealm.com.

Chapter 1
Banion

The wind blew gently through the lush, tall green grass. Wave after wave pushed and pulsed as the wind hissed through the land. Green waves moved and rustled as the breeze pushed through the grassland. The beginning of fall was at hand, and a light chill rode the gales that pushed from the snowcapped mountain range to the north.

A lone man crouched near a barbed wire fence. Though he was still young in years, a mass of scars covered his tattered hands. His worn hands worked slowly to repair the fence. With a twist, the barbwire rolled over, and coil after coil was wound around the wooden post. The barbwire dug into the gray, dry-rotted post buried in a sea of green grass.

Dressed in a long overcoat, the rancher worked with a look of dispassion on his face. A blank stare was reflected in his eyes as he worked. The man was at peace, for now, but there was something still unsettled in his soul. A mass of tortured memories lay just beneath the surface, just below the blank expression, lurking and waiting like a coiled serpent about to strike.

The rancher worked for almost an hour. A sigh escaped his mouth as he finished the repairs. He removed his wide brimmed hat and wiped his brow. The rancher's brown, long hair was a tangled mess of dirt and sweat. The cool wind struck his face and dried the sweat. Closing his eyes, the rancher let the sounds of the wind rustling through the grass fill his mind. It was a soothing sound, and he smiled as he felt the warm sun upon his brow. Slowly, the man opened his eyes and let the bright light flood in. Squinting, the rancher put his wide brimmed hat back on his head and tipped the hat forward to cover his dark brown eyes. He stretched and moved towards his horse, a magnificent animal with rippling muscles and a hint of madness in its eyes. The black steed snorted and shook its head at the rancher's approach. Stretching his arm forward, the man slapped the animal gently upon its neck. It neighed and shook its head.

With a feeling of weariness, the rancher laid flat on his back. Cool air washed over him as the sun beat down upon him. Though still warm, slight chills filled him. He took a moment to soak in the peace of the day. His eyes closed, and the only thing that filled his mind was the sound of the rustling grass. Drowsiness washed over him, and the rancher fell into a peaceful slumber.

As the day wore on in the frontier country, the sun began to move away and long shadows began to creep across the land. Awaking from his sleep, the rancher sat up and looked about. He gave a loud sigh and stretched. Slowly he breathed as he brushed the sleep from his eyes. Banion stared around, perplexed, looking for his horse. When he couldn't locate the animal in the nearby vicinity, Banion rose to his feet in search of the mighty black steed. Something was wrong. Banion caught sight of his mount just down the hill, bucking and neighing in panic.

The rancher was startled, and moved quickly down the hill. Suddenly his black horse neighed and reared back a few steps, shaking its head in fear. Banion looked at his horse silently. The horse knew something was wrong and that instantly put the rancher on edge. Staring at the steed with a quizzing look, Banion followed the horse's eyes and felt the pit of his stomach drop away.

To the east of Banion was smoke, smoke snaking into the air. Banion thought it was an illusion at first. The horse reared again as it felt Banion's fear rising in his heart. The rancher felt a chill run down his spine. Suddenly, rage and anger, old rage and anger, hiding just beneath his skin, where they had hid for so many years, boiled to the surface. The coil of snake was unleashed. A jolt of adrenaline hit his system. A look of rage covered his face. His jaw tightened, as did a heavy set of scars on the right side of his face, scars that were the only testament to a past filled with strife.

With a leap he moved towards his horse. The horse eyed him with a frantic look. The animal could feel his fear and anger. Banion jumped onto the horse and kicked it hard. With that, the animal and Banion sped away towards the smoke. For where there was smoke, there was Banion's home. Just to the east of the pleasant meadow was where Banion lived with his beloved wife.

The horse thundered through the grasslands. As he rode, the wind whipped through the grass. Waves seemed to follow the charging rider as he made his way closer to the smoke. Like an arrow piercing the grassland itself, the black horse thundered its way through, cutting a hasty swath.

The smoke was getting stronger. It was now apparent to Banion that the entire town of Birthrock, Banion's home, was being burned. The worry for his wife threw him into a frantic frenzy. His mind was in a panic.

Lily, the rancher's wife, was the only thing on which Banion could focus. Her soft smile began to flood his consciousness. The rancher shook his head to get rid of the image. What he needed to do right now was to focus on the threat, an unknown threat at that.

Birthrock was a frontier town set on the western edge of civilization. It was founded only a few years back, when homesteaders from farther east had struck out into the wide world to secure a home and future on the frontier. Birthrock was home to about a dozen families, mostly ranchers and farmers. Birthrock was a peaceful town. The thought of the entire town being burned was a mystery to Banion. Why would the entire town be burned?

Thoughts of horrid fates began to course through his mind as Banion and his mount charged onward. Indian tribes commonly raided small towns on the edge of the frontier. But Indians never seemed to burn the towns they raided…

Flames could be seen as Banion hit the edge of town. Several dead townsfolk were lying in the center of the street. Smoke stung his eyes, and Banion tried to track any possible threats as he entered Birthrock. As he rode onward, the dead townsfolk came into view. Gunshot wounds, dozens of gunshot wounds covered the bodies. Banion's mind was in shock. The amount of gunshot wounds could have only been caused by *automatic* weapons.

'That's impossible…' Banion thought. 'No one in the frontier has automatic weapons…' He had not seen such guns for years and years, not since he was still living beyond all thought of civilization, in the great wastelands of the southern reaches of the world.

A loud burst of gunfire tore the silence of his thoughts. Four bullets struck his horse. The damage to his mount was severe and the horse crashed to the ground. Neighing and bucking, the mighty steed fought for life. Banion was thrown from the horse, and he crashed to the ground only a few inches away from several corpses, whose blank expressions looked back, motionless. He rolled away and pulled a shotgun from his saddlebag. The weapon was mighty indeed, and Banion loaded an entire magazine of ten gauge shot gun shells into the weapon. It was no ordinary weapon; it was a remnant from Banion's tortured past. The weapon was ready for battle, and Banion, the snake, coiled and prepared to strike.

Another burst of gunfire rattled from one of the smoke filled buildings. Banion's horse could not withstand another volley. When the horse was again pelted with gunfire, it let out a gurgle and departed the world. Smoke still stung Banion's eyes and he tried desperately to find his attacker.

"Faber ruthes dala yungier." A hissing voice rose from behind him. The voice was haunting, and filled with the sting of darkness. Someone had flanked the rancher and caught him off guard. An explosion struck the ground near the rancher. The blast threw Banion, launching him forward.

Disoriented from the attack, Banion spun around with weapon ready. A red robed stranger moved through the smoke and fire. Like a mirage, the robed man mysteriously vanished into the flames. Banion thought he was hallucinating. It wasn't the first time he had seen such things.

"It can't be!" Banion said in rage, scanning the ruins of Birthrock for the robed man.

The blast had left the rancher exposed in the open, no longer concealed by his dead mount. Knowing that finding cover would mean the difference between life and death, Banion rushed towards the opposite side of the street.

Several more bursts of gunfire rang out as Banion ran for cover. The smoke obscured him from his attackers. The bullets all harmlessly missed the rancher.

The sound of laughter, a constant, rhythmic laughter, rolled out from several of the burning buildings. Each laugh was identical but came from different parts of the battleground. The laughter seemed to drive Banion into a deeper rage.

"Not again!" Banion screamed as he fought to remain in control. Driven by a long-forgotten anger rising from the very depth of his past, the laughter drove Banion into a focused state. Banion was no longer a rancher, he was a killing machine. A machine fueled by the insane laughter around him, the same laughter he had heard several times as a child.

Several forms finally moved out from buildings across the street. The smoke was still thick, but the forms seemed familiar to the rancher. White, pasty bodies with piercing red eyes could be seen in the thick rolling smoke. A chill shot down Banion's spine. The attackers were definitely from his past.

Shouldering the weapon, Banion opened fire. Blast after blast hit the strange attackers hunching forward with submachine guns in hand. The first blasts harmlessly ricocheted off the pasty white forms. A metallic clang and sparks were the only effects of the gunfire. The ghostly white automatons eyed Banion with empty mechanical eyes. With jagged movements, the metallic soldiers each raised their submachine guns. Bursts of weapons fire rained towards Banion. By the time the robotic death machines had opened fire, Banion was already gone, already on the move. All of the enemy fire was in vain; Banion was too quick. Using the smoke as cover, he took aim once again and opened fire.

Banion's aim was true, and several shotgun blasts struck a pasty white robot. Sparks and oil erupted as Banion's assault brought one of the attackers to its knees. With a splash of oil and a spray of hydraulic fluid, the robotic death machine rocked back and forth. Slowly, the mechanical soldier bled out.

One attacker was slain, but another took interest in the deranged rancher.

From the dark smoke came a sinister form. With red eyes shining and a wicked grin, the robot raised its weapon and pulled the trigger. The weapon froze mid-air in an ominous silence. The deadly machine stared blankly, its red eyes dully rolling back and forth across the battlefield. It took the machine a moment to discern that its gun was ineffective. Finally the robot understood that the weapon was out of ammunition. It took a second for the thought to traverse the wiring in the robot's brain.

A second was all that Banion needed. He used his advantage and took careful aim. The robotic soldier was rocked by five shotgun blasts. Spinning from side to side, the robotic death machine sparked and sputtered as the wounds took their toll. Within a few seconds, Banion had reduced the machine to a pile of twitching garbage.

The rancher was satisfied for the moment, but his glory was

short lived. Another explosion ripped the battleground. A blast of fire struck Banion in the back as the explosion hit him. A searing jolt of pain scorched his body. The smell of burnt flesh, Banion's flesh, filled his nostrils. The pain was so intense Banion almost blacked out. Bright spots filled his vision as he fought to remain on his feet. Staggering back and forth, the pain was too much. Falling forward, Banion lost his weapon. Dizzy from the pain, he rolled onto his back and struggled against the darkness invading his consciousness. With a shaky hand, the deranged rancher fumbled for his revolver.

A red robed form moved from behind a burning post; a black hood was the only aspect of the attacker's face that Banion could see. With a broad movement, a sword was pulled free and the red robed attacker charged the fallen Banion.

Taking shaky aim, Banion pulled the trigger three times. The first bullet missed, but Banion managed to get the weapon under control for the last two shots. The second shot rammed into the gut of the attacker and the third rammed into the sternum of the red robed man. Blood, a deeper color than the sinister robes, began to soak through. The red robed attacker ceased his assault. The sword fell from his hands. He staggered back and forth for a few seconds, and then fell to the ground dead.

Banion was still in pain, but managed to rise to his feet. Scanning the territory around him, Banion held his weapon ready. No more attackers were present in the ruins of Birthrock. Staggering, Banion moved through the town. More dead townsfolk could be seen, all covered in blood. Stumbling in pain and half dazed with adrenaline, Banion moved towards his house.

A form could be seen through the smoke. A body was lying on the front porch. Burning timbers and a broken form were the only things Banion could see in his battered condition.

Terror and sorrow began to fill Banion. He knew all too well whose body was on his front porch. Trembling violently, the revolver dropped from his hand. Banion fell to his knees. Lily, Banion's beloved wife, was clothed in a white dress drenched in blood. She lay silently in front of him in the burning ruins of his former home. On his knees, he crawled like a wounded animal towards his slain wife. Finally, frustration and sadness overcoming him, he drew closer to his wife and stared in shock. Banion reached forward and clutched his wife. He was distantly hoping that she would move or breathe. Deep down, he knew she would not stir. With shaky hands, Banion brushed aside Lily's hair. He caressed her softly. Tears began to fill his eyes. Stroking her hair, he wished more than anything that she would respond to his caress. To no avail her lifeless body did not respond.

Banion was a man who had never known peace until he met Lily. Sweet Lily. She was a rose amongst all the weeds Banion had known. She had saved Banion from himself. Banion had existed for so long without any hope. Sadness and misery were the only things he had known. Lily had brought him back from the edge. She had taught him to love, care, and look for the kindness in all things. For the first time in his life, Banion had known peace in the arms of Lily.

A knot formed in the back of his head. Stress and sadness were taking over. Banion shook uncontrollably. He formed a fist and pounded the wood beneath him. He bent over and placed his face on her stomach. Tears soaked into her dress.

He would never be able to hold her again. He would never be able to caress her long black hair again. He would never be able to have a cozy dinner with her. He would never be able to look at the stars with her again. He would never hear her loving voice ever again.

Banion pounded the ash-covered porch with both hands. The sadness turned to fury. Hope was lost. So much for peace and love. The world was only filled with death. Rage exploded through Banion. Anger took him. Banion rose from the porch. Flames leapt around him. When he rose to his feet, Banion was no longer a man; he was a specter of death, a man without home or reason, a man destined for vengeance.

Chapter 2
Jared

The setting sun pushed towards the western horizon, an event that had occurred day after day without a record of such things. Slowly, the yellow light erupted into an orange glow as the edge of the world devoured the sun. The further it dipped below the horizon, the more vibrant the color became, first a fiery orange then dying off into a glowing red.

As the sun disappeared from the world, its warmth receded and a chill began to rise. A slight breeze started to stir, carrying the icy might of the coming darkness.

Traveling fast and low, the wind whipped across the barren landscape. As it rushed through the blasted land, the wind stirred endless dunes of shifting sand, which moved and slithered. The gale intensified, and a cool blast of air rolled across the forsaken landscape. As the wind raced, the sand hissed and changed form.

The darkness grew as time passed. A black mass of shadows pushed forward from the eastern horizon, engulfing the land in gloom as it moved.

The darkness marched on across the endless expanse of rolling sand. Finally, it breached the sea of sand and crashed upon the base of a rock barrier running northward into the great desert. Shadows of the night crept upward, snaking up the rock face that stood more than one thousand feet above the sand floor.

The rock consisted of a series of mountains and mesas pressing northward into the wastelands. The Great Barrier was the mountain range that separated the western *civilized* world from the barren wastelands to the east.

Seated high above the floor of the barren wasteland was a lone figure, perched upon a rock spire at the top of the Great Barrier. Night advanced without mercy, plunging the wastelands into an icy blackness. Stars, pinpricks of light, forced their way through the dark veil. The air became cooler and a lone boy, nearly a man, sat more than a thousand feet above the writhing sand floor of the dunes below. Secluded in his thoughts, he stared towards the eastern waste now shrouded in darkness.

The young man sat motionless and eyed the rolling dunes uneasily. There wasn't much time left. Soon, his whole life would change. Only a few days left to enjoy the only home he had ever known. The lone man gave a loud sigh and stared hopefully eastward, pushing any thoughts of failure from his mind. He would succeed where many others had failed and died.

"And there you are, young Jared, still staring eastward, onward to your doom." An aged man moved forward from behind the young man who was crouched upon the rocks, staring down into the desert expanse. "I wish you would reconsider. You and young Tani are the best our tribe has produced in all my long years."

Jared, nearly seventeen years of age, turned around to eye the old man with disdain. "I will not fail. Beyond that void of sand has got to be *something*." The young man shifted his weight and stared at the old man. With light tan skin and a ponytail tied behind his head, Jared was very youthful, almost child-like, in appearance. No wrinkle had yet dug a single trench in his face. His strong muscles bulged and he exuded an air of arrogance. Squinting and scowling at the aged man, the young man considered him with disgust.

"I trust I have told you many times the stories of the eastern wasteland, young Jared. Many of the youth exiled from our village traveled and ran the gauntlet of the eastern wastes. You know that not a single young one has ever returned from the east. The dunes are endless and filled with deadly peril. You also know our scouts have traveled five days east and have never come back with any news of civilization, only endless sand." Master Mogi had a concerned look upon his face as he spoke. Age had taken a hold over the old weaponsmaster. He was a squat man, dressed in the robes of a village elder. His forehead was bald, and long gray locks hung about his shoulders. Experience infused his presence, and he held a piercing gaze to everyone he encountered. All of the young ones for the last forty odd years had been trained by the wise Master Mogi. Jared was one of his latest trainees and disciples.

"Eastward is *my* goal. What would you have me do? Travel to the great forests of the north? Maybe waste my exile in the comfort of the Primal Lands?" Young Jared was arrogant, and his tone said as much.

"I have told you many times that in all my years, I have never seen a better swordsman than you. But your pride will be your undoing. You are good but have never yet tasted the bitter chill of combat, real combat. I don't want to lose you to the wastes. You have a promising future in Scarskin when you return from the exile." Mogi was irritated by young Jared's bravado, but it did not matter. Jared was too headstrong to give any ground on the matter.

"And when we return from the eastern wastes, scribes for generations will sing our praises. We will be the things of legend! Think of it, never has a single member of our tribe survived the trek across the eastern expanse." Jared smiled and his hand drew the blade at his waist. The young warrior eyed the sword with a look of pride. Jared was good in close combat, and he knew it. There was not a single person in Scarskin who could rival his prowess. None of the elder warmasters could hold their own against Jared in swordplay.

"I can see that you are willing to risk your own life for your silly crusade, but are you willing to sacrifice young Tani as well? Are you willing to sacrifice the life of your best friend and the most talented shaman this village has ever produced?" the aged man's tone grew angry as he spoke.

Jared looked away from Mogi, retreating into himself. For a few moments, there was total silence between the two. Finally, Jared spoke. "Tani *knows* the risk."

Mogi shook his head in disgust. "You keep saying that Tani *knows* the risk? Does young Tani even know your intent? Does he know that you are sending him to his doom?"

Jared's brown eyes flared with anger. His arrogance was getting the better of him. "The risk is my decision to make!"

Mogi snorted and took a moment to consider the situation.

"There are things that our elder scribes cannot comprehend in the ancient texts we have recovered from the wasteland. Our brightest shamans are mystified by devices unearthed from the endless sands. Tani can make sense of anything he sees. In all my years, I have never seen a more intelligent and talented person than Tani. His intellect makes a mockery of even our most prized elders. Can you understand what our people stand to lose if Tani never returns home to us? The boy was able to read ancient text ever since his eighth year. I have seen him solve mathematical equations that no one in the history of our village has ever understood. I have witnessed the boy create fire and explosives that rival even our most skilled crafters. Not only will Tani lose his life on your insane quest, but our home, our village, will also lose the brightest hope for a good future. And all of this for your pride?"

"It's not about pride." Jared spoke almost in a rage.

"Then what is this about?" Mogi quizzed the young warrior before him.

"It's about the unknown. It's about surviving where so many of our people have failed and died. It's about exploring the great endless void of the east. I am the best swordsman you have trained and Tani is the brightest scribe our village has ever produced. We can open up the world for our village; we can open up the world for Scarskin. We will be heroes," Jared concluded, defiant. Yet, though he remained rebellious, Jared was losing confidence.

"Heroes? In order to be a hero you must be alive. There is no doubt in my mind that you and Tani will perish in the wastes. Everything Scarskin has fought to create all these generations will be in vain. The exile was created to season our strongest and help mold them into the leaders of tomorrow. We need your help for the next generation, and Tani's help, as well. I urge you to travel any direction but east." Mogi both pleaded and scolded young Jared as he spoke.

Jared was distant, his own pride and confidence his only companions. "Travel anyplace but east, you say? That is something I cannot do."

"So be it, fool. Dead men tell no tales. This is the last time I will speak to you until you are cast out of Scarskin. Enjoy these last few days. They will be your last in Scarskin, the last days in your home." With that, Mogi turned his back to Jared and walked away into the darkness.

Jared felt fear creep into the edge of his soul. For the first time in his life, self-confidence began to slip away. Fear was his newest companion. An eerie feeling came over Jared as he stared into the darkness of the eastern wastes. Daylight was gone, and all that remained was the chill air and the hissing of the endless sand.

Chapter 3
Tani

The small adobe house concealed a lone person. A crude
wooden ladder ran through a square hole leading to the upper floor.
A candle flickered in the darkness as shadows danced upon the
white, clay washed walls. Stacks of books littered the floor, and jars
of spices and raw chemicals were strewn about.   An ancient
microscope sat near the corner of the room on a wooden crate. The
small room looked like a workshop for a blossoming mad scientist.

Secluded in his thoughts, a young man sat quietly pondering
an intense series of calculations. Mathematical and ancient symbols
alike covered the page. The young scholar rubbed his temples as he
thought about the problem at hand. His hair was short but stuck up
like quills on a porcupine. A set of circular wire rimmed glasses
covered his light green eyes.

Slowly, his eyes moved back and forth as his brain strained
to find the answer. His hand closed around an ink pen. Two fingers
were missing on his hand, fingers that he had lost long ago in an
accident. The young tribal genius tapped his ink pen uneasily upon
the yellow yucca paper. He let out a loud sigh and looked away
from the calculations. The genius was known as Tani, a word in the
tribe's native tongue that meant *hope.*

Tani had grown up protected by the tribe of Scarskin. His
value was more than any treasure, for he was a treasure in his own
right.   A quick mind and an insatiable urge for knowledge had
pushed this young man to solve and understand a host of ancient
technologies that none of the village elders could even begin to
comprehend.   While Jared was the best swordsman in Scarskin,
Tani, his counterpart, was the most intelligent scholar in all the tribe,
and he was still only a youth. Tani had untold potential, and it was
whispered throughout the tribe that he was the brightest *hope* for a
prosperous future that the tribe had produced in over ten
generations.

The young scholar smiled as a thought came to his mind.

His green eyes darted back to the calculations scrawled upon the yucca paper. The ink pen pressed down, stroke after stroke, and a series of symbols appeared on the page. The calculations came together and the answer appeared.

Tani smiled at the completed calculations and rubbed his stumpy hand. With a sigh of disgust, he stared intently at the hand that had been mangled long ago. Even though Tani was a brilliant scholar, he had the irresistible desire to burn and explode things. Intellect led this young tribal to become one of the most gifted demolition experts in all the wastes. He was talented, but when he was young, an accident with homemade dynamite had left Tani's hand a ruined mess. Several fingers were blown off in the blast, and Tani, from that point onward, gained the nickname Tripwire.

The daydream subsided. Tani stretched and rose from his desk. With a dazed look on his face, the young scholar looked about his messy room. His room was littered with wiring, tools, scraps of metal, and piles and piles of tattered books, which were stacked in the corner. There was a faint smell of old paper all about his room. Fumes of sulfur wafted amongst the towers of books. He smiled softly at his room. It was his sanctuary, his home.

His thoughts began to scatter as he thought of the word: *home*. The smile ceased and his brow furrowed. A look of concern was covering his green eyes. Finally, he moved toward the stack of books. He always found comfort in the knowledge contained in them. The young scholar moved towards his beloved books, forcing thoughts of home form his mind; it was only a few days before the exile.

While crouching, the books towered over him. His stumpy hand brushed across each book in turn; calculus, organic chemistry, physics, history of the Civil War, biology, economics, electronics, and history of the living earth.

A fond look of remembrance coursed through him as calculations and great battles alike rolled through his mind. For his memory was keen and all the knowledge in those books and countless more was his, locked away behind his green eyes in that insatiable brain of his.

As he rose before the tower of books, a look of sadness brushed across his face. He loved those books, and he would miss them. Slowly, he walked away and moved towards the window by his desk. He pushed the shuttered window open and let the cool night air wash over him. The jolt of cold air was refreshing, putting Tani at ease for the moment.

He braced himself and pushed through the open window. Tani found himself on the upper level of his home. He crouched on the rooftop and looked towards the night sky. The moon had risen, and he looked uneasily at the light flooding down from it. The moon was almost full, and that put Tani on edge again. The coming of the full moon meant the beginning of the exile, the beginning of a terrifying time away from the village of Scarskin. Only a few days remained until the moon would rise full and Tani, with his best friend Jared, would be driven from their home in a ritual of passage into manhood.

Shrugging off the thought of exile from his mind once more, Tani crept across the rooftop of his home and jumped off to the sandy street below. Tani's parents were spending the evening with the neighbors, and he was none too keen to have them find out that he had snuck out. Darting away, Tani slunk into the darkness and found himself on a small trail behind the adobe house, snaking away from the edge of the village.

Small cacti and bushes lined the trail behind the scholar's house. As he moved, a person emerged from the darkness on the trail. Squinting, Tani caught sight of his friend Jared.

As Jared approached, Tani noticed a strange look on his face as he eyed his friend quietly.

"What's wrong with you?" Tani quizzed.

"Oh, nothing. I just had a talk with Master Mogi." Jared seemed cryptic and evasive.

"And what did he say?" Tani pressed.

"Nothing. He just wanted to wish us luck on our journey." Jared was lying, and his friend could tell.

"Good luck, huh? Well we could use some. The exile will not be easy." Tripwire smiled dryly.

"Yeah. Tani, we need to talk." The young warrior stumbled and slurred his speech. Jared was uneasy about something.

"Sure, Jared." The scholar raised an eyebrow and focused all his attention on Jared.

"I've made a decision about the exile. We are heading east into the wastes." Jared spoke with a lack of confidence.

"East? You're kidding, right? No one has ever come back from the east. There is nothing but endless sand."

"You've said it yourself. The eastern wastes can't go on forever. What about all of your maps? What about your theory about the ancients living out east? You have read book after book and have always came to the same conclusion. There have to be ruins of great cities to the east." The warrior was trying to convince his friend.

"I agree... but... I don't know..." Tani hesitated. Though the scholar was smart, he didn't like conflict, and had always given into Jared's demands ever since they were children. Finally, Tani sighed and spoke. "Whatever you think is fine. I just..."

"We will be fine." Jared smiled and slapped Tani on the shoulder. "The best swordsman and best scholar can't go wrong. Think of the technology we will uncover. We will be heroes. Just think, the first two to ever come back from the east! We will be elders the very day we come back from our exile!"

Tani didn't say a word; he simply nodded his head.

"Well, enough of this talk. We only have two days left before the exile. I talked to Jennifer and Hina. They said they would meet us at the springs tonight." Jared smiled.

"I could use a little Jennifer tonight." Tani laughed at the thought of seeing his girlfriend. Jared giggled and slapped Tani on the shoulder again.

"Come on, let's get some loving." Jared laughed and the two friends headed off towards the hot springs. As they walked, they talked about Jennifer, Hina, the exile, and the thought of leaving the only home they had ever known. Fear crept slowly into the back of their minds. It wasn't every day you were thrown out of your village and forced to live in the wastes for over an entire year.

Chapter 4
Mineera

The blood had already begun to clot around her nose. Red ooze comprised of warm blood and grime was smeared in her long, dark hair. Lacerations on the woman's back had stained her crimson robes a darker shade. Every inch of her body ached.

Whimpering softly, the woman closed her eyes and gritted her teeth against the pain. She moaned and shook in agony on the cold stone floor. The pain was so severe, bright blotches of light filled her vision. She was on the verge of unconsciousness.

Through a mass of dark hair matted frighteningly around her face, she opened and closed her bright blue eyes, one of which was almost completely blood-shot after she had been beaten repeatedly in the head. The woman's complexion was dark, giving her a unique look, bright blue eyes shining out from dark tan skin. Her facial features were refined and nearly perfect, creating an impression of noble blood. All in all, she was a beautiful woman despite her current condition.

The pain was tremendous, and her fortitude against it began to whither. Wracked with the horrid pain of her torture at the hands of the maniacal Priesthood of the Fallen, she begged silently to anyone who would listen. Her whimpering in the dark became a plea for the pain to stop. No one was with her in the cell, but shock had taken over from the torture. Somewhat delusional, the red robed woman was on the verge of unconsciousness.

The bright flashes of light rang through her head more strongly. The wounds from her torture began to throb more intensely. A dizzy wash of pain rolled over her. In the distant thoughts of her fading existence, she wished for death as a way to abate the horrid pain. There was no recourse from it; the pain and damage to her body drove her deeper towards a state of madness.

Her dark skinned hand moved and touched her hair. Warm blood still seeped from wounds on her scalp. Clots had matted other parts of her long, black hair. With tears streaming down her face, she opened her eyes. Bright blue eyes stared around in the darkness. She whimpered again and rocked back and forth on the cold stone floor.

"Please…" Tears streamed down her face as the pain dominated her senses. "Someone help me."

As if from a dream, a bright flash of light filled the room. Her delusions were growing and had turned into hallucinations. Pain throbbed in her temples, and it felt as if her head was going to explode.

A pinprick of light appeared ahead of the woman. It hovered in midair, and white, searing light exploded from it. The pinnacle of light rose higher in the cell, bathing it in an eerie white glow. The light pulsed and rocked back and forth, as if a searchlight was scanning the cell. Finally, the light stopped, and the woman squinted in its brilliance.

A shape emerged from the light and stepped before the imprisoned woman. The shape writhed and bounced about. Within a few moments, a few moments that seemed like an eternity, the shape coalesced into a human form before her.

With a leap, the battered woman sprung away from the form that emerged before her.

"Mineera," the spectral form spoke. The woman was terrified and reeled back, trying to escape. In a futile attempt, the woman crawled across the floor, whimpering. With each movement, pain flooded her mind and body. The pain from her torture was so severe she could barely move.

"Mineera," a loud voice boomed. The form moved forward.

Still filled with fright and wracked with pain, Mineera whimpered and scrambled for the corner of the prison cell. When she reached the corner, she huddled in a pitiful ball of misery. Clutching her knees against her chest, the woman resembled a horrified child.

"Mineera…" The voice was less frightening but intense nonetheless.

Mineera quivered and pulled her fragile sanity into focus. Carefully, she raised her head and stared at the glowing white form only a few feet away from her. The sight was pleasing, and somehow, the pain of her wounds seemed to lessen the longer she gazed upon the heavenly visage.

A peace filled the woman. Mineera stopped whimpering and moved towards the light. It was so soothing. The more she looked at the light, the less fear she felt.

"Mineera! Hear me for my words are true. I need you." The voice spoke softly. Her ears could not hear the words but she could hear the voice in her mind.

"Who are you?" Still dizzy from the pain, Mineera spoke, and a trickle of blood dripped from her open mouth.

"The One who created this world has sent me to you. Before the time of your master existed my lord. Lost in time is The One who created this world. For few today remember his love and peace. Suffering and anger control his garden. Such sacrilege cannot exist forever."

"What do you want with me?" Mineera was close to losing consciousness.

"What do I want with you? I want you to become that which you have always yearned for in your heart. For suffering and anger is not your path. Though forced to worship demons, you always felt something was wrong, did you not?" the voice boomed in Mineera's mind.

Mineera began to cry softly. The emotion was raw and she could not contain it. "Yes," she whimpered. "I have always felt something was not right."

"So as the angels of old fell from heaven and became your master, you shall rise from the pits. I call upon you, risen demon. You shall go forth and do my master's will. The One is the true master. Peace and wisdom is his grace and gift. You will be his champion." The spirit spoke softly.

"But why me? I don't understand."

"Ever since you were a child, we have sent you visions of your future. Through the cloud of evil we broke through to you. There is someone you must save or all is lost. He is the key to the end of all this misery."

As the specter spoke, Mineera was chilled to the bone. All of her life, a single dream had plagued her nights. A dream about a man dying at the hands of an assassin. Somehow, Mineera was to prevent this. But how did the spirit know of her visions? Suddenly, she realized the ghost was telling the truth, but in her condition, sanity was a fading ally.

"I dream about the future often…" Mineera spoke softly as pain thudded through her head. "But I can't change what I see. Everything I dream of comes to pass, and there is nothing I can do about it. I can't change the future. My visions are of *what* will happen, not what *can* happen." Mineera was confused and quizzed the ghost before her.

"You must find the strength to change what you have seen. It rests on your shoulders," the spirit boomed in a loud voice.

"I am to be put to death when the sun rises. I am a traitor and my life is forfeit. The Reaper Kai will see my end. I betrayed them to save the lives of the innocent. Now I am to die for my beliefs." Mineera was frustrated as she spoke to the wraith before her.

"It is your kind heart and your compassion that have gained favor with The One. He will make sure you survive so as to save the man from your dreams. If you believe in hope and wisdom, you will be saved," the ghostly form comforted Mineera.

"How am I to escape?" she quizzed, hope fading.

"Do not trouble or fret. The ones you betrayed have many enemies. One such enemy will be your savior."

"So be it. I only wish justice and peace. Many say there is no evil without good. Our world is devoid of good. If it is your will that I be your messenger, so be it, shade." Mineera lowered her head toward the strange vision before her.

"Go in peace, child." With that, the ghostly form stretched its arm forward and placed it on Mineera's bowed head. A blast of heat coursed through her body. Dizziness washed over her like a drunken wave. The blast of heat welled up inside her body. The wounds on her back tingled. The blood stopped flowing from her body. The warmth increased in intensity. The pain turned into a burning itch.

The room grew silent. The light disappeared, and all was still. Mineera rose from the floor of the prison cell. A chill and a sense of awe flowed through her. Where there were once wounds and pain, there was only calm. Her wounds had completely vanished. Gripped by a sense of humility, she fell to her knees and clasped her hands together. She threw her head towards the heavens, and a single tear rolled down her cheek.

"Thank you…" She spoke in reverence, caught in emotion,

her voice nearly a whisper.

The prison cell was dark and cold, but a new fire had sparked in Mineera's heart. For she had once worshipped dark powers and demons, she had taken a single step towards the light, and the spark she felt in her soul was cherished beyond anything she had ever known.

There was no more fear of death. Mineera believed in The One. She knew that this god would not let her die. When the sun rose, she would not die at the hands of an executioner. Somehow, she would escape and save the mysterious man from her dreams. For the safety of this stranger was key to ending the misery and death caused by the dread Reaper Kai, the same Reaper Kai that had unleashed a hoard of soldiers now laying waste to the northern provinces.

Chapter 5
The Crusade Begins

The cold night was far from over. A chill wind was blowing from the northern reaches of the Darken Realm. *The Darken Realm,* Banion thought, an apt name given to the continent of America after the fall of Man ages ago.

No one knew exactly how man fell from grace and the world ended in ruin in ages past. After many centuries since the apocalypse, the earth was still marked by the conflict. The winds were dry and the land blasted by the insatiable force of the blistering sun. Radioactive regions were still dangerous, toxic to anything that lived, a testament to the uncontrolled weapons created by the ancient peoples. Earthquakes, hurricanes, and wild tornados had also decimated the continent, further wiping away any hint of former civilizations. All in all, the Darken Realm was a battered semblance of the former glory that the ancients had toiled so long to build. As thoughts of the ruined earth flowed through his mind, Banion became suddenly aware of the natural world around him.

The only sound that Banion could hear coming from the darkness beyond his campsite was the wailing of a coyote that had topped a small bluff and was howling at the rising moon. The gibbering of the creature was unsettling as its sound echoed amongst a series of small bluffs that formed a crude beginning to a newly forming canyon.

Banion huddled near a small fire. He rubbed his hands together as the rising heat gave him comfort from the icy night. The rancher pulled his long, brown coat close to shield himself. As the chill of the night air settled over the land, the rancher's thoughts began to drift back to his past. As his mind wandered, he was caught in a trance, thinking about the events that had transpired in his home. Banion's gaze was distant as he daydreamed about his former life.

The rancher sat back and gazed at the fire. Bright orange flames licked and ate the wood as the fire fed its hunger. As he sat in the silence, a tear rolled down his cheek. He sighed, trying to fight back the flood of sadness rushing through his consciousness. It was a losing battle for the rancher, and the duress was too much to handle. More tears began to roll down his face. Finally, unable to contain his grief any longer, Banion began to sob uncontrollably.

Thoughts of his wife Lily began to fill his mind as he drifted further towards madness and despair...

For years, the lonely mercenary had roamed the southern wastes of the Darken Realm. Reputed to be the best gunfighter in the wastes, Banion O'Neil was a force to be reckoned with. Working primarily for the southern kingdom of Rasheed, Banion had performed many missions to stay the onslaught of chaos and the encroachment of less desirable peoples hailing from the battered ruins of America.

The legend of Banion O'Neil began many years before he was a full-fledged mercenary laying waste to the dregs of humanity. It was whispered that this gunman had a dark past, stemming all the way back from his childhood, before the time of his 'uncle'. Lore about the crazed mercenary abounded in the wastelands. Some said he was originally born from one of the great northern tribes, beyond the terrible deserts, in the frigid regions of the north. Others said he was a ghost, a wraith of evil born from the festering inhumanity of the barren, lawless wasteland. Many believed he was not of this world after witnessing his intensity in combat. Many whispered he was a savior sent by the old gods to reclaim the world for their own selfish intentions.

The most prominent folklore surrounding Banion O'Neil was the stories about the Great Revolt, as it had been come to be called in recent days. It was told that this crazed gunfighter began his bloody road to adventure by catalyzing an uprising in the town of Dune Station. It was rumored that Banion's 'uncle' was slain in the insurrection, and that his death pushed young Banion over the edge. After the revolt of Dune Station, young Banion disappeared into the wastelands for many years, until his reemergence as a hired gun for the kingdom of Rasheed. Since then, the mere mention of his name in pleasant company sent a tremor of fear into the air.

The revolt in Dune Station ripped young Banion away from

the last remnants of his childhood. As a man, the crazed gunman roamed the wastes and backwater ruins of old, his heart heavy with grief. There were few that could rival Banion's courage or intensity. Many villains and rival gunslingers fell before his crazed battle fury.

Death and conflict were the only fuel that kept Banion alive. He was an out of control mercenary with a twisted sense of justice. That is, until the day he passed through the small town of Birthrock. On that day, everything in his world changed.

With a dry liver and a thirst for a drunken stupor, Banion found himself in the local saloon in the town of Birthrock. It didn't take long for the locals to vacate when they heard who the newest patron was. No one wanted to mess with Banion or even be around him. People had a habit of turning up dead wherever Banion traveled.

The saloon owner ran the bar with his oldest daughter Lily, who had been helping him run the establishment since the death of her mother three years earlier.

With her pulse racing and heart stuck in her stomach, Lily wandered over to offer the sinister gunman a drink. What she found was something no one could have expected.

She was hesitant at first, trying to avoid his gaze. Finally, their eyes met and something happened; it happened to both of them.

Lily gazed into a black chasm. Banion's eyes were lifeless and devoid of all humanity. She stared in horror and Banion stared back. There was a strange sense of familiarity awakened by what she saw in those eyes. Instead of looking upon Banion in terror, her gaze shifted, and the warmth of her heart shined through the darkness. Banion shuddered at her gaze. It had been a long time since someone had looked upon him with so much kindness. The fear was leaving. Lily looked at Banion and knew that deep down, he was a good man, driven to madness by his dark past. Trembling fiercely, she stretched out her hand and placed it on his shoulder. Banion shuddered at her touch, and his eyes grew sad. Tears began to well up inside him as he pulled away from her. Like a wounded animal, Banion staggered to his feet with wild fright in his eyes. He backed away slowly and fled the saloon.

Lily followed with hurried steps and burst from the saloon. When she emerged through the doors, Banion had mounted a wild black stallion and was charging away down the main street of Birthrock.

She clasped her hands together and shook her head in disbelief. Banion had fled from her kindness, but he would return.

Banion found himself returning to the saloon again and again. In time, Banion and Lily grew close, and he learned to love. The darkness and shadow lifted, and the crazed mercenary had a home, a real home.

Thoughts of Lily washed over him like waves of grief. Each passing pulse drove him deeper into despair. Each wave pulled him closer to madness. A tense knot formed at the back of his head. His hand clenched into a fist. He struggled to remain in control. Control was lost. Hope was abandoned. A sneer covered his face as his eyes went dark. Madness consumed the rancher. He felt normal again, he felt the way he had his entire life, in an endless state of loss with no hope of salvation.

His gaze rose to the heavens above. The stars glittered above and tears rolled down his face. Warm tears chilled in the cool night air as Banion taunted the heavens. Frustration took over, and Banion lost all control.

"Why me?!" Banion screamed at the night sky. "What have I ever done to deserve your wrath?"

His mind raced, flooding with dark thoughts. The anger was growing, and dark fantasies took shape. The red robed Reaper Kai consumed his consciousness. All his life, they had taken everything from him. First his mother, then his 'uncle', and finally his wife fell to the wretched Reaper Kai and their robotic servants.

The fantasies became grim, and Banion visualized brutalizing the Reaper Kai. Wicked images of mutilating their bodies found a way into his mind. The tense knot at the back of his head grew tighter as a wicked smile graced his lips. The madness inside his mind was intense, and the only thing making him feel better was the thought of butchering his enemies without mercy. The smile increased, and his eyes grew even darker.

The madness was too much to bear, and Banion finally broke into a maniacal laughter. The laughter rose and echoed through the blowing grass. The coyote on the ridge retreated as the raving lunacy spooked the creature of the night.

Insane babble and angry taunts were shouted into the

emptiness of the night air. "I will get you all!" he screamed. He broke into laughter. "I will get you all! Every last one of you! Woo hoo!" He jumped up and down, leering. "I will slaughter all of you!"

An omen of ill intent occurred in response. A bright light, glowing orange, appeared to the northeast of Banion. Banion's arms fell to his sides. The orange glow was all too familiar. To the northeast was the small town of Pridehome. Banion was taunting his enemy in earnest, and his enemy had responded with ominous intensity. Pridehome was being burned. Banion shook his head in disgust as silence took him. He no longer raved. He said a silent prayer for all the poor souls now being slaughtered by an enemy with no mercy.

The Reaper Kai offensive was fully in progress. The entire north was being invaded by thousands and thousands of robotic death machines. The Biogtech were on the loose and their insane demonic masters would never be satisfied until all other races were exterminated.

Suddenly, a chill rolled down his spine. A sense of clarity flowed through him. His insane quest to destroy the Reaper Kai would not be in vain. He would destroy them all, somehow... Banion made a pact with himself: if by his will or without, he would make sure the Reaper Kai would be eradicated.

The orange glow increased in size as the town on the horizon was fed to the Reaper Kai war machine. His long years of experience kicked in. His daydreams were fading quickly. A single thought filled his mind: the enemy was known to send scouts ahead of the main forces. Banion eyed his own campfire with dismay. He quickly put the fire out and recovered his possessions.

Banion's quest was now focused. He knew he had to get support and warn others that the Biogtech army was in full advance.

"I must get to Rasheed," Banion said softly to himself as the flames of death engulfed the frontier town of Pridehome.

Chapter 6
The Battle of Darkpine Prison

A dull glow rose from the eastern edge of the forest. With each passing minute, the sun moved closer to the horizon. As the sun sought to breach the edge of the world, its warm glow intensified. Orange and red tones erupted from the horizon.

The old forest was silent. Pine trees, ancient and strong, rose high into the air, lightly brushing the sky. For miles and miles they perched, tall and strong. From ridge to ridge and valley to valley they spread, silent but proud, the true guardians of the forest.

A stream meandered through the heart of the ancient wood. Slowly, it crept and bubbled. Finally, with a rumble, the water crashed over a series of rocks which formed a high waterfall at the western edge of the forest.

The top of this magnificent waterfall was the location where the dread Reaper Kai had chosen to erect its notorious prison facility. The term 'prison facility' was a tame way to describe this place of horror, for those imprisoned seldom lasted a month. It was a place of death, used by the Reaper Kai to torture its enemies until they broke in spirit, mind, and body.

The sun moved forward, and the time had come. The execution of a high-ranking Reaper Kai diplomat was drawing near. Simultaneously, a prison break intended to liberate the traitorous diplomat from the horrid facility was about to be set in motion. The enemies of the Reaper Kai were lying in wait at the perimeter of the fortified prison.

"Tactical team One, respond." A large form was huddled behind a stand of bushes, speaking into a radio headset. Across the stream from the hidden commando was the prison facility.

"Tactical team One reporting. In position and ready." A low but clear voice could be heard in the headset.

"Acknowledged, team One. Tactical team Two, report." The large form shifted in the bushes. He was breathing heavily, adjusting his weight as he waited. With a grunt, he shifted his weapon off the rocks.

"Team Two reporting. In position and good to go." Another voice sounded in the headset.

"Team Two, understood. Team Three, respond." The hidden soldier peered out from the bushes as he spoke. Large round yellow eyes scanned the prison facility. His thick copper brown hide, marked with reddish purple blotches, stank like a musty river. A maw filled with sharp teeth was revealed in the dim light of the rising sun. His form was enormous as he huddled in the undergrowth of the cool forest. The soldier was not human, and was a formidable presence on the battlefield.

"Team Three responding and in position. Ready for your word." Another quiet voice resounded through the headset radio.

"Team Three, acknowledged. All teams prepare and go on my word." The copper brown skinned beast of a soldier spoke into the headset. "Listen up. The prisoner must be taken alive. I repeat, the prisoner must be taken alive. Our entire mission depends on it. Look sharp and give 'em hell, boys. Green light to strike. I repeat, green light to strike." As the leader finished his commands he rose from the bushes.

Like a mythical beast, he rose from the bushes and the undergrowth. Slowly, he stood upright. Standing tall, he was nearly the height of two men standing one upon the other. He was wide, as well; three men across could not surpass his girth. Muscles rippled underneath his coppery brown hide. Yellow beastly eyes scanned his surroundings. His snout was broad, and his nostrils flared. Large teeth erupted from his open maw. For this leader was not human, but a mutant, and a beast at that. The Darken Realm had created a host of mutant aberrations, some by chance, some by design, and this creature was a spawn from that horrid era. The leader of the commando team was none other than Globulus, the warmaster of the kingdom of Rasheed, a mutant hybrid hippo.

Walking like a man, the giant coppery brown skinned mutant hippo moved toward the prison with frightening speed. Globulus looked as if a human had been blended together perfectly with a beastly, primitive hippo. In both hands he carried a giant rotary machine gun. With a look of determination, the mutant hippo charged onward. As he ran, the signs of past battles could be seen scribed upon his body; horrific scars covered and marked his hide.

Globulus was obviously no stranger to combat.

A loud blast ripped from the tree line. The rocket-propelled grenade slammed into a guard shack at the front of the facility. The explosion splintered the guard shack, turning it into a heap of shattered glass and smoldering wood. Two guards were shredded in the attack, which sent their broken bodies high into the air.

A loud siren sounded seconds after the first explosion. The front gate was solid steel, and assault team Two was already en route with a set of demolition charges. Gunfire exploded as two heavy caliber machine gun nests lit up the assault team. The two bunkers near the front gate laid down a hail of gunfire. Laughter could be heard from both the towers. Biogtech death machines manned the gun nests and cackling in glee as they gunned down the assault team.

Team Two was scattered within seconds. Several members of the team were cut down immediately by the harsh gunfire.

"Team Three, I need sniper support. Take out the gunners in those bunkers," the mighty hippo boomed into his headset. As he yelled, he thundered towards the southern bunker with his rotary minigun in hand.

"Your will be done, sir," the leader of team Three responded.

Three well placed shots rang out instantly. The first shot slammed into the neck of the southern towers gunner. An explosion of sparks could be seen as the head of the robot was blown clean off. The second shots pierced the chest of the gunner in the north bunker. A splatter of oil erupted as the robotic soldier began to spin around in circles. The laughter continued as the robot lost hydraulic pressure, finally collapsing and ceasing to stir.

With both of the machine gun bunkers neutralized, the remainder of team Two placed the demolition charges on the front gate. The team retreated to safety and a large explosion rocked the landscape. Shrapnel and melted pieces of steel rained down after the blast.

"All teams advance," the mighty hippo warrior commanded as he ran full force towards the shattered gate. His one-ton of solid muscle shook the ground as he thundered forward.

Three tactical squads advanced on the smoking gate. Screams and yells could be heard coming from just inside the facility. All teams broke through the gate and continued their assault on the prison facility. The interior courtyard erupted into a heated battle.

Red robed Reaper Kai initiates prayed to dark powers as the very force of their will and hatred were focused into a chaotic flurry of psychic attacks. Bursts of fire and wisps of shadow shot from their fingertips. Several commandos were killed while still running through the gate. All teams spread out along the wall as they entered. Snipers took up positions immediately in the courtyard. Loud fifty caliber rifle rounds slammed into Reaper Kai and Biogtech alike. Many prison defenders were slain by the precise shooting attacks.

The courtyard continued to fill with enemy soldiers, and the commando teams were holding their own by taking up defensive positions in the courtyard. Several team members hid behind trucks, while others found cover behind generators and other thick metal relics.

The mighty hippo leader entered the courtyard last, taking cover behind a generator. Bullets hummed and ricocheted off the machinery. Commandos returned fire. The hippo, Globulus, took cover long enough to regain his composure and come up with a new plan of action.

"Teams One and Two, remain in the courtyard and support our actions. We need to lay down enough cover to cross the courtyard. Those double doors lead to the lower levels and the cellblocks. Team Three, come with me," Globulus screamed into his headset. All three teams complied immediately, and the assault was on.

"Covering fire!" the hippo yelled as the full force of the assault teams opened fire on the Reaper Kai defenders. Automatic weapon fire hummed as hundreds of rounds were exchanged.

Globulus led team Three and ran full gait across the courtyard. Biogtech soldiers laughed in glee as they took aim at the commandos breaching the courtyard. Weapons fired, and loud blasts reduced assault team Three to only a few members. Several died and collapsed in the center of the courtyard.

The mighty hippo leading the assault had been shot several times, but his thick hide had absorbed the trauma.

Team Three breached the door at the end of the courtyard. The interior was dimly lit with Old World light bulbs. The hippo never wavered in his attack. He led his troops down a series of stairs and passages. No resistance could be seen until the team hit the very bottom of the facility.

As Globulus rounded a corner, automatic weapons fire tore down the hall. Several rounds struck the mighty mutant hippo hybrid. Most embedded in his thick hide, but a few broke the skin, and trickles of blood rolled from the wounds. The hippo roared and brought the full force of his gun to bear.

The rotary barrels hummed intensely as dozens and dozens of well-placed machine gun rounds ripped into the pasty white robotic soldiers holding a position at the end of the hall. Three Biogtechs fell to the ground, convulsing in pools of hydraulic fluid. The other commandos took up positions on either side of their hippo leader. They crouched and fired quick bursts of gunfire at the remaining Biogtech soldiers.

"Mator bu wu darlar!" An ominous hissing sound resounded from behind the death machines. One of the commandos flanking Globulus began to gag. The sinister Reaper Kai priest, hidden at the end of the hall, was using his psychic powers to choke the life out of the commando. Blood trickled from his mouth as the soldier clutched and grasped his throat. A crunching sound could be heard as an unseen force crushed his throat, collapsing his wind pipe.

Globulus advanced slowly as he sprayed the hall with machine gun fire. The remaining robotic soldiers could not survive the assault, and collapsed into piles of metal and wiring. Remaining calm even while listening to his gagging companion dying behind him in the hall, Globulus halted his fire and rounded the corner at the end of the hall.

As he rounded the corner, a hunched figure in red robes hissed at the hippo. Globulus never halted, never wavered. He raised the mighty machine gun and aimed at the evil Reaper Kai initiate. The Reaper Kai drew an axe and charged the hippo. The hippo took aim and pulled the trigger. Twenty rounds of gunfire struck the red robed psychic, shredding his body into a miserable storm of gore. The body crashed to the ground with a splatter.

The commando instantly stopped gagging and rose to his feet, taking a few shaky steps. The psychic attack had halted just as soon as the Reaper Kai had died. Clutching his throat, the soldier took several quick breaths as the color returned to his face.

"Thanks..." the soldier said in a weak voice. The mighty hippo simply nodded.

The remnants of assault team Three entered the cellblock. They passed dozens and dozens of helpless prisoners. The hippo ignored their pleas for freedom. Wretched forms looked out from the barred cages and cells. Dirty and diseased hands stretched out with hope of mercy. They found none. Globulus continued on without looking at the wretches. His objective was not to rescue all the prisoners; he needed to rescue but one.

At last, the hippo found his way to a cell with a woman sitting quietly on the floor. She was dark skinned and wore the blood red robes of a Reaper Kai. Globulus halted and spoke to the woman. "Mineera of the Reaper Kai?" he quizzed her.

"Did The One send you?" the woman asked, and began to laugh dryly.

"What?" Globulus regarded the woman with an odd look. "Are you Mineera?"

"I am, master hippo," Mineera said in a dull tone. She stared at him intently, as if Mineera was looking at a ghost. Globulus did not like that look one bit; it made him feel uneasy.

"You have got to be kidding, sir. We came here to rescue a damn Reaper Kai? We lost a lot of good men, and I'm still not sure the three of us will make it out." One of the commandos spoke as the red laser sight of his weapon came to rest on her crimson robes.

Mineera continued to laugh dryly.

"Why the hell are you laughing, witch?" Globulus boomed as he spoke to the prisoner. With each moment, his reluctance to let her go was increasing.

"In a vision, my rescue was revealed to me." An odd look was on her face as she spoke, as if part of her had just come alive. A strange realization formed in her. An angel had chosen her. Everything the angel spoke of was coming true. Mineera would not be executed when the sun rose.

Globulus hesitated. A series of loud explosions could be heard in the courtyard above. The blasts brought Globulus back to reality. With a hesitant hand, he opened the cell door. The red robed woman rose to her feet and stepped out into the dim light in the hall. Dried blood and gashes were evident upon her clothing. Strangely, her flesh was intact, and no wound could be seen on her skin or body.

"What the hell do we need this witch for, Globulus? Why all this for her?" a commando asked slowly, with hatred in his eyes.

A wicked smile covered her dark skinned face, her light blue eyes sparkling from under her hood. "I am a traitor. I have information to use against the Reaper Kai in the coming war."

"Coming war?" the commando repeated with a look of terror on his face. "What war?"

"A war against the Reaper Kai," Globulus said, eyeing Mineera with suspicion.

"May our ancestors help us…" the soldier uttered as he turned away and moved towards the entrance to the cellblock.

Gunfire zinged into the cellblock as several Biogtech soldieries entered the cellblock and attacked. More enemy troops had advanced upon the prison break in progress.

"Get this collar off my neck and hurry." Mineera pulled her robes down, exposing an electronic collar attached to her neck. Globulus was puzzled, but managed to free it from her neck. The collar was known as a crasher, a device that inhibited psychics from utilizing their powers. A psychic wearing such a device could not concentrate long enough to channel spiritual energy, hence rendering them ineffective.

"We need some help, or we're gonna be overrun," a commando yelled as he fired several bursts down the hall at a squad of advancing Biogtech soldiers.

Mineera smiled darkly and started walking towards the Biogtechs in the hallway. Globulus was horrified, envisioning the psychic maiden being slain by gunfire. As she entered the hall, the soldiers halted their attack. They were not programmed to attack one of their masters. The Biogtech squad giggled and lowered their weapons.

"Open fire! Slay the traitorous bitch you foul machines!" A hiss could be heard as a Reaper Kai priest issued his command.

The robots responded and raised their weapons. Mineera dropped her head and began to meditate. A strange blue haze, almost looking like a bubble, erupted around the woman. Dozens and dozens of bullets were fired at the traitorous woman. Mineera held her hand up in the air before her. The bullets tore down the hall and rammed into a blue transparent shield of psychic energy surrounding Mineera, hitting the shield and stopping dead in the air. With a clatter, the bullets fell harmlessly to the ground. Mineera had successfully turned aside a torrent of bullets as if it was a drizzle of rain.

"What the hell?" Globulus exclaimed as he saw Mineera stop the gunfire. Though every Reaper Kai had some psychic ability, Mineera housed a considerable amount of power, far beyond the majority of the dark order.

The robots halted their attack and drew hand weapons. They advanced slowly down the hall, giggling with each step, their pale white faces bearing bright grins. Mineera raised her head and brought her hand forward. A spark of energy erupted from her fingertips. A bolt of white energy raced across the hall and struck the robots. The electrical attack was so severe, most of the robots melted in the blast, while the remainder rocked back and forth as a shower of sparks erupted from their charred bodies. The entire squad was reduced to a puddle of melted plastic and charred wiring.

"Foul bitch, we need no executioner this morning! You will die by my hand!" a hissing voice erupted from the darkness as a red robed Reaper Kai rounded the corner with a sword in hand.

Stretching her hand forward, Mineera channeled energy, and a hand axe rose from the floor. It floated mid air for a brief second then flew into her hand. Globulus and the commandos looked at each other with raised brows. They were stunned; all they could do was watch the battle erupting before them.

The Reaper Kai charged and sounded a mighty war cry. Mineera remained calm, clutching the axe tightly in her hand. The blow of the sword slashed across Mineera's chest, but she was too fast. She sidestepped the attack, and brought the blade of her axe across the shoulder of the Reaper Kai. The blade bit flesh, and the evil psychic cried in pain. He whirled around and made another hasty, viscous slash. This attack, too, was unsuccessful, and Mineera counterattacked by driving the blade of the axe into the Reaper Kai's chest. Her assault was fatal. With a whimpering cry, the Reaper Kai fell to the ground and died.

"Let's go," she said, and the stunned assault team looked on with confusion. They followed in a daze as they surveyed the destruction the psychic maiden had caused. "There is another exit that leads to the bottom of the falls. Going out through the courtyard is too dangerous."

Globulus and the two commandos nodded.

"All teams fall back, mission complete. I repeat, all teams retreat," Globulus screamed into his headset.

With that, the team traveled deeper into the prison. Within a matter of minutes, Globulus, Mineera, and the two commandos were outside Darkpine Prison. The survivors of the raid made a hasty escape into the Darkpine Forest, with their traitorous Reaper Kai companion in tow. Unbeknownst to Globulus, the four of them were the only ones who would escape the sinister prison alive.

Chapter 7
Ominous Tidings

The cloth backpack was filled with but a few items. Several canteens made from cow bladders. An old pair of battered goggles and a white cloth hood used for surviving a sandstorm. A porous reed mask to cover one's nose and mouth during sandstorms. A blue and red sleeping mat made from reeds and cloth, wrapped tightly in a roll. Rations of cheese, hard bread, and jerky, the only foods to be taken on the journey. A long tan cloak used to conceal one's self in the open desert. And finally, a small wooden box made by his girlfriend.

Jared looked quietly at the possessions in his backpack. A sense of loneliness overcame him as he surveyed the items that he was to take on his long trek across the world. He placed the bag on the floor and looked over at his friend Tani.

A collection of tools was wrapped loosely in Tani's bag. A soldering iron with a junk battery unit. An ancient book on physics. Assorted electrical devices, including detonators, a radiation detector, and a small Old World compass. Twelve sticks of dynamite, Tripwire's own blend, were wrapped neatly in a bundle. A roll of wiring used to detonate the explosives. The desert survival equipment and rations were also packed away. Tani's pack was filled to the brim and bulged. He viewed his pack and smiled, as would a fat man indulging in a banquet.

"That's all you're taking?" Tani said in a quizzing tone.

"Yeah." Jared was distant as he spoke.

"What's wrong?" the young genius quizzed his friend again.

Jared retreated towards the back of the small adobe house. He shook his head. "That's all the gear I need."

"Ok. You're sure nothing's wrong?"

"Yeah..." Jared sighed.

"You're nervous about the Exile?" Tani pushed his glasses up his nose and squinted at Jared.

"Me? The Exile? No way." Jared became cocky and hid

his fears deep down. "I am looking forward to it. The world will never know what to do when we are let loose." Jared chuckled. Tani responded with a smile.

"Mogi won't talk to me." Tani spoke in a low tone, avoiding eye contact with Jared. The young genius knew Master Mogi's unwillingness to talk had something to do with Jared.

"Bah. We don't need him," Jared scoffed.

"We don't need him? Are you crazy? He has been with us every year since we were five. He taught us everything we know about the wasteland. He taught us everything about fighting and survival. Now we don't need him? What did you say to him?" Tani was becoming irritated.

"We had a difference of opinion, that's all." Jared ended the conversation by grabbing his gear and exiting the small adobe house.

Tani shook his head and rolled his eyes. He grabbed his bag and left the house. With that, the two hit the streets of Scarskin.

Scarskin was a primitive town with promise. Many of the buildings were made out of wood and earthen adobe clay. Mostly square with wooden frames and clay mud exteriors, the buildings of Scarskin were made to weather the harsh desert environment. The clay kept the houses cool during the day and warm at night. Most of the houses were single roomed homes, but many had several levels, with the sleeping quarters up top and the living area on the bottom floor. Tani's house, for instance, was larger, since his family held more prestige in Scarskin. His father was a scribe for the council of the elders, and their house showed their status.

The village of Scarskin was constructed upon a large mesa high above the battered earth. A crude and narrow cobblestone trail snaked up the southern side of the mesa, and served as the only way into the village without scaling the sheer rock wall of the bluff. Each switchback on the road was fortified with a gate used to keep out invaders in times of war. Platforms were built above each gate, and used to rain down explosives on enemies trying to breach the perimeter of the village. The defenses were formidable, and not a single enemy had ever breached them and made it into the village. For a primitive town, Scarskin was located in one of the most easily fortified positions in all of the wastes.

The village was at the southern edge of the mesa, and was

populated by nearly twenty thousand people. Many travelers from the lands just north of the village would frequent Scarskin. A peace existed between three villages in the region. It was not uncommon for members of any of these villages to settle in the region near Scarskin known as the Yucca Flats, a weakly fertile section of land that was protected in a circular pocket, nestled in-between the mesa of Scarskin to the east and low lying hills to the west and north.

North of town, on the mesa, was a series of hot springs that produced a strange host of chemical sludge, slowly pushing up from the crust of the earth. This chemical sludge was used by the alchemists of the village to create various explosives and other wondrous potions.

The western portion of the mesa was strangely fertile. Another natural spring crept from the earth near the center of the mesa. Its continuous flow brought a consistent supply of clean, healthy water to the village. Due to its location, the spring was diverted to the rest of the mesa, allowing the citizens to grow a variety of crops including corn, wheat, and barley. The food supply on the bluff was the factor which gave the village its biggest advantage. Many towns had their food supply unprotected, and in times of war, the invading army would lay waste to the food supply. The village of Scarskin, on the other hand, could withstand long sieges without any interruption to the food supply, since it was high upon the mesa, out of harm's way.

The streets of Scarskin were constructed from light tan cobblestones. Bright colored tents lined the streets of the shopping district. Many traders from other parts up north rented spaces in Scarskin to sell their wares. Many exotic meats, vegetables, and fruits hung from racks in the market. Arms merchants sold an assortment of metal hand weapons: swords, axes, knives, spears, bows, and arrows. Armorers sold a variety of cured leathers and other armors sculpted out of thick scaly hides taken from the corpses of dead desert behemoths.

The peoples of Scarskin wore cloth and leather clothes, typically leather pants and skirts with cloth shirts and blouses. The men wore all earth tones, primarily tan and brown, while the women wore bright colors such as red and the highly prized purple.

As Jared and Tani made their way through the crowded streets of Scarskin, many villagers looked on and whispered as they passed. A woman of nearly fifty, with light tan skin and a face full of wrinkles, eyed them with a look of sadness as they passed.

Tani could not help noticing, and he took a minute to stop by her fruit stand. The woman gazed at him softly, tears welling up in her eyes.

"You remember my son Rori? You knew him, didn't you, master Tani?" She smiled and pushed a red fruit towards him.

"Yes, I remember him," Tani said softly, while Jared turned his back to the old woman in disgust.

"I heard you and master Jared are going east." The aged woman was very direct as she spoke. The look of sadness increased with each passing moment, as her thoughts drifted to her son Rori.

"Yeah, we're heading east," Tani said quietly as he turned, seeking Jared's support. The arrogant young Jared was not interested, and continued to scorn the old woman.

"My little Rori went east on his Exile. It's been nearly four… no, nearly five years. I know he is still out there, and can't find his way home." Tears welled up in the old woman's eyes as she spoke.

"Five years is a long time…" Tani's sentence fell short. He didn't know what to say.

"When you see him, could you bring him home? His father and I still miss him very much." With that, the woman regained her composure. Hope filled her mind.

"Yeah, if we see him, we'll bring him home," Tani promised, but the promise was a hollow one. Those Exiled who did not return after a few years or so were never heard from again. The elders claimed these young were not strong enough, and the desert claimed their souls.

"Oh, bless you and your ancestors, master Tani!" she declared excitedly, pushing several red Strawenfruits towards Tani. He accepted them silently and moved off down the street. When he turned back, the old woman waved to him excitedly.

"What were you doing, Tani? Her son is dead. No one lasts that long in the wastes without returning." Jared's voice was harsh.

"He did go east," Tani remarked.

"And what does that mean?" Jared's tone became more hostile.

"I just wanted to comfort her. I know five years is too long for an Exile." Tani shook his head. "I felt sorry for her. I had to give her some hope."

"Yeah, I know. Hey, Tani, I am sorry. I'm just a little rattled. Tomorrow is the day." Jared conceded a little fear to his friend.

"Yeah, I am a little scared myself," Tani said.

"I didn't say I was scared, just a little rattled." The young warrior's tone was arrogant.

"Well, anyway, I am a little scared." Being a scholar never meant Tani couldn't harass the ones around him. The sarcasm was lost on Jared.

"Let's head to your house. Our parents should all be there now. Jennifer, Hina, and their parents will be there soon. Let's not be late for our going away party," Jared said, and the two headed off to Tani's house.

Chapter 8
The Exile

A bright bonfire spewed forth a massive updraft of smoke into the dark sky. A flash of burning ash rolled and heaved upwards in the black smoke. The enormous fire crackled and lit the night. From its height upon the mesa, the bonfire could be seen for miles.

Around the fire were the people of Scarskin. This night was a sacred night to the tribals and they celebrated with the full force of their muster. Music rolled through the night and the village was awash with a fury of festivity. Small wooden flutes and an assortment of drums could be heard from miles around. The tempo of the music was quick and intense. The shadows moved as female dancers dressed in war paint leapt around the bonfire. Their forms writhed and leapt as the thudding of drums drove them into a fervor.

Though the celebration was one of life and renewal, it was mired with a silent fear, the fear of the unknown, and the sting of anticipated loss. The celebration was that of The Exile, a rite of passage to manhood where the youth were cast from the village, forced to walk to tattered wastelands and blasted landscapes of the ruined earth. For twenty full moons would pass before an Exiled youth could return to Scarskin. Twenty moons of days spent away from the safety of the village in the unforgiving wastelands. The fear of loss was hiding silently in the minds of every tribal of Scarskin. Ones lost to the wastes were never heard from again, and such mysteries were enough to drive even the hardiest of souls to madness. Youths that returned after the passage of twenty full moons were welcomed back into the village as adults, ready to take their place in Scarskin society. Those who returned before the passage of the twenty moons were known as Shagrats, cowardly folk that occupied the lowest rung in Scarskin society, forced to live at the edge of the village in a shanty town made from the refuse of others.

The shadows flickered, and all the tribe stared uneasily at the podium near the south end of the bonfire. Two tribals sat motionless as the fear of being exiled from home stirred inside their very souls.

Tani sat wide-eyed and stared around him with frantic glances. Jared was trying to hide his fear, and so elected not to make eye contact with anyone, not even his parents or other family members. Master Mogi stood in the crowd defiantly and glared at the two intensely, still angry about their decision to travel east into the great wastelands.

As frantic Tani scanned the crowd, he noticed many of the tribals had a look of fear in their eyes as well. Many of the men in the tribe stared on in trepidation, and Tani knew why: they were remembering being cast out of the village when they were young.

The young scholar glanced at his family, and caught sight of his mother and father. Tani's mother was sobbing, and his father tried to comfort her. The young genius was born from a scribe and a handmaiden, skilled in the arts of basketry. Neither of them was overly intelligent or physically powerful, but they were both good people. That sense of goodness was passed down to young Tani, along with his father's quest for an educated life.

As Tani stared at his mother crying, sadness welled up inside of him. Fighting back tears, the young genius hid his sadness and quickly looked away. Rolling his eyes upwards, he tried to fight back the tears tugging at his senses. The thought of never seeing his parents again filled young Tani with an ominous silence. It was quite possible that he would never see his parents again, or that they would never know his fate. The Exile was long and fraught with peril. It was not uncommon for those Exiled never to return.

Jared was lost in his own thoughts. Fighting back his own tears of fear and sadness, the young warrior focused his gaze right on the wooden podium in which they sat. The music and chanting roared in the background. His mind began to drift, and the fear became terror. The terror transformed into a childish rage. His mind could not function. Jared and his best friend were about to be Exiled from *their* village. Shaking like a frightful child, Jared clasped his hands together, trying desperately to regain his composure. The stress was almost too much to handle.

Jared shook his head in disgust; he knew better than to travel east, but his pride could not be injured, it was the only thing he had left. The courage was gone now; all he had was an insane commitment to do the impossible, to travel east into the wasteland, east, from which not a single Exile had ever returned in the entire history of the village.

Mogi stared intently at the tribals, as did many of the elders. Each was dismayed by the youths' decision to breach the mighty eastern waste. Not a single elder believed either would ever return.

Several roasted sheep were the main course at the banquet. Lightly spiced and roasted to perfection, the juicy meat dripped and sizzled in the fire as it was rotated on a spit. Exotic fruits from the northern Primal Lands were eaten by young and old alike. A fermented thick frothy beer made from cactus pulp was being consumed in major quantities. Even the children of the village imbibed of the strong brew. Cacti Brew, as it was known to the tribals, was a pride-honored legacy of the tribe. No other village in the region had mastered the lost art of fermentation and, Cacti Brew was a high-end export of the village. A cask of Cacti Brew could be traded for three sheep.

Tani ate his meal slowly; his mouth was dry and he could barely eat. The anxiety he felt was consuming him instead of young Tani consuming the meal. Jared played with his roasted sheep and pushed it around the ceramic plate, trying to avoid the gaze of the elders and his peers alike.

The banquet held in the honor of the two youths was nearing the end.

"All be still!" Master Mogi yelled in a harsh voice. The crowd responded immediately, and not a single person spoke. As Mogi yelled, nausea began to rise in the pit of Tani's stomach. Jared trembled slightly and tried to control it; the young warrior could not let anyone see his fear.

A creed and tradition that had existed for more than forty generations was beginning. The tribals had no real religion, so The Exile was the closest thing to it. Every person in Scarskin knew to be quiet and respectful of the ceremony.

"As it was in times of old, so shall it be this night." Mogi spoke slowly and stared at the crowd. He rose to the podium and stood between Jared and Tani.

"We, the tribe of Scarskin, were born from the mistakes of a civilization long ago. We, the tribe of Scarskin, were born from the desert. We, the tribe of Scarskin, are children of the desert." Mogi's voice boomed and many of the audience whispered the sacred Exile creed. The whisper sounded like the hissing of a snake.

"Wisdom from our ancestors has taught us to learn and grow from the desert. So shall it be this night. We are about to send our young into the fray. We are about to cast out some of our children so they can learn from the desert and return as men..." He paused momentarily and regained his composure. The pause in his voice was one of hesitation. The audience knew all too well that Mogi expected never to see the two youths again, and his hesitation to continue said as much. Many eyes in the audience became fearful and distant.

"The ancients left great wealth in the desert. They left their knowledge, and this is our heritage. Not only are the youths to learn and grow to become men, they are to return with knowledge of the ones that gave birth to us so many, many moons ago." As Mogi spoke, Tani looked on with trepidation. Tears welled up in the corner of his eyes. He fought to remain in control of his emotions.

"So let it be. So let it be known, the two youths that will leave this night are Jared of the Dunerunner Clan and Tani of the Ploughvender clan." With that, the two youths rose to their feet and stood on either side of Master Mogi.

"As custom permits, the elders of this great tribe will in turn give each Exiled a single gift to help them on their journey." Master Mogi's look of sadness was quickly becoming an expression of respect.

He moved to the side of the podium and recovered two items for the youths. "This is one of the only times in my life that I will depart from tradition." As he spoke, a hush overtook the crowd. It was very rare for a village elder to make a change in the Exile Creed.

"It is no surprise that both Jared and Tani are very special. I have never seen a swordsman to match young Jared in all the time I have walked this earth. Nor have I seen a more talented scholar than master Tani. It would be a great loss to this village to lose you both." Mogi turned to each of the youths in turn as he spoke. The village was as quiet as a tomb. No one spoke as they stared in awe. Many had never seen an elder acknowledge a youth before an Exile, but to acknowledge two youths so strongly was a thing of legend.

"The first elder of our tribe was known as elder Maverick McCoy. He was the one that formed this tribe ages and ages ago.

With a heavy hand, he smote his enemies and brought peace to these lands. So that we never forgot the struggle to rise from the ashes, he named this village Scarskin. For after the dark times of the ancients there was much strife." The elder spoke and the entire village exchanged looks of amazement. It was forbidden to speak of the dark times of old. It was forbidden to speak of when man used plumes of fire to level great cities. It was forbidden to speak of the dark history, for many elders feared it would happen again some day…

The words were ominous and each tribal of Scarskin knew that this would be a day to remember for all their days.

Mogi spoke again, and everyone listened with a chill in their heart and stomach. "Elder Maverick McCoy was wise in both battle and knowledge. He created the Exile so that in time, our tribe could rise above the other tribes in the desert. The technology of old, lost in the desert, was to be our fuel to make us survive above the others. And as you all know, not a single army has ever breached our defenses. This is a testament to Maverick's wisdom. Those returning from The Exile, generation after generation have recovered lost technologies that have saved us time and time again from invasion."

Mogi turned to Tani and looked directly at him. "Master Tani is a genius. His ability to use technology is formidable, and our future survival rests upon his ability to decipher the texts of old."

Mogi then turned to Jared. "Jared is a warrior of immense skill, and the future of our tribe also rests in his hands. Our tribe has never exiled two more potent individuals, let alone during the same Exile."

The tribe was quiet. Never had an elder given such high praises.

"However, the path they have chosen is fraught with peril." Mogi sighed and gathered his words carefully. "The two youths have chosen to travel east, a task not easily completed. For all the generations that have existed in our tribe, not a single Exile has ever returned from the eastern expanse. Not a single person from the east." Mogi paused and looked down.

"As a result, the elders have agreed to give them each a treasure beyond imagination to help them on their quest." Both

Jared and Tani shot each other odd glances. Never in their lives had an exile been given an ancient treasure from the Vault of the Elders.

"The founder of this tribe, Maverick McCoy, carried an old world blade that is said to be indestructible. It is one of Scarskin's most prized treasures. The Scar Blade is not only a weapon of old, but is a part of our heritage, the weapon carried and used by Maverick himself to quell the horrid abominations of the desert. The mighty weapon has not seen battle since Maverick's death some forty generations ago. The Scar Blade will be given to master Jared. For his skill deserves a weapon of legend." Mogi took a step back and revealed a scabbard of steel. With a quick move he slid the blade free from the scabbard. A light blue metal blade shone brightly even in the dim light. Many in the crowd gasped. All had heard the legend of the blade, but only the elders had seen the weapon.

Jared was wide eyed as Mogi handed him the legendary blade. The Scar Blade was surprisingly light, and a bright blue shimmer rose from the metal. Jared bowed to Mogi and the crowd of tribals around the podium. The gift was so magnificent that Jared could not even speak.

Mogi left the stunned Jared and grabbed a device from one of the techno elders.

"Many devices and trinkets of old have been studied for generations. This is one such device. Harvested from an Exile nearly twenty generations ago, this device and its use have still eluded even our most wise. In the old tongue it is called a 'computer'."

The crowd was unable to comprehend the device. None knew of its use.

Tani gasped; he had read of computers and pored over many books about them. Never in his wildest dreams did he imagine he would ever see one.

"The Techno elders believe this is the greatest techno gift that they can give to anyone, let alone an Exile. Master Tani, this computer is your gift for the Exile. The elders have fashioned several fuel cells for it, enough to last you until you and Jared return." The elder handed the small laptop computer to Tani.

"Thank you..." Tani was so stunned and elated over the gift, that he lost all thought about the Exile. He popped the computer open and began to look it over. "The keys are written in ancient tongue, but I can read them! Look at the symbols! Just like from my books!" His excitement quickly ended as Mogi and the rest of the tribe stared at him silently. "Sorry... It's just really neat..." Tani turned bright red, intensely embarrassed.

Master Mogi let the crowd relax, and a silence settled over the center of Scarskin. The bonfire crackled, and a baby cried in the darkness.

"I, an elder of the Scarskin tribe, acknowledge the rites of old. It is with happiness and great sorrow that I cast two of our young into the desert. We must pray to our ancestors that they find the strength to be brave and strong." As Mogi grew silent, the crowd responded to his speech.

"All be it with them," the crowd hissed.

"As we are children born from the desert, when we die we return to the desert. Let us pray that the young ones return to us before they return to the desert."

"All be it with them," the crowd hissed again.

"It is an act of love that I now turn away from you, so that you acknowledge that you are not welcome before my presence until twenty full moons have passed." With that, Mogi looked at each young one in turn, then with a slow gesture, he turned his back on both of them.

"All be it with them," the crowd hissed as they all turned away. Friends, family, and loved ones all turned away in unison.

The stunned friends looked at everyone they had ever loved. Not a single one looked at them. No father, brother, sister, mother, or lover looked at them. A hollow sense of loss filled them both. The message was clear; Tani and Jared were no longer welcome in Scarskin. The two were no longer welcome in the only home they had ever known. A tear rolled down Tani's cheek, and Jared shook his head sadly.

Jared and Tani grabbed their gear and headed toward the village gate. Within minutes, the two companions left the village of Scarskin and headed east into the wilds of a desert that had consumed so many of the young from Scarskin. As they were traveling under the light of a full moon, they each paused to look at the moon above them. The waxing and waning of the moon was their new enemy. It was a force that kept them from the only home they had ever known. Twenty full moons, alone in a world growing darker and darker just beyond the eastern horizon…

Chapter 9
The Badland Rock Spires

Tan stone spires rose high into the sky, part of a ridgeline of battered rock snaking northwards beyond view, beyond the endless sands of the great eastern waste. Like a half buried skeleton, the rock formation poked out of the sand in many locations, giving an imaginative viewer the impression that a mighty desert beast had died many years ago, and all that remained were the sand-washed bones. The Badland Rock Spires, as they were called by the tribals of Scarskin, represented the edge of the world. Elders from the tribe often sent scouts eastward, and the Badland Rock Spires were the furthest that the scouts dared to travel.

It was whispered amongst the tribe that the Badland Rock Spires were haunted by the dead youth from the Exile. Many scouts reported seeing fleeting glimpses of young men walking amongst the spires, until, in the blink of an eye, the forms would vanish without a trace. These legends of the cursed desert spires stood the test of time and survived through the generations. It was a place of ill omen, a place said to be a prison for the dead, a place that held all those youths who were not strong enough to return home from the Exile.

The rock spires hid a network of passages and caves. From time to time, the shifting sands would reveal hidden pockets in the stone. Scouts would often speak of finding buried caves that led deep into the earth, filled with human remains and the skeletons of strange beasts, mutants distorted by continual genetic damage from living in the contamination of the apocalypse.

The sun was leaving the world, heading always towards the west. The day was drawing to a close, a premature close. Darkness was about to wash over the wasteland early.

A strong wind was blowing in from the western reaches of the desert. The intense fury pulled the sand into the air, creating mighty plumes of swirling chaos. The cloud of swirling sand ascended higher and higher. Within the span of a few minutes, the flurry of sand had become a moving wall of terror. The sandstorm rolled across the wasteland with frightening speed, sending the wall of blowing sand crashing into the stone spires.

A choking flood of dirt stung the eyes of the two companions. As the storm hit, Jared and Tani made haste, placing goggles over their eyes and covering their faces with a cloth hood and a crude filter. The hood covered the entire head and faces of the two tribals save for the dirty goggles peering out into the grubby darkness. Using hand signals, Jared ushered Tani onward into the maelstrom of sand and dirt.

The blowing sand and wind assaulted the two as they fought their way through the deadly storm. The rock spires that the two had been heading towards disappeared, as the sun became a dull ball of light. The dirt and blowing sand were so thick that the two companions could only see a few feet ahead. Almost falling over from the force of the wind, Tani fought to remain on his feet. Jared turned back to help him, and the two tribals trudged onward.

It seemed like an eternity in the darkness and chaos of the blowing sand. Seconds seemed like minutes and minutes seemed like hours. Struggling against the harsh storm, Jared and Tani finally fought their way into the heart of the Badland Rock Spires.

Once they reached the rocks, the wind subsided substantially. Using the spires as cover, the two tribals found their way into a peaceful courtyard of rock protected against the mighty storm that raged in the desert.

"The Badland Rock Spires," Tani said in a dull tone as he pulled the cloth hood from his head. The young genius rubbed the dirt from around his goggles, and his green eyes scanned the courtyard of rock.

"This is as far as the Scarskin scouts have ever traveled. Five days east from Scarskin," Jared said in a dull tone as he removed his own desert survival gear.

Tani remained silent; he had heard the tales of the cursed spires many times.

The desert wind howled through the rocks. Blasts of sand forced their way into the courtyard. Surrounded on three sides by rock rising hundreds of feet into the air, the rock courtyard was a haven from the world around them. Just beyond the courtyard was open desert and a chaotic rush of sand.

"I never thought we would see the Spires," the young scholar said, still rubbing sand from his eyes. "Ever since I was a child, I heard stories about the edge of the world."

"This isn't the edge of the world. I don't believe it and neither do you. Many times you have told me that the ruins of great cities have to be out here somewhere." Jared sat on the sand and pulled his pack open.

"Yeah, I know, but what if I am wrong?" Tani was tired from the days travel and was sullen as he spoke.

"You're not wrong. Come on, you've told me many times that the ancient maps revealed large cities in the eastern regions."

"Yeah, you're right. But no one who goes beyond the spires ever returns. Even Master Mogi spoke of scouts disappearing out here in the spires, not to mention going beyond them. Maybe the sands have swallowed all that the ancients created, and this is the worst decision we have ever made." Tani spoke softly between sips from his canteen.

The winds whistled through the entry to the courtyard. With each passing second, the whistling changed pitch, creating a haunting wail. Tani shivered at the sound. He pulled his knees towards his chest and rested his chin on them, letting weariness take him.

Tani closed his eyes and took in the sounds around him. The wind whipped through the rocks.

"*Help me...*"

Tani opened his eyes abruptly, launching himself up against the back wall of the courtyard.

"Did you hear that?" he asked, wide eyed. The rational scholar had given in to the irrational. Folklore had clouded his mind, and he believed he heard a voice in the wind.

"What?" Jared's tone was confused.

"Did you hear that? The voice?"

"Come on, Tani, knock it off," the young warrior countered, feeling irritated and thinking his companion was trying to have fun at his expense.

Tani let the matter drop. Uneasily, he stared at the whirling wind. Fighting off his fright, Tani forced the stories of the Badland Rock Spires from his mind. He shuddered in the wind and pressed his back up against the stone wall of the mighty spire. Tani felt that his nerves were just about shot. Maybe he *did* imagine the voice in the wind. After all, the two had traveled for five days straight through the desert, and it had been a lonely venture. The two had not encountered a single creature or person as they made their way deeper and deeper into eastern reaches. Not a single trace of life greeted them as the made their way to the Badland Rock Spires.

"We have only been out here a few days, and it already feels like a lifetime." Tani sat on the warm sand and listened to the storm rage outside the stone courtyard.

Jared looked up at the top of the stone pillars that surrounded the sanctuary in the rock. As sand blocked out the sun, a swirling mass rolled around the top of the rocks. The light patter of sand falling could be heard. Individual grains got caught on the mighty stonewalls and trickled down the wall like a flow of water. Slowly, the sand rained down from the top, and Jared watched dully as endless grains flowed down the wall, creating small dunes of sand at the base of the rocks.

As Jared surveyed the small dunes forming at the base of the rocks, a strange sight caught his eye.

"Hey Tani, come look at this," Jared said excitedly as he moved across the courtyard.

Tani moved over close and crouched beside him. Both of the tribals felt a shot of adrenaline hit their system. Several half covered tracks could be seen around the edge of the walls. The tracks were large, and they weren't human.

"We're not alone," Jared said in a haunted tone.

Tani shivered and stared about him, feeling the hair rise on the back of his neck. "I don't like this," the young scholar said quietly. The voice he *had* heard returned to his thoughts. Maybe he *did* hear something.

"What do you think made them?" Jared quizzed the young genius.

Tani took a moment to study the tracks. Suddenly, a look of clarity dawned on his face. "Notice how the tracks are side by side and not staggered?"

"Yeah I see, so what?" the warrior was mystified.

"They're side by side. That means whatever left them walks on two feet, but not like we do."

Tani's words seemed to confuse Jared even more. "They're

not human. What left the tracks then, Tani?" Jared quizzed the young genius once again.

"If it's not human… then it has to be some sort of mutant."

As Tani's words hit Jared's ears, it was apparent the young warrior was set on edge.

"Mutant? You can't be serious. The tales and legends of mutants from Master Mogi were just stories, weren't they?" Jared was getting a little scared.

"*It's so dark, I can't find my way home…*"

The wind howled, and Jared spun around with his hand on the hilt of his mighty weapon. The warrior had heard a whisper in the wind.

Tani looked wide-eyed at his companion, and saw Jared's hand quivering just above the mighty Scar Blade. "What's wrong?" Speaking softly, Tani looked toward the entrance to the courtyard.

Shaking off the numbing fear growing at the edge of his sanity, Jared's mind retreated from the growing terror, and looked back at the strange tracks in the sand.

"It looks like the stories were true, Tani. Something lives out here in the spires, and it isn't human. Our scouts never reported anything like this." Jared spoke softly.

"The worst thing is we are stuck here until the storm blows over," Tani said hesitantly, scanning the entrance to the stone courtyard. "We had best be on our guard."

Tani and Jared moved to the back of the sanctuary and rested. The afternoon wore on slowly as the sandstorm tore mercilessly at the ancient stone spires. Eventually, the sandstorm ended and the sky darkened with the setting of the sun. Oddly enough, to the west, the stars did not shine. A patch of black void blocked out the night sky. An ominous quiet fell over the wasteland. The harsh desert sand-storm was the herald to something much worse. The tribals sat in silence and peered at the night sky as flashes of light grew closer. A thunderstorm, a true rarity in the wasteland, was rolling in. The tribals watched in uneasy fascination as their minds wandered to legends of lost spirits and mutant terrors stalking about in the darkness of the Badland Rock Spires.

Chapter 10
The End of Innocence

The tall stone rock spires were silent once again. The horrid sands had stopped their assault against the great stone monoliths of the desert. The sky was clear of sand, but now dark storm clouds mounted and rolled in from the western expanse. The shadows took over, and the stone spires began to cool.

Tani was spooked by strangeness of the day; he couldn't dismiss the feeling that he had heard a voice in the wind. Try as he may, young Jared could not deny the voice that he had heard in the sandstorm. This paranoia was growing, and the two tribals were uneasy.

Tani looked on in horror at the coming of the rain. In most deserts, the rain meant life, a way to renewal. Rain in the wastelands was something totally different. Radioactive sludge would fall from the heavens, contaminating anything it touched. Tani knew of such things, and was none too happy by the advance of the storm clouds.

"We need to find shelter from the rain," Tani said, his voice urgent.

Jared also knew of the danger and nodded silently.

Though the stone courtyard was protection from the sandstorm, it was open from above, and would not shelter them from the rain. Jared and Tani fled, searching frantically for a new hiding place.

A tall fissure split the rock face ahead of the two companions. Twisting downward, a slope of sand descended into the darkness of the fissure. The two followed the fissure and found themselves in front of a large gaping cave.

Both held their ground and stared with dread at the darkness before them. Their hair stood on end, and a chill rolled through them.

Could this be one of those caves... a cave from the stories... a cave that held the corpses of hapless desert adventurers?

The thought bounced around in each of the tribals' minds.

The first few drops of rain began to fall from the sky. The imaginary threat of shades and ghosts haunting the Badland Rock Spires was overwhelmed by the reality of being drenched in radioactive water. For the moment, the tribals would have to bury their fears to survive the coming rain.

Wretched water from the sky began to soak the desert sands. As the torrent of filth crashed into the desert, Tani crouched and recovered an electrical device from his pack.

Small pools had already formed in rock depressions, and the young genius flipped the switch on the face of electrical device. A quick series of clicks was emitted from the device. Tani shook his head slowly, and Jared gave him a quizzing look.

"It's as we feared. The water is contaminated. We should do our best to avoid it." Tani spoke in a low tone.

The tribals moved back from the edge of the cave and crouched near a stone wall. Looking deeper into the cave, Jared noticed a stagnant pool of water. He moved back to the pool and viewed it with dismay. More tracks, not quite human, could be seen all around the pool. A vile smell filled his nostrils as he got closer to the pool. Clumps of wet sand with a greenish tint lay next to the water.

Motioning the scholar over to the pool, Jared covered his nose with his hand. As Tani viewed the green clumps of wet sand, the stench was overpowering.

"Smells like vomit, or more precisely, bile." Tani had an uneasy look on his face. "Whatever drank this water must have gotten sick from it. It's a scary thought that the only water out here in the wastes is contaminated. The creatures out here must suffer from intense genetic damage and subsequent mutation."

"Mutants…" Jared mouthed and looked around. His hand moved to the Scar Blade sheathed at his waist.

Fighting the fear rising in their stomachs, the two tribals retreated from the stagnant pool and settled down to rest. Jared was terribly uneasy, but was too headstrong to admit it. Tani, in contrast, wore the worry on his face. Unable to speak, the tribals drifted into their own worlds.

The rain fell from the heavens intensely. Foul radioactive water flowed and became streams of filth. As the cave was located at the bottom of a hill, the water collected at its base. Pools formed, and the two simply watched with dull fascination. Desert storms were rare, but when it did rain, flooding was common.

Lightning flashed, and Tani was startled. Jared simply smiled at his fearful companion. The patter of water was somewhat soothing, and Jared drifted into a light slumber.

Tani jumped to his feet suddenly and pulled his dagger free. "Jared!" he yelled in fear.

Jared was jolted back to reality. His light slumber was shattered by Tani's yelp and a piercing scream. A loud crash of thunder covered most of the scream. Jared thought he was imagining things again. Tani shuddered as a chill rolled down his spine. Another series of piercing screams could be heard near the entrance of the cave. Jared jumped to his feet and drew the mighty blue Scar Blade free from its ancient scabbard. He had not imagined the last wailing set of screams.

A bloated white form lurched into the cave. Radioactive rainwater dripped from the mutant beast as it moved. The creature was much taller than a human, and was covered in irregular folds and globs of yellowish-white putrid fat. The maw of the great beast opened, revealing a jagged set of rotten teeth, black as the night. A foul green steam erupted from the mouth of the beast as it screamed again. Thick white puss dripped from one of the creature's misshapen eyes. Green moss grew around its left leg. An old wound was festering, and the smell of rotting flesh filled the cave.

Tani stumbled backwards as another white mutant moved into the cave. Jared held his ground with a dull expression on his face. Fear had filled the youth. He watched in sick fascination as the two mutant beasts lumbered towards them.

The rotten beast assaulted young Tani. It swung its fat, puss filled arm at the young tribal. The young genius was adrenalized by the conflict and moved back to avoid the clumsy attack. The creature roared in frustration, thick green bile dripping from its mouth and hitting the sand with a sizzle.

The other mutant also moved to attack the young genius. Tani was cornered and backed up against a wall. The two mutants were closing fast, and he was running out of options.

"Jared!" Tani yelled. Jared was still stunned.

Even though the young warrior was the best swordsman

from Scarskin, he had never seen real combat. Fear had taken over. Jared's mind could not comprehend what he was watching.

It took a moment for the haze to dissipate.

Finally, his mind cleared and urgency took over. Filled with adrenaline, Jared moved forward and made a clumsy attack. He hacked at the back of one of the mutants. The attack tore a large gash in the back of the beast. Normally, Jared was trained to make one–hit kills with a blade, but at that moment, he could not think clearly.

The beast roared and swung around. As it did, its clawed hand caught Jared in the face. The claw tore in, and Jared gritted his teeth. The blow was so severe he almost lost consciousness. Warm blood erupted from the open wounds on his face. He staggered back and forth as dizziness took him.

The beast took the advantage and moved forward to finish off young Jared. The warrior regained his control just in time. The attack polarized the youth; he was no longer filled with fear, but with a determined will to survive. The expert training the warrior had received from Master Mogi took over. With a deliberate set of attacks, Jared assaulted the mighty mutant.

As Jared swung quickly three times, the mutant suffered three mortal blows. Puss and fat erupted from its wounds. The creature staggered and clutched at the open cuts. With a crash, the beast fell to the ground in a pool of white fluid. It twitched but once before death took it.

Tani retreated along the wall as the remaining mutant terror closed in for the kill. Slowly, the mutant staggered onward; its half rotten leg slowed it considerably. Another piercing scream filled the cave as the frustrated beast chased the quick Tani.

Jared focused on the battle, and moved to engage the mutant. With a deliberate blow, Jared drove the mighty Scar Blade through the rotten leg of the beast. The ancient blue blade shimmered as it sheared clean though the green rotten leg.

Howling in pain, the beast crashed to the ground. Angered by the loss of its leg, the mutant was overtaken by a wild battle frenzy. It swung its claw and grabbed Jared's leg. With a tug, it pulled him off his feet. The tribal crashed to the ground. The puss covered Scar Blade hit the sand. The mutant pulled Jared toward it and he was unable to recover his lost sword.

Jared struggled to break free from the vice like grip of the beast. The beast drug the warrior across the sand. It screamed in glee as its mouth opened. Jared was horrified as the mutant pulled him closer to the steaming green mouth filled with jagged black teeth.

Tani took his dagger and plunged it into the chest of the beast. The attack was vicious, but did not faze the beast at all. Thick fat and puss protected the mutant from the attack.

Jared kicked several times as the beast tried to bite the young tribal. The struggling bought Jared a few extra seconds, time which proved crucial for his companion.

Tani uttered a war cry and picked up a large rock. With a shout, the young genius brought the rock down on the skull of the mutant. Bone broke as the skull was smashed. The beast howled one last cry. With a shudder, it died.

Jared kicked the claw free from his foot. He stumbled back and recovered his ancient blue steel sword. Tani fell back on the ground and breathed slowly, wide eyed with fear.

Jared was a mess, and his blood soaked face was still bleeding. Tani moved over and covered his friend's face with a rag. The makeshift bandage stopped the flow of blood within a matter of minutes.

With their adrenaline exhausted, the two rested quietly as the storm raged outside the cave. The stench of the dead mutants was intense, but it didn't seem to bother the two; they were both in a trance, a dreamlike state, as their fragile minds frantically tried to comprehend what had just happened.

The rain stopped, and the wretched flow of water ceased. The two tribals from Scarskin rested, but did not sleep. They did not speak because speech was unnecessary; they didn't need to; they both knew what the other was thinking. They knew a terrible line had been crossed, a line that could not be erased or forgotten.

Chapter 11
A Dream of the Future

Mineera, Globulus, and two Rasheed commandos sat quietly at a table near the back of the tavern. The blood red robes Mineera wore covered her face from view. Weariness had taken control of all at the table, and not a single word was spoken between the four. Half-eaten meals lined the table and a blank expression lined the faces of its occupants.

Mineera, dark Reaper Kai witch, suddenly rose from the table. "Be at the ready, we are under attack!" No one had yet attacked them, but Mineera seemed to have some sort of precognition about the event.

Globulus and the two soldiers were confused and remained in their chairs. All three thought the dark psychic had lost her mind.

Suddenly, a blast of gunfire rose through the dark tavern. All other patrons hit the floor. The gunfire struck and shattered the mighty hippo's beer stein. The shattered pottery crashed around on the table. Instantly, the mighty hippo rose and pulled a sawed off shotgun. The huge and beastly hippo was so large that he palmed the weapon as a human would palm a pistol.

"To arms!" Globulus yelled as he leveled the weapon at several gunmen who had burst through the front door of the tavern...

Mineera awoke from the dream with a startle. She sat up and gasped in fear. Looking around, the psychic found that there was no gunfight. Instead she found herself next to the sleeping Rasheed soldiers who had helped break her out of the infamous Darkpine Prison. The cloak of night still hung over the world.

Globulus stared at Mineera intently in the darkness of the campsite. He was still wary of the woman, and looked at her uneasily. "What were your dreams filled with, witch?" Globulus asked in a low tone. His mighty sharp teeth glittered dully in the orange glow of the campfire.

"An attack, master hippo…" Mineera was still rattled by the prophetic vision she had just witnessed in her dreams. As she spoke, her tone was low and mysterious.

"You have many visions? I have watched you when you sleep. It appears that you are tormented relentlessly in your dreams."

"I am, master hippo. I dream of many things… wars, atrocities, and countless other horrors, all things that I feel powerless to stop." Her gaze, mysterious once more, fell on the fire.

"What good is it to see the future and not be able to change it? Your gift sounds more like a curse," Globulus declared, staring at the red robed psychic traitor now huddled by the fire.

Mineera warmed her dark skinned hands in the dim light of the fire. She smiled softly as she felt the warmth of the flames. "I have dreamt all my life of the future. I have never been able to stop or alter any of my visions. They are what they are: a portrait of the future that cannot be altered."

"So what was the vision you conjured, witch?" Globulus still didn't trust her, but he talked to her, anyway.

"A vision of all four of us… in an attack… in a tavern." The dark skinned psychic maiden turned to face the mighty mutant hybrid hippo. Though her blue eyes were barely visible in the dim light, Globulus noticed that they were filled with compassion.

"How strange that such an evil creature is sitting here beside me," Globulus said as he stared at her compassionate eyes. "An attack, you say? Can you tell where and when, witch?"

"No… But I can tell when the vision begins in real life. I can give a warning then." Mineera was cryptic, and the hippo simply snorted and continued to stare at her.

"Doesn't sound like a good warning to me. We could be dead by the time you utter this warning."

"Well, it's not perfect. I can't control what I see."

"Any other helpful visions? Perhaps you have had a vision of me sitting quietly on a pier in Rasheed sipping a nice cool ale." Globulus scoffed and scorned the woman's visions.

"No, but I have had dreams of *him* again…" Her voice trailed off and her stare became distant.

"*Him*?" he quizzed.

"A man from my dreams, a stranger, a hero, who will

somehow save this world." She was remembering the vision she had seen all her life. Ever since she was a child, the same vision had returned again and again, always the same.

"Tell me about this savior, witch, for my interest is piqued."

"I have dreamed of him all my life. He is a man filled with hate and sorrow. A great scar runs down the right side of his face. His eyes are dark and distant, filled with a rage that will never be quenched. The grief of his loss can never be quieted, as his soul has given in to rage and anger. Where he was once filled with compassion, only a husk that is shattered and bruised beyond comprehension remains. For this is the man I have dreamed of all my life, and this man is destined to die in front of my very eyes." She was distant and shook her head sadly. "And all my dreams come to pass, I can never change what I see. This stranger will die, and his passing will bring about the victory of the Reaper Kai."

"Hmmm." Globulus was enthralled and chilled by the story of the strange hero. "Have you met this savior?"

"No, only in my dreams," she stated with a look of sadness in her eyes. "So much pain I feel in him... I only wish I could save him from both death and himself."

"Where is this person supposed to die in your vision? Can you tell where you are when he is to die?" the hippo quizzed, still enthralled by the tale.

"The site is familiar. I believe he will perish within the very walls of the palace of Rasheed," Mineera answered, remembering both her vision of the future and the many times she had stayed in the palace of Rasheed as a diplomat of the Reaper Kai.

"Rasheed, eh? This is grave news, witch. If your vision comes true, this stranger may perish very soon, for we will quickly be back at the safety of Rasheed." Globulus nodded at the woman.

"Yes, perhaps time is running out for this stranger," Mineera said and yawned. Weariness had overtaken her, and she retreated to her sleeping mat.

"Have still dreams, traitor of the Reaper Kai," Globulus said as he stoked the fire. He turned his large head and looked at Mineera and spoke again. "And have a vision of me resting quietly on a pier with a nice, cold ale. For if your gift of prophecy is true, nothing could prevent me from an intoxicated afternoon at home."

Mineera smiled and fell into a deep sleep. She did not have

any dreams save one, a dream that had filled her existence ever since she was a small child. Mineera dreamt of an angry, courageous man dressed in a long overcoat who would somehow save the world from the dread Reaper Kai...

Mineera was running through a dark palace with high vaulted ceilings. White columns rose and met the heights of the roof above. As she ran, a vague feeling of familiarity coursed through her.

Up a circular staircase Mineera ran, round and round until she reached a stone landing atop the twisting stairwell. Her surroundings were a rush of images: torches hung along the dark marble hallways; the palace was strangely silent; no guards stirred; there was a faint smell of incense.

Making haste, she finally came to a wooden door. Her heart pounding both out of fear and fatigue, Mineera pushed the door open quickly.

With an explosion of panic, a man sleeping near the door sat straight up and turned his head towards the open doorway. The man's face was scarred, and his dark eyes were like an icy black pit filled with surprise and immense anger. His hand moved and grabbed a silver revolver from under his pillow.

A gunshot rang out. The man turned just in time to see a shadowy figure on the balcony. A burst of blood erupted from a wound in the center of his chest. Clenching his teeth, the scar on his face contorted in a twisted mass of pain. The man in bed clutched the wound and his eyes rolled back. The gun fell from his hand. The assassin on the balcony jumped into the palace garden below, hidden by the shadows of the night.

"Mineera..." he gasped as the woman stood stunned in the doorway.

She ran to his side and pressed her hand into the warm bloody wound on his chest, tears running down her face. She was panic-stricken, and try as she might, she could not stop the flow of blood erupting from his chest.

"Don't leave..." she whimpered, and his hand clutched hers. "Damn it, don't die."

Her love was strong, but death was stronger. The man's eyes grew dark, and his hand fell from hers. He ceased to stir, and sadness welled up in her fragile soul.   Mineera's grief was overwhelming as the deranged rancher died in her arms.

"Banion…" Mineera whispered in terror, cradling the lifeless body.

Chapter 12
The Road South

The rancher who had lost his home and reason to live lay slumped with his head on a wooden table. His empty beer mug had been unceremoniously knocked over, with the dregs of the beer forming a rancid pool on the worn wooden table. It wasn't that Banion was a slob, or a drunk; he just didn't care. The entire focus of his life had been replaced by something sinister; a vengeance that no amount of beer could quench.

The tavern in the small town of Pontiac City was empty. The deranged rancher had spent a quiet afternoon dozing in the sun on the deck of the saloon between the rounds of beer and whiskey shots. He was in a daze, but for the time being, the pain of his loss had subsided.

His large brimmed hat shielded his eyes from the harsh sun. Lazily, he looked around the frontier town. Maybe two hundred people lived in the small town of Pontiac City. It was a traditional town built long after the holocaust, with a rustic cowboy theme embedded in its culture. The town was a crossroads, marking the border between the 'civilized' world and the outlands nearing the great wastelands. Pontiac City harbored mostly cattle ranchers and farmers making a peaceful living. Where many of the towns were known to harbor desperados and violent mercenaries, Pontiac City was different. Quite simply, it was a nice place to live. The most exciting thing that happened each year was the Long Ranch cattle drive, in which over two hundred head of cattle were driven south for the winter. Other than that, the town was dull.

Banion's dark brown eyes were glazed from the brew. He sighed many times and stared out towards the north end of town. As he rested quietly in the bright sun, a formation of lost souls appeared on the northern horizon, heading directly towards the town of Pontiac City. Sitting up, his eyes focused on the ragged crowd moving slowly towards the town.

"Refugees..." Banion slurred. "I guess it's time to sober

up."

Hundreds of refugees in a long, drawn-out formation were trudging forward, their faces displaying a multitude of emotions. War was upon the land, and the first wave of many was on a pilgrimage from a shattered north.

"Want another ale stranger?" a short, wimpy man appeared behind the deranged rancher, speaking softly.

Banion did not reply. The barkeep eyed him suspiciously, but did not say another word. The news on the street of Pontiac City was that the dangerous mercenary gunman had returned to town. Not a soul would tangle with Banion; he was too well known in the northern reaches.

As if in a dream, Banion gazed dully as the formation of people drew closer and closer. As the horde of lost souls became clearer, the mass became individuals. A battered crowd of men, women, and children trudged onward towards the outskirts of town.

The locals of Pontiac City came to the street to watch as hundreds of refugees poured in, stinking like animals and hardly human in their dress. Stories of a war-torn north were circulating within minutes of their arrival. Already, many of the refugees were beginning to recount the Reaper Kai invasion. Fear beset the inhabitants of Pontiac City.

A wild look of hatred covered Banion's face. The war torn rabble was all too familiar to the legendary gunfighter.

A small girl of nearly eight stood quietly in the street, sucking her thumb with a blank expression. The girl's clothes were a mess; her pink dress had been burned in several spots. A thick mass of clotted tissue was on her exposed shoulder in the place where her dress had been burned away and her shoulder charred. She was clutching the hand of an aged man with distinctly different features. It was very apparent that the young girl had lost her entire family and the aged man was just some kind soul that had taken pity on the youth.

Banion's gaze drifted through the crowd. Each refugee had their own unique story with the same outcome: pain.

A young man, finely dressed, was dragging a wooden chair behind him. Banion chuckled at the sight. The chuckle wasn't out of spite, but born of something entirely different. The finely dressed man had definitely lost his mind as a result of what he had gone through, and this made Banion feel a twisted form of kinship with the man.

Banion retreated into his thoughts as his drunken stupor inhabited his fragile mind. A little boy with tears in his eyes and a burned teddy bear in one hand staggered through the crowd trying desperately to find his parents, to no avail; both of the boy's parents had been slain when Plough Stead fell to the robotic armies of the Reaper Kai. The boy was clearly in shock as his little mind fought to find his parents in the mass of people. Finally, a woman crouched down before the boy and took the fearful child into her arms. It appeared the woman was a close family friend, who had decided to take the child in.

As Banion stared at the little boy, dark visions from his own past began to take shape in his mind. Memories of his mother filled him...

A little boy walked back from the edge of the forest. Crunching through the pine needles, he kicked a pinecone and smiled. He almost stumbled, and fought to keep his burden intact, as his small arms were filled with dry branches and kindling. Barely six years old, the boy emerged from the woods and moved through the streets of the village nestled in the northlands of the world.

A crisp chill was in the air. Winter was on the doorstep, only a few days after the Season of the Witch celebration, an event held to honor the great civil war waged long ago against the enemies of the empire.

The boy was in good spirits, and he smiled while running through the streets of the north woods village. As he rumbled onward, pieces of kindling fell from his arms. With a laugh and a bolt of excitement, the young boy caught sight of his mother outside their cabin. He giggled and ran faster.

With a warm smile, young Banion's mother greeted her young son with open arms. The excited Banion dropped his kindling and launched into his mother's arms. She tickled him mercilessly, and he broke into a frantic laughter.

"Ah, Banion," she giggled. A smile was on her face as she lifted the youth off his feet. With a great hug, she spoke once more to the child. "How did a mother get so lucky?" she began to tickle him and he thrashed and giggled.

"Can I have a cookie, Mom?" He gazed at his mother with soft puppy-dog eyes. "A cookie? Well I don't know… you made a mess of the firewood. Pick it up quick and get inside. I'll think about that cookie."

She was graceful and slender, with long, brown, flowing hair that fell about her shoulders, a charming smile, and a pretty delicate face; Banion's mother was a vision of tender love and compassion.

With the hope of getting a homemade cookie, young Banion ran into the house and unloaded the firewood near the hearth.

Suddenly, there was a loud blast. An explosion could be heard, and a curl of smoke rose from a ball of fire near the walls of the forest village. Banion's mother was alarmed by the sound and rushed out the door of the house.

Little did they know that an ancient enemy, one thought to have been eradicated, was about to make a debut after hundreds of years of silence.

"Stay here!" she ordered the small child. Gunfire could be heard, and an odd, mechanical laughter rose from the edge of the village.

Young Banion was shocked by the sounds and sought refuge under the kitchen table in their log cabin. Seconds turned into minutes, and the sounds of conflict grew closer. Worried, the small Banion O'Neil rushed out into the streets in search of his mother. Young Banion was unfortunate, for he reached the streets just in time to see his mother…

With a deliberate shudder, Banion's daydream ended as he shook himself from the nightmare of his past. A tear rolled down his cheek as he whispered a word that only he could hear: 'Mom'.

Banion struggled to expel the horrific vision and remain in control.

"Damn, it hurts…" he whispered as the haze of alcohol coursed through his veins. Even in his drunken stupor, the pain was still there, raw and bleeding, like a needle in his mind.

The refugees crowded into the tavern and any other place they could find in Pontiac City. The town was in an uproar as all the inhabitants clambered to the center of town to hear about the war in the north.

"So the rumors are true?" someone in the crowd shouted.

"The Reaper Kai are really on the attack?"

"The attack? Look at us!" a woman refugee shrieked in response. "Look at us!" The woman's shrieking turned to sobbing and she broke down in a pitiful huddle.

The crowd stared on in horror, and all was silent.

Panic swept the streets. If the northern towns had fallen, there was nothing to stop the Reaper Kai and their robotic army from invading other towns further south. There was news that a militia had formed, and was making raids and guerilla attacks against the Reaper Kai forces. But the militia was too small and too ill equipped to face an enemy of such magnitude. It was only slowing down the main force, not making a significant impact. After all, what could a handful of poorly equipped guerilla fighters do against an army numbering in the thousands?

Finally, the mayor and sheriff of Pontiac City were summoned, and they addressed the refugees in order to gain information about the situation unfolding in the streets.

With a shaky step and a pale face, the mayor took a stand atop the fountain at the center of town. He stood high up above the people, clutching his hands together to ease the tension he was feeling.

"The people of Pontiac City have no quarrel with the Reaper Kai. They will not attack our town. They have no reason to do so." Mayor Grub spoke slowly, his voice tense.

"We had no quarrel with them either!" a refugee yelled from the crowd. "They burned our homes and killed all they saw!"

"My entire family is gone!" a frantic woman screamed in anger and grief.

"We have no reason to fear an attack. We are peaceful," the mayor protested.

Many of the refugees scoffed at the ignorant mayor.

"This town will fall as the others did." A calm voice rose from the crowd. It was direct and devoid of all humanity. The crowd turned to the dark garbed mercenary known as Banion. Many knew of him, and the crowd listened intently to his words, for he was a legendary gunfighter, the stuff of myth and story.

"You cannot know the intentions of the Reaper Kai," the mayor whined.

"I know their intentions. Their goal is absolute. They care nothing of our lives and our peace. They want our land and our very souls." Banion spoke confidently as he addressed the crowd. "They will not stop until every race is eradicated from the Darken Realm. They will create a demonic paradise in which to worship their dark gods for all time. We are nothing to them. They will not stop. They will not barter. They will attack Pontiac City, and they will burn it to the ground and enslave all the survivors."

"You are not in charge here, Banion O'Neil. This is our town, and we will send a diplomat to reason with the Reaper Kai. In the end, we will be spared, and we will live in peace," Mayor Grub spoke in defiance of Banion.

"No, I am not in charge here, but neither are you. You are not in control of this situation, the Reaper Kai are. Their long sleep is over, and their wrath has come." Banion's voice was ominous and full of foreboding. "I urge all of you to evacuate this city and flee further south to the safety of Rasheed. There you will be protected from the Reaper Kai. I urge you all to leave as soon as possible. The enemy is swift, and this city will fall quickly. The Reaper Kai army is pushing its way slowly southward. I fear we have less than a few days before this town falls, as well."

"If you do not stop your poisonous words, mercenary, I will have you arrested!" Grub shouted at Banion.

A laugh erupted from Banion. "You do not have the strength to imprison me. And even if you did, I am not the enemy. The army of mechanical soldiers marching south is."

Banion turned his back to the mayor, and pushed his way through the crowd.

The crowd responded to Banion and Mayor Grub in different ways. The majority of the crowd took Banion's advice, and set out immediately towards home with the intention of leaving. The refugees nodded in agreement with Banion and also decided to continue on to the south.

At the sight of panic filling his citizens, Mayor Grub yelled to the crowd. "Do not trust a mercenary from the wastes! Banion is scum and his words are poison. Stay here and we can reason with them! They have no reason to attack us! Do not fear!" The Mayor swayed many of the crowd, causing them to change their mind. The mayor was right in their eyes. Who was this Banion anyway? A crazed madman? A mercenary that killed for money?

"I don't need to trust a mercenary! I can trust what I saw! The Biogtech army killed many and burned my home!" a refugee yelled in anger with his fist raised towards the mayor. "Trust me and my loss. You must flee," the man shouted at the crowd.

As indecision plagued the crowd in the street, Banion retreated back to the tavern. As he entered, the sheriff of Pontiac City followed him, and sat beside him at the bar.

"What are your plans?" the sheriff asked as he eyed Banion with suspicion. In some places, Banion was a hero, while in others, he was known as a deadly killer.

"I'll stay in here in town until the scouts of the Biogtech army reach us. I'll gauge the might of the army heading south. I must have a better understanding of the enemy if I am to convince King Toil of Rasheed to go to war against the enemy." Banion was filled with anger at the thought of the Biogtech, army but he had a clear plan.

"We aren't gonna make it, are we?" the sheriff asked Banion bluntly.

Banion did not respond; he didn't have to. His silence spoke volumes. Pontiac City was doomed.

Chapter 13
The Deep Nothing

Eight days of travel had taken their toll on the two friends from Scarskin. The endless dunes and burning desert sun were wearing out the youths. The prospect of never escaping the hell-forsaken wasteland was also becoming a reality.

The desert was a relentless foe. The sand dunes were now a menacing threat. Each night, the desert winds would erase any record of their passing. As the days wore on, the dunes looked more and more alike. Had the youths been here before? Were the tribals traveling in a circle? These and other doubts were mounting.

The endless tan dunes of shifting sand were Tani and Jared's only companions since they had left the Badland Rock Spires. The days of travel seemed like an eternity. The Badland Rock Spires were the highlight of the journey thus far, and a horrid highlight at that. From time to time, young Tani would find himself daydreaming, staring off into the desert. The weariness from the long journey, isolation, and the fiery heat of the desert had made Tani, on more than one occasion catch sight of more mutant terrors lumbering across the dunes in search of fresh blood, the blood of the tribals. With a shake of his head, the tribal genius would shrug off the mirage, and take more shaky steps onward, deeper into the desert.

The sun of the eighth day of travel had reduced the tribal's trip to a slow crawl across the burning sands. They progressed step by weary step, slow and deliberate.

It was midday when the sand dunes dissipated, decreasing in size. Beyond the dying dunes was a giant flat expanse. The sand still clung to the floor of the world, but the valley was strangely calm, and oddly enough, not a single sand dune could be seen for miles. This strange sight caught both of the tribals off guard. They could both tell that something unnatural was at work. How could the monstrous dunes be flattened for miles?

"Hold on a minute, Jared," Tani said with an odd tone in his voice.

"Yeah… something isn't right," Jared agreed, his expression concerned. "What happened to the dunes?"

"This landscape is strange. Look at the sand," Tani pointed, as his mind analyzed the road ahead. "Instead of dunes, the earth has been flattened. What could do such a thing?"

Jared squinted into the flat expanse and caught sight of something else which was unusual. Small depressions were in the ground ahead, large circular patches where the flat-combed sand had sunk a few feet.

"What is that?" Jared pointed at one of the circular depressions.

Tani adjusted his wire-rimmed glasses and his brow furrowed. The young genius was inspecting the depressions in the sand with an intense absorption. "I'm not sure," he responded.

"I can't make anything of it." Jared was still concerned, and his hesitation was mounting. "Should we travel around them?"

"The expanse before us is huge. It would take hours to travel around it. With our supply of water dwindling, I doubt we have the luxury of wasting any time." There was a sting in the scholar's voice as he spoke. Jared heard the jab about running out of supplies and brushed it aside.

He let out a large sigh. "Let's get this over with." The young warrior took a step forward into the flat expanse of sand.

Hesitantly, they moved, steering clear and giving wide berth to the circular depressions in the sand. Within a matter of minutes, the tribals were inside the flat expanse. Jared led the way, with Tani only a few paces behind him.

"We are running out of supplies," Tani said, still irritated about the dwindling provisions. After all, the young genius knew better than to travel east into the great wastelands, but he had been too timid to say anything until now. The exhaustion of the last eight days of travel had taken its toll on Tani's psyche, and he was now irked enough to complain.

Jared did not respond. They had both avoided the conversation for days. There were only about another day or two of provisions left.

"We will find food and water soon." Jared spoke with confidence.

"Really?   You see a town out here or something?"   the scholar was sarcastic, and Jared rolled his eyes as Tani spoke.

The two companions continued on in silence for half an hour.   Neither of them spoke of the despair they were both beginning to fear.   The thought of running out of provisions was becoming a real threat.   Less than two days of food remained, and there was no end to the desert in sight.   Suddenly, Jared interrupted the long silence.

"Coyotes are smart, right?"   Jared was smiling, his gaze transfixed just south of where the two were traveling.   There was a glimmer in his eye as he stared at a patch of sand.

"Yeah, I guess," Tani replied in a somewhat mystified tone. He was growing weary of Jared, and simply rolled his eyes in disgust.   The young scholar was in no mood for games.

"A coyote would not be caught out here in the desert without a close supply of water, right?"   Jared pressed.

"Yeah, I guess.   What are you getting at?"   Tani was irritated, but decided to listen with half an interest and half a care.

Jared bolted several steps south. He moved with glee in his eyes.   Something had caught his gaze.   Tani saw the hope on his face and became interested.

Jared moved quickly, and then stopped, grinning widely. The young tribal shifted back his ponytail and pointed at the ground before him.   Crouching down in the sand, he smiled again.   Jared looked back at Tani and pointed to a set of tracks in the sand. "Maybe not a coyote after all, but a small dog or fox of some sort."

Tani was excited by the find, and rushed to his companion's side.   They both stared at the set of fresh tracks in the sand.   The tracks pushed towards the northeast through the oddly formed flat open expanse.

"They lead through a patch of earth with those strange gouges in the sand."   Tani spoke in dismay, pointing at the odd indentations in the sand.

"Oh, don't worry so much! Those pits are nothing to worry about. All we need to worry about is where the tracks lead. The beast is probably on its way to water. We can follow it," Jared responded excited.

With that, the tribals moved off towards the northeast, tracking the desert coyote.   Their pace quickened, and they were almost dashing after the trail of tracks. Quickly, the two moved with a sense of accomplishment. Hope filled them as they both fantasized desperately that the tracks would lead them to water, and maybe even to some food. An hour passed, and the two companions followed the tracks deeper into the strange valley. The further they pushed, the more frequent the indentations in the sand became.

The burning sun mocked and taunted the youths. It shone bright upon them and assaulted them without mercy. The heat was almost unbearable and the weary tribals were sweating away drop after drop of precious water. The temperature rose to a burning point, and the two were in a trance from the heat. They simply watched the tracks with dull fascination, hurtling faster and faster after them. The tracks meandered back and forth, leading Jared and Tani deeper and deeper into the valley.

Like a shattered dream, the tracks ended abruptly. Both the companions halted uneasily and stared about. Scanning ahead, both noted that the tracks ended at the edge of one of the strange pits littering the valley floor. Blinking as if a perverse magic trick had occurred, Tani and Jared looked around them, wondering where the tracks had gone, where the animal that had left them had gone. Their search was to no avail; the animal tracks had vanished in a single step.

"It's as if the desert swallowed the animal whole. Look at how the tracks end at the edge of this pit. What do you think it is? Some sort of sink hole?" Jared stared around him in confusion. In every direction, they could see more of the depressions in the sand. The depressions became suddenly sinister. Panic set in, and both of the tribals whirled around in a circle. Everywhere they looked, more pits spread out beyond them in every direction. They were surrounded by the strange depressions in the sand.

"I have an odd idea, Jared..." Tani's voice trailed off.

Suddenly, the sand began to stir. There was a tremor, and both companions fell silent. A bulge appeared in the sand at the center of the pit. Two large pincers erupted from the sand at the center of the hole. An insect head emerged, and a set of antennas flipped outward, probing the air and sand. An odd chattering erupted from the submerged creature as its mandibles ground together.

The tribals fell silent and dared not move. They did not even dare to breathe. More bulges appeared on the ground. The sand rippled all around the two. As if many burrowing beasts were on the way, several rippling trails of sand approached from all directions, each bulge emanating from a nearby depression in the sand.

The two remained motionless with fear, eyeing the bulging sand in terror. The bulges moved towards them, and then suddenly stopped.

"What do we do now?" Jared asked in a low tone.

As Jared spoke, the creature in the pit moved up the slope toward him. The bulges in the sand moved once again towards the companions. Strange clicking could be heard as more subterranean terrors moved closer and closer.

A wild thought came to Tani. His green eyes scanned the strange insect creatures with suspicion. Finally, his eyes lit up, and he motioned to young Jared.

Jared understood the signal and fell silent. With fear rising in his heart, he scanned the territory around him while his hand dropped to the hilt of the mighty Scar Blade. As soon as the young warrior fell silent, the bulges in the sand stopped moving towards them.

Tani had an idea: the beasts probably hunted by sound or vibration in the sand. His green eyes moved to each pit in turn. He nodded, and another thought came to his mind: each pit was a lair in the sand. Each pit was the home of a subterranean menace. The creatures must have smoothed the entire valley. It was some sort of homemaking. Irregular shaped dunes would make it difficult to discern the direction of movement, while a flat, open stretch of sand would aid the creature in hunting its prey. It all made perfect sense. Jared and Tani had wandered into some sort of mutant insect colony, and this valley was their hunting ground. When the two spoke or made noise, the creatures were lured from their lairs to feed.

"Fascinating..." Tani's mind was swimming as he thought about the insects now stalking them. *"Evolution at its finest. What a miraculous creature."*

The two companions remained silent, standing motionless on the sand. Patience was their ally. They waited for what felt like ages, until, at last, the bulges in the sand moved back to their respective lairs. The mighty insect only a few yards away slunk back into the center of the sand pit.

Using a primitive set of signs and hand signals, Jared and Tani communicated. They both decided to remain quiet for a time, and then leave the pit slowly and quietly.

It seemed like an eternity but they were willing to hold their ground for as long as necessary.

Tani motioned to Jared and Jared nodded in recognition, understanding that the time had come to move away slowly and softly. They had only taken a few steps when the beast reared up once again from the center of the pit. The strange clicking noise erupted once more, and the sand stirred. Many other insect beasts began to tunnel towards the two. Seeing the advance of the subterranean menaces, they stopped instantly. When their own movements stopped, the bulges in the sand stopped as well.

The situation was not getting any better. Tani shook his head in dismay and Jared pointed to his sword at his waist. Tani's expression grew horrified as he looked at Jared about to pull his blade. Tani shook his head, 'no!'

Jared had a wild impulse to fight all the beasts with his blade. The plan would be futile, and Tani convinced him of this by using hand signals and a stern look of horror. Not knowing what else to do, the companions stood motionless again for a time.

The sun disappeared from the world behind the western horizon. The chill of the night began to cool the travel–worn companions, granting them mild comfort. Though they were no longer sweating, their peril was by no means diminished.

As the darkness took the wastelands, a wind rolled from the western expanse. The sand stirred and swirled about. With a hiss, it rolled and heaved.

As the wind pushed the sand and the hiss rose in the waste, the bulges in the sand began to move in random directions. The noise was too much to bear or interpret, and the strange creatures were confused. The beast in the pit moved back and forth, not knowing what to do.

Tani had a gleam in his eye. He spoke softly to Jared. "The wind is distracting the beasts. Walk away softly, but do not run. While the wind blows, they are distracted by all the noise and they can't hunt." As he talked, the beasts did not draw near, moving about in seemingly random directions instead. Jared agreed to Tani's plan.

With slow steps, the two moved softly. Taking caution to avoid the pits, the tribals from Scarskin pushed on.

The wind continued, and the two companions escaped the lurking menaces in the sand. Within an hour, they left the flat valley and the pits hiding the insect beasts.

As they exited the valley, they paused briefly to turn around and survey the valley. They both shook their heads and let out a sigh of relief.

"It's a good thing the wind started blowing," Jared said triumphantly. Tani simply wrinkled his forehead and shot his friend a look of disgust. "I was about to slay all the beasts!" Jared said in an arrogant tone.

Tani shook his head. "Yeah, good thing!" his tone was sarcastic, and Jared didn't appreciate it much.

"Now what do we do?" Jared asked, with a hint of embarrassment.

"Well, the coyote was heading northeast, so I say we travel in that general direction. The coyote was probably in search of food or water."

"Yeah, that's what I was thinking, too." Jared had not actually thought the same thing, but he was too proud to admit otherwise. In reality, Jared had no course of action whatsoever.

"You were thinking that, too?" Tani pressed his friend with a furrowed brow.

"Well, yeah," the warrior affirmed. Tani rolled his eyes.

The night had fully engulfed the desert. With weary feet, the companions traveled two more hours, wanting to put as much distance between themselves and the accursed valley. The tribals made camp and rested uneasily until the sun once again rose in the east.

Chapter 14
Despair in the Desert

Burning sun, endless days of heat without shelter. The wastes had become a prison for the two tribals from Scarskin. It was a prison made of their own weary thoughts and empty desires. Desires to drink water and be safe from the burning air and grueling climate, desires to be home and away from the harsh world.

Neither Jared nor Tani had spoken the entire day. When the sun rose, the two companions each finished the last of their rations. The water was nearly gone. Only a few cool sips remained in Tani's water bladder.

The sun was nearly in the center of the sky. Tani was angry and resentful as he walked behind Jared. Thin lines of sweat continually rolled down Tani's face, and many drops fell and collected inside his wire-rimmed glasses. With annoyed sighs, the young scholar would remove his glasses and wipe them dry with a dirty rag from his pocket. The process would begin again, and Tani fought a constant battle just to keep his own sweat from collecting upon his glasses.

Staring with contempt and loathing, Tani trudged onward, trying to shake off the thought of strangling Jared for getting them into this situation.

"I cannot believe we are out here! In the middle of nowhere! For what? Why the hell are we out here?" Tani's mind was filled with fury as angry thoughts bounced around his mind. It would be a miracle if they survived the desert. The young scholar's anger was turning to an adolescent rage. He stomped onward without saying a word. *"We are going to die out here!"*

Jared was scared, but didn't want to admit it to himself or Tani. The young warrior had finished the last of his water an hour ago. Already, his lips were beginning to crack and wither under the heat of the desert. The young warrior tried to force the thought of water out of his mind. But the more he tried to discard his desires for a nice cool, wet drink, the more it drove him crazy. Each passing moment propelled him further and further towards a fantasy world, a world focused on a swim in the local Scarskin waterhole.

Finally, the young genius spoke angrily. "We need to rest." The statement was assertive, not open to debate.

"Fine," Jared rasped in an equally angry tone.

"Mogi is insane. He recommends traveling in the desert during the day. What a ridiculous idea. If we traveled at night, we wouldn't consume as much water!" Tani was irked, and decided to take it out on someone who wasn't there.

"Yeah," Jared sighed. "But he always said the desert is a dangerous place to travel at night with sink holes and such."

"Yeah," Tani said, resting quietly on the sand. There was an ominous pause in his voice. He stared dreamily into the open desert. Finally, he spoke. "We are going to die out here."

There was another moment of complete silence between the two. The realization had also filled Jared. The young warrior also believed the lack of supplies was going to kill them. The thirst was already beginning to take Jared. It had only been an hour since he drank the last of his water, but the thirst was already consuming his every thought.

"We can last another day without water." Jared was uncertain but tried to sound cheerful.

"The desert can suck every ounce of moisture from a body in less than two days. The victim is essentially desiccated and mummified. With any luck, our dried husks will still be laying out here when the next idiot from Scarskin decides to travel east," Tani blurted out harshly.

Jared didn't respond. His own blood was about to boil over, but he was too proud to admit that he was wrong. It was a mistake to travel east. Jared could admit it to himself, but not to his best friend. Fear of dying in the desert was taking over.

Sighing heavily, Jared said, "Let's ignore Master Mogi today. Let's set up the shelter and sleep out the rest of the day. When the moon rises..." As he thought about the moon, he fell silent. The moon was the symbol of their strife. The two had to be exiled twenty moons. He laughed slightly. 'Twenty moons?' he thought. They weren't going to survive long enough to see the first full moon rise. "When the moon rises, we will set out again. We will head northeast, in the direction of the coyote tracks we found yesterday. With luck, we will find shelter and water."

Tripwire, the young genius did not respond. He was quietly setting up the white tent. The two companions proceeded to take quick naps here and there throughout the afternoon.

The day wore on slowly. The tent was little comfort against the harsh temperatures of the baking desert. Off and on, they thought about their doom, but did not speak of it.

Finally, their harsh enemy, the sun, crashed below the western horizon. The blazing desert rapidly dropped in temperature. The two companions rose from the tent and made ready to depart in search of water and food.

Tani tilted back his head and drank the last few gulps of his water. As the cool water rolled down his dry throat, he wondered if it was the last water he would ever drink. He shuddered at the thought, and returned his empty water bladder to his pack.

With dazed looks, the two companions stared at each other in the dim light, neither of them smiling.

Jared led the way, and Tani followed a few paces back. Heading northeast, the two continued in the dim light of the moon. It was a crescent moon, and the two stared in dismay at its presence. The moon seemed to mock them. It was a silent enemy, which waged a constant war against their moral. For they must see twenty full moons before they would be welcomed back to their home in Scarskin.

Jared was weary, and suffering from a dull, throbbing headache. The lack of water had turned him into a walking zombie, staggering as if each step was his last. His joints ached, and his blood seemed to thicken. With each beat of his heart, the throbbing in his body seemed to intensify. Each step seemed like a marathon. He staggered onward, dizziness filling him. His conscious mind began to fail, and he walked onward without realizing that he was beginning to die of thirst.

As Tani worried about Jared, a sick set of scenarios played out in his mind. *Which of the two would die first? Would Jared be the first to go, leaving Tani to stagger onward alone? Would the young scholar succumb the harsh desert environment first? Would Jared bury him if he died first?* Tani shook his head, forcing the thoughts from his mind. Fear was the last thing the two needed.

Slowly the young tribals walked through the cool, but dry

night air. Even though the temperature in the desert had dropped greatly, the tribals still thirsted fiercely. With numb thoughts, Jared and Tani pressed on.

A few more hours passed, and Jared could barely move further. He swayed back and forth from time to time, almost on the verge of collapse. The young genius hurried to his side and supported him. With hope gone, the two continued to move onward slowly through the chill night air.

Jared was on the edge of ruin. Tani was wearing thin trying to help his weak friend continue. The moon was past its apex, and was heading to the horizon and the dark lands beyond.

Suddenly, a strange glimmer emerged in the young genius' eyes. A frantic panicked mania covered Tani's face. A shrill laughter echoed through the night air. Tani laughed hysterically, falling to his knees and groping wildly at the desert sand.

Jared collapsed on the cold sand and looked oddly at his companion. The young warrior was barely able to walk, let alone comprehend the bizarre behavior of his companion. Tani turned to Jared, and in the moonlight, held a small green root between his fingers.

The zombie-like, blank expression on Jared's face turned to disbelief, and a look of excitement coursed through him. Mustering the last of his strength, Jared rose to his feet and moved to behold the small green plant in Tani's hand.

"A Creeper Sprig!" Tani said excitedly. Jared was elated as well, and for good reason. The two tribals had both seen Creeper Sprigs all their lives. And they both knew that Creeper Sprigs only grew close to the town well back in Scarskin.

Hope had returned. Suddenly, Jared caught the scent of moist air nearby. Moving quickly, the two friends crested a tall dune and looked down upon a welcome sight. In the dim light of the setting moon, the two beheld a great pool of water, surrounded by a stand of mighty desert trees.

"Bless the ancestors!" Tani exclaimed.

Jared stumbled down the hill, and Tani followed close behind. The two reached the edge of the pool and Tani knelt down, hurriedly rummaging through his backpack. A small electrical gadget emerged from his pack and was set near the water, emitting a slow series of clicks. Tani clapped his hands together.

"Background radiation only! The water is clean! It's not contaminated!" he shouted in excitement.

As soon as the young warrior heard his friend speak, Jared plunged his entire head into the pool of water. The cold blast was reviving, jolting the youth back from the verge of death. Yelling wildly, Jared plunged into the waters and let the icy blast restore him to life. Splashing about like a child, he scooped several mouthfuls of water and drank them down quickly.

Tani fell to his knees and ran his fingers through the water, his mind elated by the find. With a broad smile upon his face, he scooped water with both hands and drank a refreshing gulp of water. The instant it hit his throat, his soul sang. The fear was gone.

Hope had returned. With the fear of death a fading memory, peace filled their hearts. The dismay was gone and tragedy was avoided.

"We made it!" Jared yelled in excitement, still splashing around like a fool. "You hear me, Mogi?" The young warrior yelled into the night. "We made it!"

Tani smiled and sat near the edge of the pool. The insane journey through the burning wasteland was far from over, but the tribals had succeeded where so many others had failed. By some miracle, the youths had escaped the dangers of the desert and made it to an oasis, a paradise secluded in the barren, ruined wastelands. It was victory.

It didn't take long for the euphoria of finding the oasis to wear off as the fatigue of a long day set in. Drowsy and exhausted from a long day, with the anxiety of death abated, the tribals rolled out their sleeping mats and fell into a deep slumber.

In their dreams, a sense of accomplishment filled them. They had made it across the burning waste and had pushed further east than any of their tribe ever had.

Chapter 15
Prince Jared of the Scarskin Tribe

Jared awoke suddenly to find a polished, razor-sharp spear point pressed against his throat. He sat up slowly to find dark skinned nomads clothed in white surrounding him. Tani sat quietly a few feet away with his hands on his knees. The contents of their backpacks had been strewn all about. Over a dozen strong warriors surrounded the two.

With dark brown skin and dark brown eyes, the nomads stood silently and defiantly. Long white flowing robes covered their bodies. Round white cloth headdresses adorned their heads. The spears they wielded were wooden save the point, which was steel and very sharp. The warriors were obviously desert worn and accustomed to traveling in the open wastes.

The nomads continued to rummage through the tribals' belongings. Tani's gear was strewn about. His explosives and his laptop were near the water; apparently, the nomads didn't know what they were looking at. His other electrical devices were untouched as well, and had been spread about on the sand.

The nomads then got to Jared's pack and belongings. It didn't take long for a warrior to find the ancient sword that Jared carried. The warrior looked oddly at the finely crafted scabbard. With a tug, the blade slid free. Its blue metallic sheen erupted as it cleared the scabbard. A gasp of excitement rolled through the crowd.

All of the warriors pointed and talked amongst themselves. Their speech was an unintelligible chatter of clicks, chirps, and grunts. They were clearly excited by finding Jared's mighty weapon. Immediately, excitement rolled through all the nomads and they clambered around to catch a glimpse of the strange blade. Chattering in his strange language, the nomad holding the blade shouted and turned away from Jared. Within a matter of seconds, a tall man garbed in blue moved into view with a petite dark skinned woman.

The man was larger than the others, and clothed in blue and white desert robes. His eyes were harsh, and did not waver. The chieftain stared at Jared with suspicion. With a serious look, the nomad chief stroked his long gray beard and grabbed the mighty Scar Blade from the nomad warrior. He grunted as he inspected the legendary sword of Scarskin. The tribals remained prone upon the sand and looked at the chief with concern. The leader was tough, strong, and not one to be messed with. He was definitely in charge of the situation, and the two tribals knew it.

Tani's eyes widened as he stared at the nomad leader. As if in a dream, the young genius caught sight of a firearm on his belt. Tani stared intently; he had read about guns, but had never actually seen one. A fascination washed over him as he stared at the gun strapped to the nomad leader's waist.

The chief regarded the two tribals at length. He looked at each in turn, summing up young Tani first and young Jared second. Finally, the chief held the mighty Scar Blade and moved towards Jared with a look of suspicion. His advisor followed, and they stood very near Jared. Jared regarded them indifferently.

The nomad chief stared intently at Jared while his female advisor moved forward. The advisor was a small woman dressed in a white blouse, blue skirt and a bright purple flowing sash about her waist. A collection of scrolls, maps, and a telescope hung from her belt. The advisor's face was lean, and beginning to crack with age.

"Batug wutag alang gallae," the woman spoke in the direction of the tribals from Scarskin. Jared looked oddly at Tani. Tani shrugged, unable to decipher the language.

"Shano grutbeiden alles ratonhula," she pronounced once again, staring at the two from Scarskin.

"I don't know what she said, but it sounds like a derivation from an ancient tongue," Tani said to Jared while staring at the woman. "It seems familiar, but I can't quite figure it out."

"Ah, you speak Drokanish," the woman stated finally, her voice heavily accented.

"Umm, I guess," Jared answered in a confused tone.

"We thought all the Drokans had been eradicated." She eyed them suspiciously.

"We are not 'Drokans'," Tani said, trying to pronounce the unknown race as the woman scribe had pronounced it.

"Then where else could you be from? We are at the very edge of the world. There is nothing for many days travel in any direction. From what land do you hail?" The scribe spoke while the nomad chief stood silently, listening intently to the conversation. There was a vague sense of recognition on the chief's face as he listened. It was apparent to the tribals that he understood the conversation, at least partially. Between exchanges, the advisor would still translate for the chief.

Tani shot Jared a glance of warning, and Jared heeded the distress in his friend's stare. He wavered a minute, then finally spoke. "We are from the south," Jared lied.

"The south?" She pressed with an uneasy look in her eye.

"Yeah, the south," Tani confirmed. Since the two tribals did not know with whom they were dealing, and they didn't want to give away the location of Scarskin. Jared and Tani were both uneasy with the nomads who were still surrounding them with spears at the ready.

The chief spoke in his native tongue to his advisor. She looked thoughtfully at her master and then finally nodded when he was done speaking.

"My master wishes to know if you are a king." She looked directly at Jared while holding the mighty Scar Blade in her hand.

A wild idea formed in Tani's mind. Without warning, the young genius blurted out a quick response. "Yes, he is a prince, a very powerful prince from our nation in the south," Tani interjected, as Jared stared at him uneasily. "I am his advisor and scribe."

"Do your servants always speak for you, prince?" the woman pressed, still unconvinced by the lie. Her eyes narrowed as she stared at young Jared.

"Uh..." Jared wavered. "He is allowed to speak for me when he sees fit." Jared's face was turning bright red.

"I see." The woman advisor eyed them.

The chief moved forward and spoke in his native tongue; he grabbed the sword from his female scribe and returned it to Jared. Neither of the tribals understood what the nomad chief had said, but he seemed less suspicious of the two. Seeing the gesture of their leader, the nomads lowered their spears and allowed Jared and Tani to rise to their feet.

"You must be the son of a king," the scribe translated the

king's words. "I have never seen such a weapon in all my years in the desert."

Jared nodded in respect to the chief as he took possession of the mighty Scar Blade. Tani mirrored the gesture, first to the chief, and then to the female scribe.

"We noticed you are devoid of provisions." The chief spoke quietly to Jared in a heavily accented and choppy tone. The chief had a basic understanding of the tribals' language, and was making an attempt to communicate. He continued to let the scribe translate the majority of his speech. "If you will tell us of your journey, you can feast with us tonight in this oasis."

Though Jared was young and somewhat arrogant, he was very respectful of the chief, bowing before him as he spoke. "Your invitation is most welcome."

The chief boomed with laughter and moved forward. He placed his hand on Jared's shoulder. He issued a command, and his nomad guards knelt down and placed all of their gear back in their respective packs. "I hope you are not too offended. We are suspicious of all travelers, especially at the edge of the world. Come, we will rest through the heat of the day!"

As they walked, Jared turned to Tani and spoke under his breath. "You were right all these years, Tani. People do exist beyond the eastern waste."

"I have never been so happy to see people in all my life, Jared," Tani responded, and his words spoke volumes. The nomads had startled the two tribals earlier on, but they were filled with hope to find people living east of the great wastes.

Jared and Tani followed the nomad chief and his entourage. They walked behind a stand of tall green plants, and found that nearly a hundred nomads had made camp in the shelter of the oasis. About fifty camels were tethered around the waterhole. Many white tents had sprung up. Small children ran and splashed in the water. Women roamed about with wicker baskets, chattering in their native language. Strong men garbed in white stood around the edge of the camp, each with a spear in hand.

Jared and the scholar Tani were ushered into a dark blue tent in the center of the camp. The tent was large and cool on the interior. It was early morning, but the shelter was welcome, no matter the time of day.

Exquisite woven rugs lined the floor of the tent, which was also furnished with wicker chairs and pillows. A basket of red fruit was near a mighty chair in the tent. The chief moved to the wooden throne and sat down. As he did, several servants rushed forward and offered him both water and meal. The chief waved his hand; Jared and Tani sat on the pillows near the throne. When the female advisor joined them, she smiled and chose to sit right next to young Tani.

The day wore on at a comfortable pace. Young Jared and Tani felt better the longer they spent in the company of the chief. It was a relief that the two had made it east across the deadly expanse. The nomads were excellent company, and they exchanged stories the entire day. Jared spoke of the white mutants they had encountered in the desert. The chief called the mutants the 'Malg', and stated it was not uncommon to come across them. Tani related the story of the strange subterranean predators in the open flat valley. The chief smiled and called the two 'clever' for escaping them unscathed.

The sun set in the desert, and the nomad tribe had a banquet to honor their new friend: 'Prince Jared of Scarskin'. After the banquet, the chief ushered the two once again into his tent. The scribe was also invited, and they resumed speaking about their travels. All others were forced to leave the tent. Only the chief, the nomad advisor, Jared, and Tani remained in the tent.

"We know that you lied about the location of your village. There is nothing south of here for many days of travel. We have never seen your kind anywhere in this area. We know you are neither from the north nor the east. We also know that the world stops here, and there is nothing west of here. The language you speak is not pure Drokan but is close to it. We are curious about where you came from," the chief said, trying to unravel the mystery of the youths, and speaking both to the tribals and to his scribe, in order to help her translate.

Jared and Tani looked at each other and nodded. "We have come across the great void. The far west is where our home lies," Tani replied, stunning the nomad chief.

"That is not possible, nothing lies to the west." It was as if the chief was seeing a ghost as he spoke. There was a look of disbelief in his eye, as if he was staring at a legendary pair of heroes.

"Our scouts have traveled many days west, and have never found anything but endless desert."

"This is madness, but it makes sense. Their garb and speech is strange, and we have never seen anything like them all the years in the desert. However unlikely, it must be true!" the female scribe said excitedly.

"How long was your crossing?" the chief asked, eyeing them curiously. "Do not worry; your secret will stay in this tent."

Jared and Tani believed him. Tani nodded to Jared, and the young warrior spoke. "Ten days it took us to cross the desert. We braved fierce storms, mutants, and starvation to get here."

"Ten days in the open desert!" The chief was astounded. "Never have I heard such a story. The desert is covered with ruins and shelter east of here. No cache of water is further than two days travel. I thought our land was bleak, but the wasteland to the west sounds horrid."

"It is. I felt many times that we should have perished out in the wasteland," Tani replied, looking at both chief and scribe.

"All this time, we felt the west was empty and devoid of life. And all this time, civilization has been continuing." The female scribe shook her head in disbelief.

"All this time, we thought nothing existed east of our village, and here we are," Jared stated.

"What brings you out to the desert? Why brave such peril?" the scribe quizzed the two from Scarskin.

"A rite of passage in our village is known as the Exile. At our age, we are cast from our village for twenty full moons. In that time, we learn about the world beyond our borders, and return home as men fit to live in our society," Tani explained, and the scribe was impressed with his speech and intellect. "We find relics of the old world and bring them back so Scarskin can grow strong."

"A noble pilgrimage," the chief nodded. "If you would teach us of your travel across the western waste, we will tell you all we know of this land."

Jared and Tani agreed, and the company of four spent the rest of the cool evening speaking of far off lands and distant cultures. A friendship was forged between the youths from Scarskin and the nomad tribe. In the end, the chief agreed to take the tribals to a distant part of the land known as the 'Frontier'.

Chapter 16
The Vision Comes to Pass

Mineera, Globulus, and two Rasheed commandos sat quietly at a table near the back of the tavern. The blood red robes Mineera wore covered her face from view. Weariness had taken control of all at the table, and not a single word was spoken between the four. Half-eaten meals lined the table, and a blank expression lined the faces of its occupants.

Mineera, dark Reaper Kai witch, suddenly rose from the table. "Be at the ready, we are under attack!" No one had yet attacked them, but Mineera seemed to have some sort of precognition about the event.

Globulus and the two soldiers were confused and remained in their chairs. All three thought the dark psychic had lost her mind.

Suddenly, a blast of gunfire rose through the dark tavern. All other patrons hit the floor. The gunfire struck and shattered the mighty hippo's beer stein. The shattered pottery crashed to the table. Instantly, the mighty hippo rose and pulled out a sawed off shotgun. The huge and beastly hippo was so large that he palmed the weapon as a human would palm a pistol.

"To arms!" Globulus yelled as he leveled the weapon at several gunmen who had burst through the front door of the tavern.

Globulus aimed the weapon at the first of three hired mercenaries. With a calm gesture, he pulled the trigger, and the sawed off shotgun boomed in his hand. The blast was well placed, and the charging gunman took the burst of pellets in his chest. His momentum carried him midway across the tavern before he died from the gunshot wounds.

The other two mercenaries spread out and fired a spray of automatic weapon fire. The two Rasheed commandos hit the deck just as Globulus took two rounds in his chest. His thick, bestial, leather skin stopped the bullets from causing severe damage; only a small trickle of blood erupted from the wounds. Grunting with a wild look in his eye, the mighty mutant hippo let the adrenaline of combat flow through his veins like a burst of wild fire.

Not caught up in the fear of combat, Mineera closed her eyes and concentrated. The rip and roar of the battle around her was pushed from her thoughts. With a wiggle of her fingers, the traitor of the Reaper Kai channeled mystic energy through her being. A pale spark emerged as her fingers rotated in a circle. The pale light rose in intensity, and a bubble of blue spiritual energy engulfed the psychic maiden. Mineera stood calmly in the center of the room. The bullets rammed into a blue barrier of mystical energy surrounding the psychic. The Reaper Kai traitor was unharmed; her psychic abilities had shielded her from the intense firefight.

As the gunfire hummed and tore the tavern to shredded flecks of splintered lumber, Globulus was on the move. He strode forward, pushing tables and chairs out of his way as he charged. With a scream of rage, the hippo mutant bulldozed through the bar. Finally, he crashed into a mercenary trembling at the sound of the charging menace. The mercenary was shocked, and halted dead in his tracks. A look of fear flashed through his eyes as his submachine gun lay still at his side. Globulus did not falter, and closed the gap instantly. With a loud grunt, the one-ton beast picked the mercenary off his feet. A grotesque crunch could be heard as the hippo throttled the hapless mercenary. Like a rag doll, the mercenary was cast to the floor with both neck and spinal column horribly mangled.

The last of the three mercenaries fled while firing a spray of gunfire. He edged backwards while laying down a suppressing fire. Mineera was not impressed. Pulling the hand axe free from her crimson robe, Mineera pulled the weapon back behind her head. With a grunt, she hurled the deadly weapon at her foe. The axe moved through the air with frightening accuracy while somersaulting end over end. The mercenary tried to dodge the projectile, but his efforts were in vain. In mid-air, the axe changed course under the unseen will of the psychic maiden, ramming into the mercenary, making him fall to the floor in a spastic whimper of death.

In the blink of an eye, all was still. The three mercenaries lay dead on the floor of the tavern. The other tavern patrons had fled the establishment in horror at the beginning of the battle. Not even the owner remained in his own bar.

The remnants of the Rasheed team looked around uneasily, scanning the tavern for more foes. There were none to be seen. One of the Rasheed commandos was dead; his lifeless body was lying against the wall. The enemy mercenary gunfire had struck him dead in the exchange.

The other remaining commando crouched on the floor clutching his chest with blood dripping from between his fingers. He had obviously suffered a deep chest wound. The blood pulsed between his fingers as he tried to stop its flow. The wound was too great, and the commando fell into a slumber from which he would never awake.

Knowing the horror of war all too well, Globulus didn't even attempt to see if the two commandos had survived. He knew they were dead simply by sight. Mineera and Globulus looked on, disheartened. The two Rasheed commandos were dead leaving only the traitorous witch and the mutant hippo alive.

"You were right, witch. I don't know how such a thing could be true, but you were right. Your vision was a portent of the future that should not have been ignored. Now, more of my companions have fallen." Globulus shook his head in despair while he eyed the red robed Reaper Kai traitor in suspicion. "Too many good men have died on your account."

Mineera was sullen, looking at the dead commandos with a mixture of grief and guilt.

"My gift is a curse. I am forever bound to my dreams of the future. No matter what I do, I cannot change fate. All I dream comes to pass." Mineera was soft spoken; the hood of her robe hid her eyes.

The mighty mutant hippo moved across the room and searched the dead mercenary team. He quickly found what he was looking for; a tattered note was in the pocket of the lead mercenary. The note was a notice of death, and Mineera was the target.

"It is as I feared. They were here for you. The enemy despises you and will stop at nothing to until you are dead." Globulus spoke with an agitated tone. In his opinion, this woman was not worth the price of all the good men who had fallen on her behalf.

Mineera could sense the hippo's feelings, but did not respond. In her heart, she felt guilty enough for all who had died to liberate her.

"We should not stay here any longer. The enemy is on our trail, and there are many more days of travel ahead of us. We will camp in the forest tonight." Globulus moved towards the door. Mineera did not follow; she stood quietly surveying the dead Rasheed commandos.

"We should respect the dead and bury them." Her voice was haunting and chilling.

Globulus halted dead in his tracks and a chill ran down his spine. "What?"

"We should bury the dead."

"Since when do the dread Reaper Kai bury the dead and pay respect to anything but their own selfish wants?" the hippo pressed with an angry tone. "Time is short; the soldiers fought bravely and gave their lives for you and Rasheed. Do not let their deaths be in vain. Our goal was your safe return to our city. If we do not make haste, the enemy will put an end to both of us, and the war will go bitterly. We need your knowledge if we are to survive."

Mineera still held her ground, and Globulus admitted defeat. "So be it," he said, and then shouted to the owner of the tavern, who was cowardly looking in the front door, "Come here now!"

The tavern owner meekly approached the mutant hippo.

"Make sure my friends are properly buried. The other three you can cast into a ditch, and let crows pick their corpses clean. Here is some money for your trouble." With that, the hippo handed the tavern owner a few silver coins. The tavern owner nodded, and Globulus stared at Mineera with an irritated glower upon his beastly face.

"They are all to be buried, even the mercenary gunmen," she decreed, and moved through the room filled with the dead.

Globulus sighed, agitated but gave in to her demands. Looking at the barkeep, he spoke, "Bury them all." With that, Globulus and Mineera made haste to escape the area before more enemy agents came calling.

The two moved into the darkness and left the border town behind them, traveling for an hour under cover of darkness before weariness took them. They halted in a small stand of trees and made camp.

"I will take watch until the sun rises, for even though I am tired beyond measure, I cannot sleep after the loss of my soldiers. Guilt and remorse are my only companions this night," the mighty hippo spoke.

Mineera did not respond, and slunk into the darkness away from the fire, hiding in the shadows and coolness of the night. Secluded in her thoughts, the psychic maiden cast her gaze towards the heavens and the twinkling stars of the night sky. The cool air brushed across her face as a sorrow filled her. She wept under the darkness of the sky. Warm tears flowed down her face. As the sorrow and guilt flooded her consciousness, weariness began to take her, and she drifted slowly into a world of shattered dreams. With a heavy heart, she fell into an uneasy slumber, and dreamt a dream that she had seen so many times before...

As the dream tore at her soul, Mineera thrashed back and forth, mumbling softly. The event was playing itself out once more, and it was taking its toll. Globulus listened to the sounds of her unrest with a sick fascination, trying to divert his attention, then succumbing once more. Mineera was a horrific accident that the mighty hippo wanted to avoid, but was too damn interesting to ignore. Mumbling softly in the darkness, she called out repeatedly in a haunting whisper. "Banion... Banion..." A chill rolled down his spine. Having spent a lifetime in the service of Rasheed, Globulus knew all too well the gunfighter known as Banion. His suspicion rose and he began to fear her. What was her fascination with the crazed mercenary known as Banion? How could she possibly know the reckless gunfighter?

With indecision filling him, Globulus shuddered in the darkness, listening to her tormented dreams unfold. She thrashed about a few more times and her dreams ended.

Mineera sat up and looked around with a dazed look upon her face. "Who are you? Why do I dream of you every night?" she asked in a dreamy voice, thinking of the dream she had seen so many times before. The darkness did not answer. The stars continued to twinkle, but did not answer.

Globulus heard the witch whisper in the dark. The madness had taken her once again, he thought. In the beginning, he had hated her, but as of late, seeing the torment inside her, he felt pity instead. He looked at her in the darkness as she spoke to the shadows. The wind rose suddenly, and the hippo thought he heard a voice in the wind, a faint voice calling to her. He shuddered, and a chill rolled down his spine. And then, all fell silent and the night continued.

Chapter 17
A Quiet Truce

For the length of two full moons, Jared and Tani traveled with the nomad tribe. They learned much about the desert and the world beyond their village. By young Tani's request, the nomads brought the tribals from Scarskin to the edge of the desert, to a realm known as 'The Frontier'.

The Frontier was a place of strife. The chief of the nomads urged the two youth to stay with them, but Tani thought otherwise. The young genius was interested in what lay beyond. The nomad chief stated the The Frontier was rich with ancient lore, but ripped by constant conflict. Nomad scouts had revealed that a war had erupted in the northern regions, and that it was consuming all the land.

The envoy of camels moved slowly through the broken landscape. The dunes of rolling sand dissipated, and the earth was a mass of cracked clay scarred like a shattered mirror. Pasty brown grasses and thirsting shrubs clung to the barren wasteland. As the procession pushed out of the heart of the wastes, green plants became more frequent. Finally, patches and clumps of thick green grasses replaced the dry, cracked earth. The clumps accumulated, and entire fields of lush vegetation could be seen ahead.

The tribals were shocked by the vision before them. Instead of endless sand and barren rock outcroppings, there were majestic grasslands in sight. A sense of accomplishment filled both the youths as their hearts were lifted by the view facing them. No longer did they have to fear death in the desert; the nomads had delivered the tribals to the edge of the civilized world, a world that Tani had dreamt of his entire life. The young genius smiled as his light green eyes surveyed the lands ahead. *"We made it!"* Tani thought triumphantly. *"We made it."*

"This is as far as we go," the chief stated in an ominous tone. He stared uneasily towards the northeast as he spoke. "It is unwise to linger at the edge of this place. The corrupt peoples of this land should not be underestimated."

"What lies beyond? I can see endless green up ahead. I never thought I would see such a lush place." Tani was awe struck as miles and miles of grasslands rose ahead of them.

"This is the edge of 'The Frontier'. Just to the northeast, beyond the road, is a small Frontier town. This is as far as we go. Fierce ancient secrets and technology abound in this land. This is a place rife with death and suffering. We seldom travel even this far." The chief spoke quietly, as if trying to avoid an unseen foe. He was clearly uneasy, and anxious to get back to the safety of the wasteland.

There was a moment of silence as the two tribals stared uneasily. The nomad tribe had become family over the last months. Both Tani and Jared felt sadness at the thought of leaving their new family. Memories of the Exile flared in their minds. It was as if it was happening all over again. The fear of being alone was beginning to mount once more. The nomad tribe was a safe, warm place, while 'The Frontier' was an unknown force that pushed their thoughts to a frigid place of uncertainty.

"I urge you not to go," the chief exhorted them. "Stay with us until your Exile is over. You will be safe, and we will teach you much of the southern desert and western reaches."

Both Jared and Tani were silent as they contemplated their decision to leave. The safety of the tribe was a calming thought. It would be so easy to stay, so easy to be protected and nurtured by the tribe. Tani became distant as he fought off the fear mounting in his thoughts. Jared looked out towards the grasslands with indecision.

Finally, Jared looked at Tani, and the young genius looked back. They both knew that they couldn't stay. Their entire goal and purpose was to open up the world for Scarskin, and living a peaceful twenty moons with the Nomad tribe went against all their plans for greatness. Every ounce of terror they had felt bounding into the eastern wasteland would be in vain. Braving the harsh world only to dive back into the cradle of safety went against all they had fought for. Mogi and the other elders *were* wrong.

Tani nodded, and Jared understood his intent; the tribals could not stay with the nomad tribe. Jared and Tani would face the peril of uncertainty rather than the safety of the familiar.

"We have enjoyed our stay with you. But we must press onward and explore more of this land. Our goal is to recover lost technologies, and The Frontier is a place beyond anything we could have hoped to discover," Jared said, nodding to the chief respectfully.

"You are always welcome at any of our waterholes," the female scribe said, bowing to Tani first, then to Jared.

"Goodbye, Prince Jared and Scribe Tani. Our hearts are heavy with your passing. Be safe," the chief declared sincerely. "Now we must be going. It is not safe to linger here at the edge of The Frontier. Farewell!" With that, the nomad tribe turned back toward the wastes.

With heavy hearts, the nomads left the youths. They had become accustomed to Tani and Jared. It was as if the youths were being exiled again, except that this time, it was from the nomad tribe, not the Scarskin tribe.

The procession of camels pressed deep into the dry cracked earth. The white garb of the nomad procession shone brightly as they moved. The chief paused for a brief moment, reining his beast around and waving a fond goodbye.

Jared and Tani watched for nearly a half an hour. Finally, the last trace of the tribe disappeared beyond a dry dirt hill in the distance.

With that, the two looked northeast and found themselves staring at a deeply rutted road. The grass along either side of the road began to hiss. A light wind had picked up, and was rustling through the tall grass. It was a sinister sound that disturbed both Jared and Tani. They eyed each other oddly, as if they had just witnessed an omen of some kind. Shrugging off the feeling, the two decided to set out.

It was mid-day as the tribals began to walk along the road. They pressed deeper and deeper into the lush rolling grass. Barbwire fences soon appeared at the edge of the road. Mighty herds of cattle grazed. Houses, small and made entirely out of wood, could be seen from time to time. Jared and Tani both felt a jolt of adrenaline hit their systems. They had both seen the things that they were seeing before. They had seen such visions in many of the books they looked at as children; books that were from the old world, as if the world had never changed out in the grasslands. It was as if the great apocalypse had never touched the land. Both of the youths were caught in a daydream, as they pressed deeper into the seemingly untouched land.

Soon, a horse and rider approached from ahead. The horse neighed and bucked his head as it traveled forward. The beast of burden had caught sight of the tribals and was trying to alert its master, to no avail; the rider was barely able to remain seated upon the horse.

A drunken man dressed in a tattered shirt and a battered hat swayed back and forth in the saddle. A gray beard covered his face, as did many layers of dirt. The man clearly had not washed in over a month. The rider approached, and Jared waved at him.

"The... whores..." The man struggled in the saddle. His eyes rolled back and forth. The language was similar enough to their own to enable Jared and Tani to understand him. "The whores are incredible!" the man broke out in insane laughter. He spurred his horse past the tribals.

Jared shot Tani a bemused look. "Too much cacti brew." Tani nodded in agreement.

The two from Scarskin pressed onward, and soon found themselves at the outskirts of a town. Several streets lined with two story wooden buildings spread before them. With a knot in their stomachs, the two moved into the town.

Wooden boardwalks bordered the roads. Horses were tethered to water troughs, and eyed the tribals uneasily upon their approach. A wisp of dust rolled around in a plume as a tumble weed rolled down the main street. Even though it was afternoon, the streets were devoid of life and activity, washed in an eerie silence. Jared and Tani shot each other looks of concern as they pressed onward. It was as if the town was abandoned.

A man sat on a porch, spitting hunks of chew into an ancient spittoon. "Damn tribals," the man said as he stared at Jared and Tani. He spat black liquid from his mouth and squinted in the sunlight. The hunk of spit and chew splashed against the spittoon in a grotesque splatter. A line of dark liquid rolled down his chin as he considered Jared and Tani with a look of hatred. "Why don't cha crawl back into the wastelands, you damn savages?"

Neither of the youths responded. They continued onward. Tani finally caught sight of the word 'Saloon' written on a building.

He motioned to Jared to go into the tavern.

The tribals pushed into the saloon, which was dimly lit and packed with a variety of patrons. Many of them wore brimmed cowboy hats. No one spoke in the saloon, and the feeling was somber. As the two entered, several of the patrons shot them dark glances from unshaven, dirty faces.

Not knowing where to go, the tribals sat at the bar, feeling very out of place and trying to act inconspicuous. The patrons eyed them with a mixture of hate and levity. Tani and Jared both felt very uneasy, and blushed as they looked at their clothes with a sense of embarrassment. Their attire was poorly constructed compared to that of the people littering the bar.

The barkeep snorted and shot them a dirty glance. Finally, he moved over and asked, "What will you have?"

"I would like some water," said Tani earnestly.

"Water? Water?" the barkeep snorted and laughed. "You hear this, boys? This damn tribal wants a glass of water."

"Yeah, that's real funny, Earl," a bar patron chuckled.

"We don't serve water. What else do you want?" he sneered at them both.

"What else do you have?" Jared responded.

"We got whiskey, rum, and ale. What will you have?" the barkeep asked in a wicked tone.

"I will try whiskey," Jared said sheepishly. The young warrior fought back the blush in his cheeks. The more he fought the embarrassment, the brighter red he became.

The barkeep filled a shot glass and handed it to Jared. "That will be one dollar, you savage."

"Dollar?" Asked Jared in a confused tone. He looked stunned, and the barkeep shook his head in disgust.

Tani rooted through his pack and recovered an ancient dictionary. He thumbed through it and found what he was looking for. "It's a type of money," Tani explained.

"I don't have any dollars," Jared said apologetically.

"No money?" the barkeep shouted, grabbing the whiskey shot from Jared. "Get out of here, you piece of desert trash! You and your stupid ass friend!"

A chuckle rose from the bar patrons.

"Shut your damn mouth, or I'll shut it for you." A man rose

from the back of the saloon. He was tall and lean, his hair long and dark. A scar ran from his right eye down to the tip of his chin. His long coat fell open as he stood, revealing a hand flexed just above his gun belt. A flash of madness was in his eyes. His gaze fell on the barkeep and did not waver. Darkness and madness were the only expressions on his face.

Several of the patrons dove under tables. Jared and Tani looked around, somewhat horrified. The barkeep was frozen in terror.

"You think you're pretty damn tough, don't you?" the gunfighter spoke, his gaze never wavering. "I grew up in the wastes. You got a problem with tribals?"

There was complete silence. The barkeep was too afraid to speak. He knew better than to cross the deranged gunfighter.

"You got shit in your ears? I said, do you have a problem with tribals?" Banion said in a nasty tone.

"No..." stuttered the barkeep.

"Give him his drink back. It's on the house," Banion stated, and the barkeep responded immediately, stammering.

"Sure, Banion, whatever you say." His shaky hand returned the drink to young Jared.

"Thank you, friend," Jared said to Banion.

Banion returned to his table in the corner of the room, sat, and did not respond.

Banion sank back into his chair. His eyes were dark and unstable, his expression uneasy. He was anxious about something, something horrible.

He ignored the tribals, his thoughts drifting to the war. The world had been silent for a few days, a few days that transformed his terror into a tremor of anger. The Biogtech army would not allow this moment of safety to last. The army was pushing its way south, and Banion knew the calm would not last long. For many days, he had sat in the bar, waiting; waiting for the army from the north to raze the backwater town of Pontiac City to the ground. But no war had come. The north had been gripped by a silence, an eerie silence. The stream of refugees had stopped nearly two days ago. But it was this temporary calm that had set the deranged rancher on edge. He knew all too well that the Reaper Kai would not rest for too long.

He knew their goal was absolute, and that they would not rest until every other race had been annihilated.

Many of the townsfolk had begun to come back from the south. They were convinced that the mighty mercenary, Banion, had been wrong. Banion knew otherwise. But in the end, he didn't care. He knew that the Biogtech army was close, and that this silence would not last.

He slammed down the rest of his ale and stared at the tribals with an odd look. Banion had traveled the world for years and had never seen garb like the one that he saw on the tribals. He snorted. *"Where the hell did these two come from?"*

Pushing all thoughts from his mind, the deranged rancher sank deeper and deeper down, letting the liquor take him to a silent place. The dull pain of his existence still throbbed, but the alcohol was soothing. And so he sat, with a somber look on his face which masked the seething hatred just below the surface.

Chapter 18
The Battle of Pontiac City

A loud boom and a blast of heat created a vortex of rising air. A bright orange swirl of fire and smoke curled around as flames erupted at its base, tearing into the wooden building. The explosion shredded the building, turning it into a mass of flaming ruin.

Tani and Jared sat straight up on their sleeping mats. Screams and the sound of gunfire rolled through the night air. Confused, the two tribals looked at one another. The two youths were camped at the edge of Pontiac City, and it was readily apparent that the town was under attack. Quickly, they grabbed their gear and made towards the center of the besieged Frontier settlement.

As they neared the center of town, a strange laughter filled the air. The cackle echoed throughout the buildings. Jared and Tani stopped dead in their tracks and looked around in confusion. The laughter was rhythmic, mechanical, and chilling.

More gunfire could be heard. Following the sounds of battle, the tribal youths caught sight of a peculiar scene. In the dim light, Jared could just barely make out a crude barricade constructed of furniture and wreckage. Many of the townsfolk could be seen behind the barricade wielding rifles and pistols.

With cautious steps, Jared and Tani slowly made their way through the town, trying to discover what was going on. At the intersection ahead of them, several townsfolk were running south through the town, screaming in terror. Bursts of weapon fire rang out, and two of the townsfolk crashed to the ground only a step ahead of Tani and Jared. Blood and fearsome mortal wounds covered their ruined flesh. Jared and Tani jumped back and took cover. Though they had fought and braved mutants in the wastes, this was a whole extra level of fear. It was one thing to see a mutant terror die, but to see another human torn and slain before ones eyes was terror unequaled.

The remaining citizen whimpered and cried in despair. Frantically, he ran and darted back and forth like a crazed animal. A crescendo of laughter rolled from the northern junction of the street. The laughter was wicked but measured, rolling in a defined pattern. Several more shots rang out. The crazed man was struck, and spun around as multiple rounds of gunfire hit his body. With a whimper, he collapsed and died. Reacting to the man's death, Jared jumped back a few steps in fear. He stumbled and fell down. On his back, Jared pushed himself backwards to put as much distance as possible between him and the corpses in the street. Tani simply stared wide-eyed at the sights before him.

The laughter was rising, and the strange unknown attackers were drawing near. The tribals were still concealed by the corner of the building, but not for long. A shuffling sound now could be heard; the attackers were getting closer.

Tani saw a dark shape from the corner of his eye. In the darkness of the night was a hidden assassin clad in brown. A shotgun moved onto the top of a water trough as the hidden man prepared to assault the strange attackers.

The Biogtech assault drones were about to round the corner where the tribals cowered, when a series of shotgun blasts tore into their ranks. A unit of six Biogtech death machines laughed and raised their weapons in an attempt to counter attack. With jagged movements, they plodded forward with their red mechanical eyes shifting back and forth. The pale white plastic bodies of the Biogtechs hunched forward as they giggled in staggered tones. They continued on, searching for the unseen attacker.

The robotic soldiers moved past the corner of the building and did not take notice of Jared nor Tani. The tribals were greatly relieved to remain unseen by the strange robotic attackers.

More shotgun blasts rang out, giving away the position of the stealthy attacker. The lead Biogtech took two blasts in the chest. The first blast harmlessly ricocheted off the steel chest plate on the robotic soldier. The second blast shredded the neck, and pieces of plastic and wiring were blasted free. A stream of oil and hydraulic fluid erupted in a spray. The robot halted and fell to the ground, twitching as oil sprayed from its neck.

The five remaining Biogtech death machines advanced while firing bursts of submachine gun fire. The concealed gunman jumped from behind the trough and leaped off towards a covered boardwalk near his position. Bullets tore into the water trough, shredding it into wooden fragments of shrapnel as the man burst into the darkness of the dimly lit street.

Dropping his shotgun to favor a submachine gun, Banion chambered the first round in the magazine and fired a burst at the Biogtech detachment. His hasty attack was in vain; not a single bullet bit a robotic soldier, and he retreated a few steps to bring the weapon under control, slowing his breathing and focusing on the fight at hand.

The two tribals now stared at the pale white plastic robots closing in on Banion. They were horrified, and tried desperately to comprehend what was going on. Finally, Tani took the initiative. He dropped to his knee and groped hastily through his pack, emerging shakily with a lighter in one hand, and a stick of dynamite in the other.

Banion retreated, taking cover behind some wooden barrels on the boardwalk. Taking hasty aim, he fired multiple bursts of gunfire at the robotic death machines. The fire felled one. The remaining four took aim at Banion.

A deafening blast ripped into the center of the robotic soldiers. The dynamite stick detonated, and two Biogtechs were ripped to shreds. A shower of metallic parts, melted plastic, and earth rained down. The Biogtechs were confused by the attack, and halted for a brief moment as the rain of rubble crashed down.

Banion took advantage of the pause, and struck out to put an end to the robotic soldiers. He rose to his feet and took careful aim at the nearest soldier. Pulling the trigger, he fired the last rounds of his clip into the pasty white robot. Maintaining control of the weapon, all of the remaining rounds in the magazine struck true and shredded the breastplate of the Biogtech. It fell to the ground and ceased its hideous laughter as a spasm of death took it.

Banion's weapon was out of bullets, and he retreated long enough to reload it. The remaining Biogtech took the opportunity to attack Banion. It laughed as it fired at the fleeing human. Jared had had enough. He was still trembling, but didn't want the courageous stranger they had met in the bar to die. With a shaky hand, he drew the mighty Scar Blade free from its ancient scabbard. It had a dull blue glow in the darkness, hungry for the kill.

With a war cry, Jared leaped forward with the ancient blade held above his head. He closed quickly on the last of the robotic soldiers. With a grunt and a yell, he drove the blade from above his head into the shoulder of the Biogtech. The blade hit steel, but did not halt. The Scar Blade drove all the way through the torso of the eerie mechanical foe. Jared cleared the blade from the robot, and it fell into two pieces, ceasing to exist.

Banion stared in awe as the soldier was cleaved in two by the youth. A bullet slid into his submachine gun as he chambered the first round of a fresh magazine into the mighty weapon. Banion crept forward and scanned his surroundings for more enemies. As no more enemies could be seen nearby, he approached the tribals cautiously. They stared at him, dazed, as Banion looked back with a similar confounded look on his face.

"Two tribals appear from out of nowhere. One is armed with explosives and the other with a blade the likes of which I have never seen in all my years. These two tribals are mere children in my eyes, but have more courage than most men twice their years." Banion eyed them both as he spoke, but he was most fascinated by Tani and his explosives. "Where in hell did you two come from?"

"I am Jared of the Scarskin tribe and this is my companion Tani the scholar," Jared said, gesturing at Tani. The adrenaline from the battle was still high, and the two youths were rattled.

As Jared finished speaking, screams rose once again from the barricade a few streets over. Banion looked at the barricade, then at the tribals, and once again at the barricade. There was a moment of silence. At last, his eyes moved back to the tribals. He stared at them for what seemed like an eternity. Banion's face was covered with inner turmoil. Finally, he spoke with hesitation. "Follow me."

Banion led while Jared and Tani followed, not knowing what to think. They reached the barricade within seconds, and saw that several dozen more Biogtechs were assaulting the town from the north. Many dead townsfolk lay bloodied on the barricade already, but they were stalwart, unwilling to yield their position to the enemy. Letting the town fall to the Reaper Kai and their robotic soldiers was not an option.

As the gunfight continued, Banion pulled his electronic binoculars free from his belt. He looked out into the darkness and caught sight of a large army, several thousand strong, wavering near the northern fringe of the town. He shook his head in despair. "It's as I feared. The army of the enemy is large indeed."

Banion pointed at the binoculars while looking at the young tribal genius.

"Night vision," Banion said as he tossed the binoculars to Tani. Tani stared out and saw the host of thousands wavering just to the north. Tani gave Jared a chance to look as well. The tribals were wide eyed with fear.

"This town is lost!" Banion yelled. "Thousands more are on the way! Retreat!"

Many of the defenders wavered. The sheriff of the town had been slain, and the mayor was nowhere to be seen. Finally, Banion rose to his feet and spoke to Jared and Tani. "The last thing I want is a couple of brats following me across the damn wasteland. Get out here and go back to your 'Scarskin'."

With that, Banion left the barricade and made haste towards the southern end of the town. Jared and Tani were stunned, and didn't know what to do. They looked at each other and shrugged. The tribals bolted off after Banion, not wanting to stick around as several thousand more Biogtechs assaulted the Frontier town.

The defenders on the barricade were confounded. Most of them stayed, not knowing or believing that thousands of additional robotic soldiers were lurking just a few miles northward. Jared and Tani ran after the crazed rancher. They caught up with him quickly, and he turned around and glared at them as they followed.

"You little shits. I told you to get out of here!" There was anger in his voice, but the tribals simply stared at him with innocent eyes. They said nothing as Banion glared at them. Finally, he shook his head and cursed at them. "Damn you! If you little bastards want this, then so be it."

It was at that moment that Jared and Tani crossed a terrible line, a line that many moons from now would continue to haunt them. They had just joined up with the most feared gunfighter in all the land and his insane quest of vengeance.

There was a quick moment of silence. Finally Banion moved off and untied a horse which was tethered with several other beasts to a wooden trough. He jumped on its back, and motioned for Jared and Tani to do the same. The tribals each mounted a horse.

Another series of explosions resounded, and fire leapt on the barricade. The screams of the defenders could be heard. The trio turned and viewed the glowing inferno and the stalwart defenders protecting the failing barricade. It was an ominous vision, seeing the townsfolk defend their home amidst the flames and hideous laughter of enemy troops. It was a memory that would be burned into the tribals' memory forever.

Banion turned his horse south and brought it to a gallop. The tribals followed, flying into the night.

"So, why do you have three horses?" Jared asked.

Banion looked back and shook his head in disgust. "What the hell was I thinking?" Banion said aloud as he looked at Jared.

"These are not his horses," Tani replied, hoping Jared would catch on.

"Not his? Whose horses are these, then?" Jared quizzed.

Neither of Jared's companions answered, and the young warrior remained dumbfounded.

The night was brisk, and soon the trio could not see the flames of the town on the brink of loss. Two hours passed, and the sun was pushed towards the horizon to the east. The trio rode on; little did they know that as the sun was rising in Pontiac City, not a single citizen was left alive. The flames of war had claimed another town in the name of the dread Reaper Kai.

Chapter 19
Truth Revealed

After nearly two days of travel from the ruined town of Pontiac City, the trio had stopped where the grasslands of the north began to disperse in the hot, arid land. With the lushness of the grasslands behind them, the mighty desert lay ahead in their journey. A long day's ride had left Banion, Jared, and Tani exhausted and travel-worn.

It was after sunset, and the cold night air rolled into the land. Jared and Tani were withdrawn, turning to stare at each other at regular intervals. An uneasy silence settled over the three.

Banion had not spoken a single word in the two days travel from the battered Frontier town of Pontiac City. Instead, he brooded, filled with darkness and anger. The tribals had attempted several times to talk to the crazed rancher, but he never responded. Their attempts at communication with Banion were met only with hateful stares or complete silence.

This dark mood had evoked anxiety in both of the youths. They had no idea where they were going, or what Banion's mysterious purpose was. This uncertainty was rising, causing both of the tribals to doubt their decision to travel with Banion. It wouldn't take them long to slip off and put some good distance between themselves and the crazed gunman. But fear was at the back of their minds, the fear of the unknown. The tribals had found themselves in the middle of a conflict, and they were unsure if it was a worse decision to travel with Banion, or to brave their unknown surroundings assailed by an open war.

As indecision tugged at both of their sensibilities, the tribals eyed each other, hoping the crazed rancher would speak. Finally, Banion moved off into the darkness, leaving the two tribals alone at the campfire.

Tani was plugging away at his laptop computer, improving his knowledge of its use. Jared watched uneasily as Banion left the camp. When he could no longer see the deranged rancher, Jared began to speak softly to Tani.

"What is wrong with him?" Jared quizzed in a low tone. He didn't want Banion to overhear if he was lurking somewhere in the darkness.

Half listening to Jared, still deep in thought about his computer, Tani finally took notice of the fact that Banion had disappeared, and answered drearily, "I'm not sure." Tani looked around hesitantly. Finally convinced that Banion was not near, he began to speak freely. "There is darkness in his eyes. When he looks at me, I feel that he is more a wild animal than a man."

"I am afraid we have come out of the desert into some sort of war. I don't know what is worse, braving this war alone and exploring, or following this madman around the wastelands," Jared said, his gaze drifting to the fire. The memories of the battle in Pontiac City were filling him with fear, but he was too proud to admit it.

"Yeah, and I'm not sure I want any part of it. The technology behind those walking robots is formidable. Even in the most advanced books I had back in Scarskin, there was little mention of such things. We are beyond any sense of sanity." Tani's tone was troubled. His gaze shifted to the fire, and he shivered at the thought of the Biogtech soldiers.

"Banion seems to be a great warrior of some kind. He is strong, but I fear for our safety. I don't think he's *normal*," Jared whispered, and peered at the darkness, scanning for Banion.

"I agree. Maybe we should consider heading out on our own. I am just afraid that we will stumble upon our own doom, since we don't know these lands, especially in a time of war." Tani fell silent for a few moments, rubbing his hands by the fire. His good hand rubbed the stumps that were once the fingers on his right hand. "I cannot hold eye contact with Banion. I fear for my life every time he stares at me. But even in his madness, I can see compassion below the surface. He is a tormented man, but I bet he is a good man," Tani whispered to his companion from Scarskin.

"Even good men can be driven to madness," Jared said, as a jolt of adrenaline hit his system. A figure had appeared behind him, emerging from the darkness like a wraith of the night.

Banion, dressed in his dark brown overcoat, considered the two youths in disgust. He glared at both of them. In the darkness, the fire glittered in his eyes as he gazed at them. Banion had overhead the end of the conversation.

"Biogtechs," Banion said as he sat down near the fire.

There was a moment of silence as Jared shot Tani a confused look.

Tani's curiosity overrode his fear of Banion and, meekly, he asked, "What?"

"The things of darkness that attacked Pontiac City are called Biogtechs. They were created by the ancients, and the dread empire of the Reaper Kai has unraveled the secrets of their making." Banion spoke in a hushed tone which filled both of the youths with dread. "The Reaper Kai and their minions are attacking and invading the entire Darken Realm. We are headed to the great city of Rasheed in the south. I have many contacts, and know the king personally. My goal..." He trailed off, considering the two youths with a snort. "*Our* goal is to alert King Toil and raise an army against the Reaper Kai."

"Oh." said Jared, with a look of amazement on his face. "What...?"

"The Reaper Kai are the masters of the robotic soldiers. Thought to be extinct for hundreds of years, the Reaper Kai emerged from the darkness and with them, an army of mindless robotic servants. Their goal is the complete eradication of all other peoples."

"Reaper Kai? Where are they from?" Tani pressed, not wanting to relinquish the communication that had sprung up.

"They were born out of the past mistakes of a mighty empire far to the north..." Suddenly, Banion became hostile, and snapped at the youths. "No more talking. Get some sleep. We have a long way to go in the morning." Tani and Jared kept their mouths shut and did not respond. "I will keep the first watch."

With that, Jared took out his sleeping mat and lay down on his back. He looked up at the darkness of the night sky. Stars twinkled in the darkness. Suddenly, his thoughts drifted to the moon. He looked about and finally caught sight of it. It was half full, and he sighed at the thought of it. *"Twenty moons,"* Jared thought. *"Twenty damn moons."*

Tani disobeyed Banion, and continued to play with his computer. His mind was fully engulfed in the ancient device within a matter of minutes. The bright screen cast a myriad set of colors on the scholar's face. His eyes scanned the screen intently, its reflection revealed in his glasses. The genius's young mind pored over the ancient keys as he read the screen intently. Since they had left Scarskin, Tani had unraveled a great many mysteries of his own. There was an ancient electronic encyclopedia on the computer. With it, Tani could study a great variety of topics. The physics and calculus sections were too simplistic, and did not provide enough detail for the scholar's liking, but other sections had piqued his interest.

He was especially enthused with the sections on history in the ancient encyclopedia. He read about ancient wars and the colonization of far away lands. Tani marveled at the technology levels throughout the history covered in the ancient computer. In the short span of a few hundred years, the world moved from an agricultural society to a sophisticated one based on a hoard of wondrous devices. These societies lost their ability to discern spiritual matters and worshipped technology, technology that ultimately brought about a series of wars. The wars were numerous, but there was no mention of the final war, the war that brought both plague and fire.

An idea began to form in Tani's mind as he read. During the colonial times, many great countries had sent their troops and explorers to far away lands. In those times, many societies of various languages and stages of development met and came into contact. Tani looked at the clothes he wore and then looked at Banion's. He smiled in the darkness.

Both Jared and Tani were explorers from a primitive land who had discovered a much wider world, filled with technological wonders passed down through the generations since the ancient Armageddon. Tani shook his head in wonder, and suddenly felt very lucky. Jared and Tani were the first of their tribe to contact anyone east of the great waste. As fanciful stories of conquest and exploration filled his mind, he thought of their own voyage into the unknown. It was an amazing feat indeed.

With a smile on his face, Tani mentally recounted many tales of valor and great deeds he had read about. He wondered if he himself would be part of such stories. What was his place? What was this war that the tribals had stumbled upon? Without their volition, they were now involved in a small part of this war.

Tani brought out his sleeping mat and thought about ancient history and tales of great explorers. There was a jolt of excitement in his stomach as he thought of such things. Secretly, he imagined the unknown. As his mind conjured wild visions of the world about them, he gazed over at Jared sleeping nearby. He finally understood the young warrior.

All of his life, Jared had hungered to journey into the unknown and be a warrior of legend. Tani had always dismissed these thoughts as foolish. But as he thought about these ideas, he was comforted. Tani himself had developed a wanderlust and an urge to do great things. Finally, he understood what Jared had felt all along. It was impossible to travel into the safety of the known world. The only thing that mattered was the adventure and excitement of the Great Beyond, and the mystery behind a journey that defied all odds.

Tani grew drowsy, but smiled in the darkness. At last, he finally understood why it was so important for the tribals to travel east into the wasteland; to travel in any other direction would have spoiled the true passion of being young, the passion to do things beyond comprehension for the sake of adventure.

Chapter 20
Desert Outpost

The sand, the tireless, endless sand, rolled on before the trio. Tan dunes, tall and proud, stretched on in every direction. The trio was beyond the safety of civilization, having driven deep into the southern wastes of the Darken Realm. The mood was sullen, and the tribals were losing confidence and patience with the deranged gunfighter. Banion had been silent again the entire day. Jared and Tani felt scared to speak, for when they did, Banion glared at them with hostility.

The ride was long, and the heat of the desert made the trip all the more tiresome. It was nearing sunset when the trio topped a ridge of shifting sand. Down below in the valley was a trade station with walls of dull white-washed clay. Dune Hollow, as the desert outpost was called, was in the center of the main route from the northlands to the southern reaches of the Darken Realm. The outpost had been operating for hundreds of years, acting as a way station and gambling den for mercenaries, nomads, and desert traders. In Banion's younger days, it had been a place to find work and drink his sorrows away.

There were five buildings in all, surrounding a guard tower in the center. Though still about a mile away, the trio was close enough to tell that nothing stirred in the trade outpost.

Banion was cautious, bringing his binoculars to his eyes. He stared about, his face dismayed. "Get ready, kids, this isn't going to be pleasant."

"What are you talking about?" Jared quizzed with a look of concern.

Banion did not respond, but stared back, his face solemn. The crazed rancher directed his horse down the dune towards the abandoned trade outpost. The sun hit the edge of the desert and began to disappear below the horizon. A chill wind blew from the western lands.

Tani and Jared followed Banion down the crest of dune.

They hesitantly rode behind the seasoned mercenary, maintaining a distance of several horse strides behind the horse that bore Banion.

A hiss of sand rose as the wind whipped against the dry dunes. Jared shivered as the cool wind blew across his neck. Fear was filling his mind. Not knowing what to think, his hand rested tensely on the hilt of the mighty Scar Blade. Tani was fearful as well, but didn't hide it as well as Jared. Tani spurred his horse forward as a knot formed in his stomach.

As they approached the perimeter of the outpost, a lonely feeling filled the trio. A wooden door creaked in the cold wind. The sand swirled around, and a wind chime chattered. A whistling noise rose as the wind tore through the open buildings. The trade outpost, Dune Hollow, was deserted.

Banion reined his horse to a halt and stared about cautiously. With a leap, he jumped off his horse. Scanning the abandoned outpost, Banion looked for signs of human presence. Finally, the deranged rancher caught sight of something. Strange tracks were half covered by the shifting sand. Banion knelt down, suspiciously surveying the tracks. He looked at Tani and shook his head, indicating that he was puzzled.

Leaving their horses untied at the perimeter, Banion motioned the tribals to follow. He pulled his silver revolver free and held it tightly while his eyes scanned the nearby buildings. Tani produced a dagger, and Jared brandished the mighty Scar Blade.

Slowly, they crept forward, each with heart pounding. Banion led the way. They breached the perimeter efficiently, only to discover a corpse half buried in the sand. Dried blood had coagulated in the sand, forming globs of clumped sand around the corpse. Horrified, Jared and Tani stepped forward to view the body with Banion. Only the bottom part of the person remained. The upper torso had been torn free and was nowhere to be seen. Banion's face conveyed his repulsion and fascination.

"Biogtechs?" quizzed Jared, staring around uncomfortably. His hand trembled as he clutched his ancient sword.

"No," Banion replied in a cryptic tone.

The trio moved into the center of the white-washed clay buildings. Doors stood ajar or were ripped clean from their hinges. More strange tracks littered the earth and spread about the outpost in all directions.

The wind chime clanged again and again. The wind increased in intensity as the sun disappeared from the desert. Sand swirled about with a whoosh, chattering as it pelted the walls. A haunting wail sounded as the strong wind whipped through the abandoned outpost.

"This place is dead," Banion said. As his voice rose, the wind increased, so it seemed Banion was speaking at a whisper. The tribals were barely able to hear his words, but they both knew what he had said. "We need to restock our provisions, especially our water. There isn't another outpost until we hit the Coal Wastes near Rasheed, and that's at least three days travel from here. Spread out and meet back here in five minutes. Try to find water first and foremost, then food," Banion spoke up in the rising wind, heading off towards a dark building.

Jared and Tani stared with fear as he left them. Finally, they mustered the courage to explore on their own. The two moved in the opposite direction from Banion. The light was dimming quickly as Jared and Tani moved into the largest building of the outpost.

Slowly, they crept forward. With a chill rising in their hearts, they pushed onward to explore the silent building.

It had once been a bar, but now it lay in ruin. Benches and tables had been pushed up against broken windows in a crude attempt to form a barricade. But the barricade had failed, and most of its components were smashed and battered as if *something* had broken through the wood. The bar was littered with broken glass and debris. Dried blood and irregular blobs of green mucous covered the floor. A sickly brown and green pool of foul smelling filth spread near the back of the bar.

Trembling uncontrollably, Jared moved on with Tani close behind. They surveyed the bar and searched it quickly. With a jolt of revulsion, the two found a bloodied human rib resting near the bar. The sight was enough to drive them both to sickness and panic. Fighting back the bile rising in their throats, they retreated a few steps and recovered their composure.

A creaking sound filled their ears, catching their attention. Floorboards were creaking. Creak. Creak. Something was moving nearby. Jared and Tani held their breath. They looked at each other with wide-eyed fear. Snap. Another board popped as something moved close. Slowly, they retreated from the sound. The darkness of the night had robbed them of their vision. Creak. Something crept closer. Frantically, the tribals looked around and saw nothing. The wind howled outside. The wind chimes sang a wicked overture. A loud snap sounded out in the darkness. The tribals looked out in the dark at a door near the back of the bar. The sound had come from behind the door. *Something* was lurking behind that door.

The two felt a punch of adrenaline hit their systems. Their senses heightened by fear, they stepped back again. The doorknob rattled. Something struck the door from behind. The doorknob rattled again and began to turn. Jared moved back, shaking. Tani stood horrified. Their thoughts were wild, and they were prepared to defend themselves from whatever terror came forth. Finally, the door creaked open and Banion moved in slowly with revolver in hand. He looked at them oddly as they stared at him with piercing gazes.

A great relief filling them, they both let out a sigh and smiled at one another.

"I found another corpse. It looks like something was gnawing on it." Banion shook his head, speaking in a low tone. "There's slick green muck all over the floor of the building."

"Same here," Tani said, pointing at a pool of green filth.

"I have no idea what happened here. I suggest we refill our canteens and ride a few hours more before we camp. I do not want to camp in this ruin." Banion said, already moving out of the bar. "I found the well house, it's over here. Follow me."

The night had fully engulfed the outpost. Shadows rose, casting the abandoned buildings into an icy blackness. Their sense of sight had been overcome by the lack of light, but their ears were overwhelmed with sound. Doors creaked as they swung in the wind. The wind chimes rattled back in forth. The sand hissed.

They made their way through the darkness and came to the well house. As they entered, Banion lit a lantern and held it over the well. Jared worked the crank and discovered the rope had been severed, and the bucket was nowhere to be seen. The trio looked on in dismay, until Banion held the lantern close over the edge of the well and smiled, pointing at an iron rung ladder set on the wall of the well.

"One of you runts gets the task of climbing down and filling our canteens," Banion declared, surveying the two tribals.

"I'll do it," mouthed Jared.

He moved to the edge of the well and threw his leg over the side. Banion pulled a flashlight from his belt and handed it to Jared, who accepted, staring at it dully.

"It's a flashlight, Jared. Flip the switch," Tani explained, pointing at the button on it.

Jared flipped the switch and smiled at the device. He placed it in his belt and climbed down into the well. The well was blacker than the night outside. As he climbed, he breathed heavily, and the sound echoed in the deep well. He pressed on, descending slowly until his foot slipped on the iron rung beneath him.

Panic flooded him as he braced himself. Despite stumbling, the young tribal managed to remain in control and regain his footing. He stopped for a moment; the rungs from here on were slick, coated with *something*…

Jared grabbed the flashlight and pointed it into the well. A confused vision rose to meet his eyes. Instead of gray stone and rock, the bottom part of the well was coated in a sickening green slime.

Shaking his head in dismay, he pressed on. It became increasingly more difficult to descend into the well. The green filth was thicker and thicker as he climbed downward into the blackness.

"There's more of that green stuff down here. It's all over," Jared shouted up to his companions who were peering into the well.

"Just get the damn water," shouted Banion in an irritated tone.

Jared reached the bottom of the well but found no water. Small pools could be seen, but nothing large enough to fill a canteen. A large gaping hole was torn in the wall of the well bottom. It was dark, and the light of Jared's new flashlight could not reveal the end of the tunnel beyond the hole in the wall. A musty smell greeted his nose. The green slime was now a thick growth, sponge-like in appearance. Fibers and tendrils of a green, moss-like substance grew out of the repellent green slime coating.

"There is no water down here!" Jared shouted. "There's a hole in the wall. The water must have drained away!"

"Damn him. Can't even get some water," Banion cursed young Jared.

"It's not his fault," Tani spoke in his defense.

"We're coming down, Jared!" Banion shouted back, giving Tani a dirty look.

The trio soon was at the bottom of the well. Banion held the lantern before him as they moved down the dark tunnel at the bottom of the well. The green sponge-like fungus grew as they traveled. As they crept deeper into the earth, long tendrils of green fungus hung down and brushed their bodies as they moved. The tendrils were now thick and strong, reminding the trio of tree branches.

Tani stopped and pulled some of the substance free, eyeing and sniffing it. It was musty and smelled like rotting death. "Some of it is slick, like some sort of secretion, and the rest of it is spongy, like a plant. It's very strange. It's almost like some sort of symbiotic relationship."

Banion continued on into the darkness. The green fungus was now a thick mat lining the entire tunnel. As they moved, the tendrils crunched under foot, while the sponge-like base squished.

After a few minutes of travel down the tunnel, it opened into a large vaulted cave. The walls were covered in a sickly green mass of the slimy fibrous growth. Dozens and dozens of smaller tunnels exited the chamber in all directions, some near the floor of the cave, others higher up on the walls and ceiling. It was as if the mighty room was in the center of a block of porous sponge. The floor was flooded with a deep pool of water. None of the strange green fungus grew in the water, which looked clean.

Jared moved forward and crouched down to fill the canteens. Tani stood close behind Jared, staring at the strange room. Banion had moved away from the water. Near the floor were several high mounds of fungus. They seemed peculiar to him, and curiosity got the better of the crazed rancher.

Moving over to the strange humps of green fungus, Banion crouched and tugged at the fibrous mass. It gave way, and he pulled it free from the mound in a great clump. As the sheet of fungus was pulled free, a stench of death filled his nostrils. He jumped to his feet and recoiled as he saw what lay beneath the fibrous layer of fungus. A human corpse was decomposing under the green lump, feeding the fungus.

"Tani, get over here!" Banion said urgently.

Tani moved over just as Banion uncovered more of the

mounds of fungus.   More decomposing human bodies were revealed. A foul stench rose in the air, and Tani bent down to retch.

"What the hell is going on, kid?"   Banion was aware of Tani's keen intellect, and was looking to him for answers. "How did these bodies get down here?"

A wild idea came to Tani's mind as he surveyed the fungus.

"*Something* is growing the fungus, using the dead bodies as nourishment for the fungus. But what is the fungus for? … Maybe for food?" Tani speculated, his tone distressed. Nodding his head, the green eyes of the scholar blinked several times as his mind ground away at the problem at hand. "Whatever consumes the fungus uses the corpses to grow it. What we are looking at it is some amazing form of life, a creature that farms biological material from decomposing animal matter."

Just then, Banion remembered the strange tracks in the sand around the outpost. "Hey, Tani, how big would an insect have to be to drag a human down here?"

"That's ridiculous. No insect gets that big…" Tani's mind bounced back to the tribals' desert crossing and the oversized mutant insects in the strange flat valley. The young scholar nodded in belated agreement with Banion's theory. "Actually, I think you're right, Banion. The tracks in the sand up there in the outpost were not from a mammal, reptile, or bird. It was more like an insect would leave."

"Jared!" Banion shouted. "We are leaving now!"

"I'm not done yet," Jared whined, confused.

"Leave the damn water and run!" Banion shouted again.

Jared stood to leave and none too soon. A chattering noise echoed through the cavern. All the tunnels lining the vaulted chamber erupted with a strange clatter of sound.

"Son of a bitch!" Banion yelled as he handed the lantern to Tani. His submachine gun came free of his long coat. Just then, a burst of gunfire tore the room. Banion had attacked something at the edge of his vision. It was large, nearly the size of a man. A strange scream roared in the darkness as some unknown beast died.

Jared and Tani were running towards the tunnel to the well. Suddenly, a torrent of green shapes erupted from the sponge-like openings lining the walls of the room. From both floor and wall emerged a horde of green forms. Squat and covered in thick green exoskeletons, each had two bright yellow eyes which glowed in the dim light. With four legs and curved, hooked arms like a pair of scythes, the mutant insect horde screamed in anger. Their small heads clattered as their black mandibles chattered. In a matter of seconds, hundreds of the green insects covered the room. It was as if a green tide had struck. The tide heaved and buckled as the chattering increased. A tidal wave of insects grew and crashed upon the floor.

Banion opened fire while backing up slowly. His bullets pierced and tore at the horde. Green exoskeletons faltered as the gunfire hammered through the chitinous armor. Yellow blood sprayed as the wounds bled.

Jared and Tani had run the entire length of the tunnel, and were below the ladder of the well. Jared was terrified as he charged up the ladder. Tani held his ground, and a plan went through his mind. Falling to one knee, he brought out a cluster of dynamite and began to fashion a fuse.

Banion moved back slowly, pausing in the tunnel to the well. His weapon hummed and many mutant insects died. For each mutant terror that fell, two more took its place. The floor had turned into a yellow-coated nightmare. The chattering became more intense as the sounds of the dying drove the insects into a killing frenzy. As Banion moved back, he reloaded several times and spent many bullets. The mantis creatures poured into the tunnel in a wild frenzy.

Banion looked back and saw Tani crouched, assembling the dynamite charges. He nodded in approval and yelled to Tani, "Hurry up! I'm almost out of ammo!"

Tani ran forward and placed the charges along the wall of the tunnel. He moved back and rolled out the detonation line. Wiring it to a battery pack, he looked up in time to see Banion passing the charges on the floor.

"Run for it!" Tani screamed.

Banion turned and ran while firing his weapon behind him. As he ran, dozens of insect warriors piled into the tunnel. Running full gait, Banion reached Tani just as the tribal detonated the explosives.

A shockwave and a loud boom erupted, and the dynamite tore both rock and flesh. The blast was strong enough to cause the collapse of the tunnel some forty feet down. As stone collapsed, many insects screamed as they were crushed by tons of rock and sand. Banion and Tani were both thrown against the wall by the blast.

Jared peered down the well, terrified that his companions had been killed by the blast. Banion was laughing while holding his head. His cowboy hat had fallen off, and Banion was wiping his own blood from a cut at the back of his head. His laughter was sinister, but also light hearted and amused. Tani looked at the crazed rancher and began to laugh himself. Banion rose to his feet, placed his hat back on his head, and pulled Tani up.

"You little bastard!" Banion shouted while patting Tani on his shoulder. "Tani is not a fitting name for you. You need something more dangerous."

"In Scarskin, my nickname is Tripwire." Tani giggled, glad to be alive.

"Tripwire, eh? Sounds good to me!" Banion roared with delight.

With that, the two emerged from the well and looked at Jared. Something was not right with Jared, and both of his companions could tell. There was a sheepish look on the young warrior's face. He seemed embarrassed and humiliated at the same time.

The trio emerged from the well room and heard a strange chattering sound. It was faint, but all three knew what it was. The desert was filled with the haunting noise. Quickly, they recovered their mounts, and bolted south through the desert. As they rode, they could see great mounds of earth west of them. From the mounds heaved insects bent on death and destruction. But the horses were too fast for them, and the companions managed to escape the valley. Glad to be alive, they rode into the night until the sun broke, putting as much distance as they could between them and the cursed outpost.

Chapter 21
The Shadow of War Grows

Young Jared was silent; he could barely look at either of his companions. During the ride, he was sullen and lost in his thoughts. It had been an entire day since the encounter in the bowels of the ruined outpost known as Dune Hollow. In the end, Jared could not escape the conclusion that he had run, turned tail and run from the danger that beset the trio. It was a feeling he could not shrug off. Jared was a coward, and no one could tell him differently.

All his life, young Jared had looked up to his father. Being a guard of the Tribal Council, Jared's father was well known for his combat skills and courage. He had protected many of the council members from assassins sent by the thugs hailing from the Primal Lands. Every attempt had failed, and the assassins met a grisly fate at the end of his spear. Jared's father was good, but there was someone *better:* his own son. The only person in all of Scarskin who could stand against him in single combat was Jared.

Jared shook his head in disgust at himself. He had always wanted to live up to his father's standards, and now that dream was failing.

Jared thought of himself as courageous, but as of late, that courage was slipping away. Ever since the two tribals came into Banion's company, Jared felt as if he was second best. Before Banion, Jared had been the leader of the two. But since Banion came into the picture, the reckless mercenary rancher was calling all the shots. Tani followed Banion's orders, and Jared was jealous. Everything Banion embodied was what Jared wanted to be. Sure, Banion was crazy, but he was strong, confident, and a natural leader.

Jared was also feeling horrible since he abandoned his companions at the trade outpost. When his companions needed him the most, Jared had turned tail and escaped up the ladder. He shook his head in embarrassment. His cheeks turned red in the hot sun.

Banion had lagged behind his companions. He watched the young warrior ride on, tracking him with a dark expression. Young

Jared was still looking sheepish, and Banion knew why. Jared slumped in his saddle while his ponytail bobbed back and forth. His childish features made Banion want to laugh.

"Hey, kid, got any water?" Banion jeered. "If not, maybe you could get me some."

Jared did not respond. He simply felt more cowardly.

Banion stared at Jared's leather boots and began to laugh again. "Hey, kid, how are your running shoes?"

Tani didn't like Banion's tone and spoke up in Jared's defense. "Leave him alone, Banion."

"Hey, bookworm, mind your own business," Banion scorned.

"Knock it off," Tani shot back.

Banion snorted and rode up next to Tani. "It's a long way through the desert, kid. Don't make me leave you both out here." Banion was joking, but Tani and Jared were horrified. Neither of them spoke. The crazed rancher began to whistle and sing as he rode. The two tribals rode silently.

"Oh I wish, I wish, I wish, I wore, a sweet dancing lady. Oh I wish, I wish, I wish, I wore a sweet and pretty whore!" Banion was crazed with mania, laughing and singing boldly. "Oh I wish, I wish, I wish, I drank a sweet draught of ale. Oh I wish, I wish, I wish, I drank a beer with a ripe stank!" Banion sang for a bit more, then fell silent.

The trio topped a tall dune and halted. Below, in a broad valley, was a swarm of ants, or what appeared from this great distance to be a swarm of ants. Hundreds of forms were surrounding a wide variety of tents. The shapes were massed together, and Banion knew immediately what they were.

"Refugees, hundreds and hundreds of refugees..." Banion shook his head in disgust and spit in the desert. "You two runts ever have seen a war? You haven't seen anything yet."

Banion drove his horse down the dune towards the enormous refugee camp in the valley below. Before them was a horrifying mass of tattered, ragged souls. Many were dressed in dirty, stinking clothes. As the trio rode through the waves and waves of lost souls, Jared stared at each one he passed. Most did not return his gaze, but simply stared away, far away, with blank looks, hearts filled with sorrow, or minds filled with anger. Jared found it hard to pass through the crowd, and his own thoughts of inadequacy were not helping his demeanor.

Some of the refugees gibbered like madmen, others wept softly even though they had no more tears to shed. As they passed through the crowd, both Jared and Tani became intensely aware of Banion. Banion rode confidently through the crowd with a dark look on his face. The tribals exchanged looks before returning their gaze to the crowd. Banion was a madman himself, and the two tribals wondered what had driven the rancher to his own state of madness.

Some refugees stared up and stretched their hands out, hoping for a scrap of bread or a moment of comfort. They found none. The trio rode through the crowd and made their way to the tents at the center of the refugee camp. Reaching the center, they dismounted and waded further into the horde of homeless and hopeless.

Banion looked around the crowd, staring to find *something*. The crazed rancher scanned all the eyes and faces of the people around him. Finally, he found a man squatting with his back resting against the support of a tent. The man was cleaning his pistol. He had a splash of gray in his thinning brown hair, and deep lines and wrinkles dug trenches in his face. As Banion moved forward through the crowd, the man squinted at him with a look of recognition.

"Well, if it ain't the sorriest piece of shit in the entire Darken Realm," the haggard man said, looking up from his pistol.

"You look even sorrier than me, Willy." Banion crouched before the man. "What is all this?" he asked, gesturing around them.

"All this? All this is what's left of the Frontier. This is all that made it. There were more, but many didn't make it," Willy said, snapping his pistol. The bolt rolled back into place on the weapon. Satisfied with his work, Willy put the weapon in the back of his torn pants.

"There were more of you?" Banion pressed.

"Yeah, hundreds and hundreds more. We pressed south past the edge of the Darkpine Forest. Not more than three miles southwest of the forest is where they hit us." Willy shook his head as he stared out at the refugees milling about.

"What hit you?" Banion quizzed again.

"Damn slavers and Splicers. Hundreds of Splicers..." The man brushed his thinning hair with his hands. "Never seen so many. Even in the Iron Kai surveillance campaign twenty years ago. The Splicers were so thick you couldn't see the earth. They came down on us fast and hard. Like a swarm of spiders those damn Splicers came. Some caught at the edge were covered by dozens at a time. They didn't have a chance."

"You look like hell, Willy." The rancher shook his head.

"You too, Banion." With that, the two old acquaintances parted. Banion motioned the two tribals to follow.

"We're leaving," Banion ordered.

"Sounds good to me," mouthed Tani as he looked around through his round wire glasses. Jared also agreed, and the trio made haste and remounted, pushing out south from the refugee camp. None of them looked back.

When they were a few miles away, Banion spoke in a hushed tone.

"It's worse than I thought. The Reaper Kai has a much larger force than I ever imagined."

"What's a Splicer? And who are the Reaper Kai?" Tani had wanted to ask about the Reaper Kai many times, but Banion wasn't receptive to conversation most of the time.

"What's a Splicer? A Splicer is one of the worst damn things you could ever imagine. The Reaper Kai use 'em to gather slaves and to control those slaves," Banion responded. "The Reaper Kai army uses Splicers to enslave those that are not slain in their initial attack. When someone is Spliced, they lose their identity and will. They become slaves of the Reaper Kai, obedient servants that follow their masters' will to the end."

"How do they work?" Tani pressed, his mind set aflame by the wonders of such a device.

"Not sure, bookworm. I've seen them, and they are mechanical in nature. They leap onto a victim and pierce their flesh. Within a matter of seconds, the victim loses the ability to fight back. Within a matter of minutes, the victim is a willing servant of the enemy," Banion added while considering young Tani.

"I have never heard of such technology. The fusing of mechanical implants with organic material is beyond my comprehension." The young tribal genius shook his head in wonder at the thought. As Tani mulled over the Splicers in his mind, Jared took the opportunity to ask his own question of the deranged gunfighter.

"Who are the Reaper Kai?" Jared asked.

"The ancient empires of the north gave rise to the Reaper Kai. Their empire is in the deep north. They are a cult which worships dark powers and evil spirits. Where the world grows cold and great forests begin is where they have made their home. The land is twisted and perverse. Some say black magic has warped the whole land that the Reaper Kai occupies." Though conversing on a dark topic, Banion offered up much information.

"We have tales in our own land about those who worship dark powers. They are cast out from our village. Our elders whisper that some can speak to beasts, and dark spirits are seen near them when the sun sets." Jared shivered as he recounted the tales.

"A member of our tribe came back from an Exile and spoke of blood drinkers who dwelt in the forests of the north," Tani added.

"Those are sinister stories, but the Reaper Kai are a reality that cannot be matched by your darkest nightmares," Banion stated.

"Where did they come from?" asked Tani.

"I don't rightly know. All my life, they have haunted my steps. First, I lost my mother to them. Then my 'uncle' was killed. Finally, they took my Lily, my sweet Lily." A dark look of poison flooded Banion's eyes as he spoke. His words became harsh, and his face twisted in anger. "I will make them pay. If it costs me my life, then so be it. I will make them pay."

Jared and Tani exchanged furtive looks. They had never heard anything about Banion's past before, and this piece of lore was almost too much to handle.

"No more talking," Banion said in a harsh tone. He was losing control, and the tribals were smart enough not to make a single sound. They followed him quietly through the desert of shifting sands on their way to the south.

Chapter 22
The Man from Her Darkest Dream

It was midday when the attack came. Mineera and Globulus were caught out in the open. A squad of Biogtechs, eight strong, led by a Reaper Kai initiate, ambushed the two travelers. The ground was open and flat save for the many deep pits which scarred the earth. A black glimmer rose from the pits, and the smell of coal wafted over the land.

"Run for it!" Globulus roared.

As the mighty hippo screamed his warning, the host of robotic soldiers emerged from a coal pit near the two. A barrage of weapon fire erupted as the squad started shooting. Mineera managed to erect a mystical barrier just after Globulus sounded his warning. The bullets roared forward and struck the ethereal barrier. Bullet after bullet rammed into the psychic barrier, leaving both Globulus and Mineera unharmed. All the bullets halted mid-air, and then fell harmlessly to the ground.

The robotic soldiers cackled mechanically and spread out, spraying more gunfire at the two travelers. Globulus was on the move, and pulled Mineera after him hastily. Both psychic maiden and mutant hippo made haste towards the south. To the south was a mine, a huge coal mine, the pride and joy of the Coal Wastes, a barren area used by the kingdom of Rasheed to harvest coal and other precious minerals. As if a mighty tree had been ripped from the earth, the mine was a jagged hole in the earth. A guard tower stood at its south rim. The watchman had already shouted a warning to the miners in the pit below at the sight of the battle unfolding between the mutant hippo, a Reaper Kai traitor, and a Biogtech assault squad.

Globulus ran at full speed while shielding Mineera with the enormous bulk of his body. Several bullets struck his thick, copper brown flesh, but barely broke the skin. The two hit the edge of the pit and made their way across a tall catwalk positioned above the mining pit. Quickly, the ground dropped away, and the two found themselves more than a hundred feet above the bottom of the pit. Black, coal-covered miners scattered in the pit bottom while looking up at the catwalk.

The minions of darkness closed in quickly and opened fire again. Globulus, still shielding the dark skinned Mineera, took the brunt of the gunfire. His body was torn and battered. Several bullets hit their mark, bringing the one-ton beast to his knees. Bleeding and injured severely in his right leg, Globulus grunted as dizziness took him. Fighting back the darkness, he staggered on the catwalk and turned around to face his enemies.

"Run, damn you! Run!" Globulus grunted as he yelled at Mineera.

With labored moves, the mighty hippo brought his rotary machine gun to bear on his enemies. With quick bursts of gunfire, Globulus fought the pain and dizziness, while spraying the metallic death machines advancing on the narrow catwalk. Two Biogtechs were mowed down and shredded into a splash of motor oil and a shower of plastic debris.

The return fire was intense. A dozen bullets struck the injured hippo. Most stuck harmlessly in his thick hide, but a few pierced the leathery skin. Two fresh wounds opened on his chest. The injuries were too much to bear, and Globulus fell into unconsciousness. Slumping against the catwalk, the hippo warrior did not stir.

The Biogtechs advanced, and the Reaper Kai initiate smiled in glee. His blood- red robes rippled in the wind as he placed his foot on the catwalk. The host of evil advanced on Mineera while she huddled near the fallen Globulus, not wanting to leave his side.

"What the hell is going on?" Banion said in a loud tone, crouching near the base of the guard tower at the south end of the coal mine.

"I don't know!" Jared said, startled and wide-eyed.

"That is Lord Globulus, the Master of Arms for King Toil. And it seems he is traveling with a Reaper Kai who is being attacked by another Reaper Kai." Banion was mystified as he trained his weapon first on the woman Reaper Kai, and then on the other Reaper Kai advancing on her.

His gun moved back and forth. They were both his enemies,

but Globulus seemed to be with the woman. His weapon continued to waver between the two. Finally, he rose to his feet and took aim. His gun ripped the air, ringing out, adding to the chaos of the battle.

Banion's attack was hasty and a little out of range. Not a single bullet hit an enemy. The Reaper Kai initiate whirled around and dove off the catwalk, leaping forward and landing at the edge of the great pit. The robotic soldiers halted their assault on Mineera and sprayed the bottom of the guard tower. Many bullets ricocheted off the metal girders and steel supports.

The hail of gunfire was intense, causing Banion and the two tribals to hit the deck. Tani threw his pack open and started cutting down the fuses on two sticks of dynamite. Jared cowered with his hand clenching at the hilt of the Scar Blade. Banion crawled across the ground, trying to catch sight of the Biogtech robotic soldiers attacking their position.

"We're pinned down!" Banion yelled while firing his weapon around the corner of the tower.

A bright flash of lightning arced across the catwalk as Mineera concentrated on slaying the robotic soldiers. With hand outstretched, a mighty blast of psychic energy ripped from Mineera's fingertips. The white blast of pure energy struck a Biogtech. The blast was so intense, the robotic soldier's upper torso disintegrated in smoking ruin. Mineera's attack was successful but costly. She felt a rush of weakness course through her as she expended immense spiritual energy.

Banion shook his head in amazement at the Reaper Kai aiding them in battle.

"Damn Reaper Kai just took out one of their own soldiers." Banion was stunned, but still didn't trust the dark skinned woman crouching near the fallen hippo. Jared simply shook with fright. Tani was looking around the edge of the tower at the advancing robotic soldiers. His stumpy hand held a stick of dynamite; the other held a lit lighter.

The soldiers advanced, with the Reaper Kai initiate at the back of the squad. Their gunfire was so precise and deadly that the trio dared not run from the safety of the steel tower.

Mineera was on her feet and staggering across the catwalk, not knowing who had attacked the Biogtechs, but thankful nonetheless. She made her way to aid the hidden attackers.

Tani had had enough, and hurled a lit stick of dynamite into the advancing robot death machines. The weapon detonated and shredded two Biogtechs, leaving four deadly attackers and one Reaper Kai. The young genius had earned the nickname Tripwire once again.

"Good shot, bookworm." Banion rose and sprayed the attackers with bullets. One more robotic soldier felt the sting of Banion's weapon, and collapsed from the battle wounds he had sustained. The battle was turning around quickly to favor Banion and his crew of tribal misfits.

Jared was filled with fright, and dared not charge several armed robots with guns. Tani was lighting his second stick of dynamite when a putrid feeling coursed through him. Nausea filled him, and he vomited immediately. A chill rolled through his body as he began to gag and cough uncontrollably. Young Tani clutched at his throat and struggled to breath. Within a matter of seconds, he crashed to the ground and writhed in pain. Suddenly, his body started to convulse and foam bubbled at his mouth. A seizure took his body and left him incapacitated, twitching like a fish out of water just before death.

"Stupid child," hissed the Reaper Kai, holding his hands above his head. The evil psychic attack was effective, and Tani was now unable to breathe effectively, let alone fight.

Banion was incensed at the sight of the fallen Tani. He blared out a war cry and leveled his submachine gun at the Reaper Kai initiate. Gunfire erupted from the weapon, and harmlessly ricocheted off a barrier of spiritual energy surrounding the Reaper Kai.

"Woe to any that oppose the Reaper Kai!" the initiate hissed as Banion's gunfire was knocked away by an unseen force. The evil initiate could form a shield of spiritual energy just like the traitorous Mineera.

The Biogtechs opened fire and almost felled Banion. Close was too close, and Banion's long coat ended up with several bullet holes.

With three more robotic soldiers and a fierce demonic Reaper Kai still standing, the battle had turned in the enemies' favor with the loss of Tani's abilities. Jared was useless against gun wielding foes, and Banion was running out of ammo and time. The enemies were closing fast.

With determination, Banion rose and calmly aimed at one robot, then the next, and then the next. With a focused series of well-placed shots, all three Biogtechs fell to ruin and ceased to move. The assault was impressive; in merely a few seconds, Banion had slain the remaining Biogtech soldiers.

The Reaper Kai initiate was undaunted by the loss of his squad. He went into a light trance and focused on Banion. With searing pain, Banion dropped his gun. A fierce pain had engulfed both of his hands. They trembled uselessly, and he fought to gain control of his own body. Banion's struggle was to no avail; the Reaper Kai initiate was too powerful, and caused an even sharper pain to erupt in his hands and quickly spread to his arms, as well. The pain was intense, and Banion fell to his knees, trembling in agony. It felt as if a mighty fire was burning his hands. The pain was so severe that Banion was unable to continue the battle.

The Reaper Kai advanced and drew a hand weapon, a wicked black blade. He advanced on the trembling Banion and prepared to slay the deranged rancher. He had advanced within a few feet of Banion before young Jared charged the red robed Reaper Kai.

With a shout, the tribal warrior swung at the Reaper Kai. Hissing like a snake, the Reaper Kai dodged the blow and retreated a few steps. Seeing both Banion and Tani fall to the Reaper Kai filled Jared with fear. His normal training and excellent sword skills would usually have enabled him to slay the opponent, but Jared was wild with fright and unable to fight effectively.

"Puny child, I shall bathe in your blood!" The Reaper Kai shouted, stretching his hand high. With a supernatural tug, the mighty Scar Blade flew from Jared's hand and ended up in the hand of the Reaper Kai. "I will slay you with your own blade!"

"Bastard son of darkness, face me!" Mineera yelled while brandishing her hand axe. The traitor of the Reaper Kai had advanced upon her enemy from behind.

The Reaper Kai spun around with a sinister black blade in one hand and the mighty Scar Blade in his other hand. "Father Vertigo will sing my praises after I place your severed head before his altar!" the Reaper Kai hissed.

"You are nothing more than a puny initiate! Do your worst,

fool," Mineera shouted, proceeding to engage the Reaper Kai in a bloody melee.

The battle was quick and fierce. The Reaper Kai attacked in a frenzy, but was unaccustomed to fighting with two weapons. Mineera took advantage of this fact, and hewed the clumsy Reaper Kai. With a quick series of strikes, Mineera tore the initiate to pieces. The bloodied Reaper Kai fell and died immediately.

Recovering quickly from the psychic attack, Banion was already on his feet, drawing his revolver. He moved forward and placed the gun sights on Mineera's skull. Mineera looked up and stepped back in fright, not from the gun but from Banion's face.

For all her life she had seen his face. She knew every feature, from his fierce dark eyes to the wicked scar on his cheek. In her darkest dreams, she had seen Banion. Year after year, night after night, the same dream haunted her. In this vision, the person now standing before her died at the hands of an assassin. It was a shock to finally be standing before a dream she had seen thousands of times.

Mineera saw his eyes and stared at them intently. Tears rolled down her face, and she smiled. With a calm gesture, she reached out her hand and moved towards him. Banion was stunned by her gesture, but years of anger tugged at his senses to pull the trigger and slay her, for she wore the robes of the Reaper Kai.

Her dark skinned hand moved forward and her robe fell away from her arm. The evil vision of a snake wrapped around her outstretched limb. Banion eyed the snake tattoo on her arm with disgust. His trigger finger tensed, and the hammer of his revolver quivered. Banion shook with rage but Mineera continued to move forward.

Finally, she placed her hand on his chest. Mineera smiled as she felt his form. This was no ghost or vision; this was him, the man from her dreams. Banion felt her hand touch him, and lowered the revolver. A sick look was on his face as he recoiled from her touch. Pulling away he stared at her with disdain. Banion's hatred was absolute. He hated the Reaper Kai in every way. Holding back his wild anger and need for retribution was testing his soul. Banion wanted nothing more than to kill her, even though she had saved them all. Shaking off the haunting rage driving his mind towards madness, he looked away from her and felt his tense hand relax a bit. She would be allowed to live, for the time being.

Abandoning the Reaper Kai woman, Banion moved to Jared, who was helping young Tani to his feet. The trio then stood together, eyeing Mineera warily.

"What brings one of your kind so far south in the company of Lord Globulus?" Banion sneered, his eyes cold and hostile. The shiny silver revolver still quivered in his hand.

She did not respond to his question, and moved away from Banion with sorrow. For her, this moment was a defining one in her life, meeting a phantom of the dream world. For Banion, it was torture not to slay her. Mineera retreated and walked towards the fallen Globulus. "Globulus needs our help," she said softly.

With that, the four moved to the catwalk. Tani was staggering while wiping vomit off his chin. Jared steadied the young scholar with a look of concern. Banion rubbed his hands, still thinking about the burning pain that had engulfed him just a few moments before, and how pleasant it would be to slay the woman Reaper Kai. Shaken from the battle, the stunned team reached the fallen mutant hippo.

Globulus had recovered somewhat, and was staring about with a confused look on his face. The wounds he had suffered still filled the mighty hippo with dizziness, but the blood had clotted for the most part, leaving only a trickle from one of his chest wounds.

"You look like hell, friend," Banion said, staring at Globulus.

"Banion? Banion O'Neil?" Globulus shook his head. A broad smile covered the mighty hippo's face as he stared at his long lost friend. "Now it all makes sense. The only person in the Darken Realm that could have saved us from this mess did. You are a happy sight, Banion. It's good to see you."

Banion helped the huge mutant to his feet. Jared and Tani gasped at the sight of Globulus. Neither had ever seen a mutant hybrid before. And neither was brave enough to talk to the mighty Globulus.

"Who are the kids, Banion? You babysitting or what?" Globulus chuckled. Almost falling over, the injured hippo steadied himself, feeling lightheaded from the loss of blood.

"Something like that, friend," Banion replied, eyeing Mineera suspiciously out of the corner of his eye.

Globulus noticed his gaze. "Don't even ask. We need to get her back to the city as soon as possible."

With that, the five companions hastily departed from the mine in the center of the Coal Wastes and headed off towards the city of Rasheed. As they traveled, they helped the injured Globulus walk.

Jared and Tani were horrified that a giant talking mutant hippo was traveling with them. Banion stared at Mineera as fantasies of slaying her rolled through his head. Mineera stared back at Banion, smiling from time-to-time, happy to finally meet the man from her dreams. Globulus walked in pain and was just happy to be alive.

Chapter 23
The Road to Rasheed

A chill was in the air. The night cloaked the campsite of the five companions. Smoke lazily drifted into the night sky as the crackling embers of the fire popped and hissed.

Jared and Tani had made their way beyond the edge of the camp. In the darkness, they felt much distress, a distress that had been building the entire day since the encounter in the Coal Wastes. The tribals had snuck away from the camp to discuss their concerns.

"What are we doing with these people? And what is that mutant?" Jared whined.

"I believe he is a hippo,." –Tani replied in a quiet tone, looking hastily towards the camp. No one stirred.

"A hippo? Well, that's nice," Jared said, rolling his eyes. "You remember what Master Mogi used to say? Never trust a mutant."

"After viewing that creature… I am not entirely sure he is a mutant." Tani spoke softly in the darkness, not wanting anyone but Jared to overhear the conversation.

"Well, if Globulus isn't a mutant, what is he?" the young warrior wanted to argue, but wasn't quite sure what was on Tani's mind.

"He walks upright like a human, has thumbs like a human." Tani's mind was racing. "It's almost as if he was *merged* with a human, you know, like some kind of hybrid."

"A hybrid?" there was a tone of confusion in Jared's voice as he spoke.

"Ah, I don't know… let's just call him a mutant." Tani was confused as well, and chose to concede to the fact that Globulus was unnatural, avoiding a closer analysis of the strange beastly hippo. "But that *mutant* is the least of my worries. I don't know if Banion or that red robed witch is worse. You saw what that Reaper Kai did to us today. If it weren't for her, we would have all been killed."

"Yeah, and that red robed witch *is* a Reaper Kai! What are

we doing here, Tani? I mean, this keeps getting worse and worse. First Banion, then a talking hippo, now a red robed Reaper Kai." Jared spoke in a hurried flurry. "We could slip away in the night," he entreated earnestly, and Tani nodded in agreement.

"Banion is insane. Just being around him has gotten us into a mess of trouble more than once," Tani said in a hushed tone.

"What have we got ourselves into? Witches, mutants, and a mad-man." Jared shook his head.

"I say we go with them to this 'Rasheed', and then part company." Tani looked around suspiciously as if he was being watched.

"I agree. Let's just go back to camp and get some sleep. I want to put an end to this day."

With that, the two tribals from Scarskin made their way back to camp. As they returned, Mineera was fast asleep, while Globulus and Banion were talking quietly.

"Where did you two little gutter rats sneak off to?" Banion asked sarcastically. Neither of the tribals responded. They simply made their way to the sleeping mats, ignoring Banion.

Banion snorted at the two as they passed him silently. Globulus chuckled, and then winced in immediate pain. With a gasp, he clutched his chest and lightly rubbed the bandages.

"Where did you pick them up, anyway? They don't look like the sort of folk you usually travel with, Banion," Globulus quizzed the deranged rancher. "The dread gunman Banion O'Neil doesn't usually travel with any company, if I remember correctly."

"Ran into them in Pontiac City." Banion's look became distant. "The night it fell."

"'Fell?' What do you mean by that?" the hippo seemed concerned.

"Sacked by a Biogtech army under the control of a Reaper Kai war band." The rancher spoke slowly, his expression becoming more withdrawn. "I came to their aid, and they insisted on following me. Good thing, too. Pontiac City probably fell within the hour after we left."

"The Reaper Kai have begun their assault already?" Globulus was angered by the news. "I thought we had more time before the attack."

"The entire north has been ravaged already. Many towns are

gone…" With that, Banion stopped speaking and fell silent. His thoughts had drifted to Lily, poor Lily.

"Birthrock?" Globulus spoke in a low tone. Banion did not respond at first. The mutant nodded, falling silent himself. He had known Banion for a great many years, and knew that he had taken up a quiet life in the north. Quiet no more; Globulus shook his head in despair.

"It was a sun-lit day. The wind was blowing. The air was dry with a slight chill. I had gone to the south field to fix a fence. I napped for a while under the shadow of an oak tree. When I awoke is when my nightmare began. The town was burning before I made it back. When I got to Birthrock, everyone was dead, even Lily." Banion's eyes were dark, and the campfire glittered in his eyes. The glitter grew more sinister by the second, turning to a burning, smoldering madness. The silence was ominous, and the mighty beast shivered as he stared into the lifeless eyes of a murderer.

"I guess you are retired no more." The statement was matter-of-fact. Banion did not look away from the fire as Globulus spoke.

"My goal is to warn King Toil and lend my aid. I surveyed the army that attacked Pontiac City, and it was formidable. Whatever the cost, they will fall by my hand or by some miracle. The Reaper Kai will not survive this." Banion palmed his revolver and pulled it out, stroking it lovingly. With a click, the chamber snapped open and Banion spun it around a few times. With a flick of his wrist, the chamber clicked back into place. Another quick motion and the silver revolver disappeared into his long coat.

The mighty hippo changed the subject. "Those two brats, why did you let them come with you? It's not your style to have runts like that in your company."

A wicked smile crossed Banion's lips as he spoke. "The bookworm, Tani, is talented. I have never seen a better demolitions expert in all my years. The best thing is, the damn kid makes his own explosives," Banion cackled.

Globulus eyed Banion oddly, as if he thought the deranged rancher had entirely lost his grip on reality.

"The other one is annoying. His name is Jared. Tani insists that Jared is the best swordsman alive. I sure haven't seen it. The kid is too unsure of himself when push comes to shove. His cockiness and arrogance will get him killed some day." Banion nodded slowly as he thought about Jared. He fell silent for a brief moment, and then spoke again. "Ah, hell, maybe he has a little promise." Banion laughed, and Globulus smiled.

"It's my turn, I guess." The hippo nodded and looked over at Mineera, who was sleeping by the fire. She was caught in a dream, and was mumbling while thrashing about like a fish out of water. "She is the lead diplomat of the Reaper Kai Empire. Or maybe I should say that she *was* the lead diplomat."

"She betrayed them?" Banion seemed amazed. His temper flared suddenly. "She is lying to you. You cannot trust her. That witch will lead you to ruin. You would do best to slay her while she sleeps, or better yet, let me kill her."

"Hold yourself, Banion. Mineera is the key to our survival. She knows of their strengths and weaknesses, and we can use her knowledge to our advantage. We can prepare our armies with her aid."

"Or she will use that knowledge to destroy you," Banion countered.

Finally, Globulus gave up the argument. He too, did not trust Mineera. "Ah, hell, Banion, you are probably right. I don't trust her at all. But King Toil is convinced that she will help us, and I am bound into his service." The hippo shook his head and sighed. "But I have to tell you, I've never seen a person more tormented. Every night, she thrashes about like that. It's as if she is fighting a war in her dreams."

"I have no pity for one of her kind. Death is the only dream they deserve." Banion was harsh in tone.

"She whispers your name in the dark of night," Globulus said softly, and a chill rolled down Banion's spine.

"What?"

"I have heard her whimper and whisper your name. She claims that you are in her dreams," Globulus stated.

"I don't understand. How could that witch know of me?" Banion was irritated, and, once again felt the impulse to kill Mineera as she slept. "Not one survived Dune Station. Not a single Reaper Kai survived the rebellion. How could she know me?"

"You don't exactly live a quiet life, Banion O'Neil. There are many in the Darken Realm that know your name. Hell, probably more know of you than don't."

"I don't like it, Globulus. She is crazy. There is no way she could know me." Banion shook his head and thought back to their meeting. "Still... there is something about her... her eyes... ah, hell, I don't know. She reached out to me with such love in her eyes... I really felt that she knew me..."

"What could it mean?" the hippo quizzed.

"Nothing. It's nothing more than a Reaper Kai trick." Banion nodded in conviction, his temper flaring.

"What about them?" the copper brown skinned hand of Globulus pointed to the two tribals sleeping on their wicker mats.

"The runts? I keep traveling and they keep following. But if I hang around you, I don't think they will stick around long. Did you see the look on their faces when they saw you?" Banion chuckled.

"Watch it, cow puncher; I can still crush you with my bare hands."

"Not in your condition," Banion laughed.

Globulus chuckled, clutching his chest and wincing in pain.

The conversation continued as Globulus became drowsy. Banion took first watch, and the mighty hippo stayed up a little longer to catch up on stories with the legendary gunfighter. The night drew on, but it was a quiet one, except for Mineera. The only sound in the night was her thrashing about and mumbling as she slept. From time to time, she whispered in the darkness: "Banion... Banion... don't die..."

Chapter 24
Father Vertigo

The flames rose from the black melting wax like a dagger, blue at the base and soaring upwards until their tips were bright yellow. Hundreds of black candles were lit in the chamber. The air was stagnant and hung heavily in the room. Strangely enough, the candle flames pulsed and danced as if caught by a breeze. No such breeze coursed through the room, and the candles were dancing on their own, caught by some unseen force.

Red robed figures moved in and out of the shadows. An icy chill flooded the room; it was a cold that could not be warmed. The dim light hid many figures clinging to the comfort of the shadows. Chanting and hissing rose from the red robed initiates slinking near the edge of the candlelight.

A figure dressed in blue and black robes emerged from the back of the room and approached a rancid alter covered in a sickening mess of dry blood and littered with broken bone. As he drew near the defiled alter, the candles burned more intensely, and the shadows in the room lifted. Surrounding the altar was a dark patronage of evil. Minions of darkness moved forward to behold their master, now standing confidently before the desecrated altar. As the red robed beings moved forward into the candlelight, a hideous visage could be seen. The red robed beings were no longer human; their hatred and their embracement of darkness had transformed their shape and twisted them into beasts.

The enclave of evil was twisted beyond compare. These minions of evil, once human, had given up their humanity to gain favor with the dark powers. Their bodies had twisted into those of deformed goats. With long snouts that dripped a foul puss and eyes that burned red as the fire, these Reaper Kai had sacrificed their bodies and souls for the sake of evil.

Horns had replaced hair, and hooves had replaced their feet. Instead of skin, a thick bristly coat of gray or black fur covered their bodies. These Reaper Kai were no longer of the same order as the lesser initiates. The foul creatures were known as the Najaszim, Goat Minions in the common tongue, and their master now stood before them at the tainted altar.

The master of evil presented a powerful presence before his mighty host of Goat Minions.

Father Vertigo was a myth in most lands. Born from darkness and bathed in sin he was. In the quiet shadows of long lost madness his name was whispered. For over seven generations of Reaper Kai had known Vertigo. He was said to be immortal, and cherished by the most powerful of demons. For where chaos was a part of evil, Father Vertigo had no part. He was a malevolent force that favored order within evil. Where there was vice and sin, Father Vertigo favored the strong who could look beyond such things and perform their duty to the dark powers.

Vertigo was short in stature but imposing. His eyes had long since rotted, leaving only black globes within his bony eye sockets. An ashen white beard flowed from a chin that was braided and forked. White rotted flesh covered his body, for that body had long since died. The power of his will and a host of dark spirits kept his physical form in one piece. Vertigo was nothing more than a shell, a vessel for evil to reside within. And it was this tattered body that held the most powerful manifestation of dread the world had ever known.

With harsh eyes and an air of confidence, the lord of hell on earth surveyed his prized Goat Minions. Father Vertigo stood before the blood stained altar and smiled wickedly at his disciples. The Goat Minions moved forward and hissed in reverence at their master. Many fell to their knees before the lord of evil. This token of respect elated Darklord Vertigo, and he urged his unholy congregation to rise.

As they rose, Vertigo held his hands high in the air and spoke to his coven. "Today is the first day of the end, my children. We are moving towards the oblivion with great speed, and our masters in hell are rejoicing in our splendor! We are about to take the first step towards the end of all that is good. Our garden is about to be forged from the blood of our enemies. With all due speed, we set our course to cleanse this earth of all that oppose our rule and our might. We alone will be the lords of this earth. And with our goal shall come the end of light. For when our mission be done, the gates of hell shall be unleashed, and all the souls shall pour forth into the garden of our design. That garden will be a paradise for all the lost souls of all the lost ages. No longer shall it be a garden of good, but a utopia for our kind and our master!"

The coven hissed in glee, and many of the Goat Minions bayed and growled with twisted, happy fascination.

"So let it be this night that we perform a ritual to ensure our victory!" Vertigo proclaimed loudly. With a look of hatred in his eyes, the Darklord pointed towards a circular stone plate resting on the floor in the center of the room.

The Goat Minions bayed and neighed in the darkness, beginning to claw at the stone plate covering the floor. With great effort, the coven of fallen souls heaved and pushed at the stone plate. The stone plate lurched inch by inch. As it did, a stench of decay and death filled the room. Inch by inch, the plate moved further. Stone ground against stone. The plate crept open and the stench increased.

As the coven of Goat Minions toiled with the stone plate, the plate was revealed to be covering an ancient well. Warm, humid, sickening air rushed from the well. Maggots and flies erupted from its edge. The floor near the hole was instantly covered in a carpet of filth. Thousands of maggots crawled from the evil well. A cloud of flies rushed forth from the depths, hovering above the opening in a black swarm.

The stench from the well was horrific, and many of the Goat Minions retreated from the edge of the pit. Vertigo did not waver, nor did he falter. He had no fear of the pit or of what resided at the bottom. For Father Vertigo had given his entire essence to the darkness, and he did not fear anything born from the darkness.

"So is our right and so is our splendor that I summon Lord Iblis to bless this pit with his power!" Vertigo yelled, raising his hands above the altar. As he spoke, a tremble rose from within the pit.

"For centuries, I have diligently followed the word of our law. And in the darkness of our past, I had constructed this pit to pay homage to Lord Iblis. For over two hundred years have I planned this night! For over two hundred years have I fed this pit warm souls! For over two hundred years have I deposited hundreds of the living so that they may die and be trapped forever within this pit! It is my right to call you forth now to do my bidding, to do the bidding of all that is evil!" Vertigo yelled in glee. The ground shook. Screams rose from the pit with a keening moan. The lost souls were screaming out in terror, screaming out in fear. Hundreds of voices mixed in the piercing wail.

The Goat Minions fled from the edge of the pit and covered their pointed ears. Only Father Vertigo stood unmoved by the sounds of hundreds in pain and terror.

"So be it. I plunge this world into darkness, and forsake all that is good and just!" Vertigo yelled intently. "Lord Iblis, I summon thee to do my bidding!"

With that, the ground shook violently. The maggots ceased to move and died. The flies fell and dropped into the pit. Screams of terror rose from the pit with greater intensity. The ground heaved. A thud rose from inside the pit. A sliding noise and squishing sound emerged amidst the screams of the damned. Something was crawling from the depths of the well. Something was climbing the sheer wall, something born from the darkness.

Suddenly, a sickly green hand, a giant, misshapen claw reeking of death, emerged from the pit. And then another misshapen arm emerged. The Goat Minions were instantly filled with a fear that they had never known before. Not a single Goat Minion could gaze at the monstrosity rising out of the well.

And then the creature rose out of the pit, and all that was holy was undone. All that was sacred was gone and torn asunder. The grotesque beast hunched in the room. None save Father Vertigo could gaze upon the monstrosity, for it was utterly unholy. Cowering, the Goat Minions backed away and sought shelter from its presence.

With terror filling them, all the Goat Minions fled the room, leaving it and the Darklord Vertigo alone.

The beast rose, and hundreds of screams filled the room. Sickly green it was, standing larger than a two-story building. Its body was twisted, and the odor of death surrounded it. The faces of fallen souls covered its body. All about the monstrosity were the faces of all that had been cast into the pit. Forever were they bound to be part of the beast's body. Open mouths wailed and screamed. Other faces looked about, wide-eyed with fear. More than a hundred faces were set into the torso of the demonic creature. Like living tattoos, the faces covered its body and screamed in anguish.

The beast roared and eyed Vertigo. For only the righteous and the very evil could look upon the monstrosity. All others would be filled with fear and flee from its presence, or cower before it until death.

"So, fool!" a loud voice boomed as the hundred faces screamed in terror. "You have summoned me forth at last. I grew in the pit for ages and ages. So hungry I was. And so good of you to feed me. So many souls are mine, but I still hunger!"

"I fed you well," Father Vertigo said in a dull tone. The Lord of Darkness gazed at length upon the hunched form at the edge of the foul smelling pit. Vertigo paused, and the beast eyed him in consideration.

"Now I command you to build a vessel for me. It shall be large enough to house me. It shall not let a single ray of the sun touch my body. Light from the sun will wither and burn my flesh. Wheels must be placed upon my vessel, my coffin, and it shall be drawn by forty oxen," the beast roared.

"So be it," Vertigo said, bowing before the creature. "And what shall I call you, lord of evil?"

"Hence-forth, I will be known to all as the Abomination, for I am an ancient beast from the land of fallen souls. Beldarmordain is my home, and my hunger grows." The Abomination roared at Vertigo, who bowed before his dark majesty.

"So be it, Abomination of Beldarmordain. The war has already begun, but we will need your service soon," the dark father said dully.

"War shall it be, then. I hunger for more souls. I need the fresh splash of blood in my jaws. What city shall I lay waste to?" The Abomination spoke as its hundred trapped souls wailed.

"A great city in the south. A city named Rasheed. Our army is already moving, and our spies and assassins are already at work," Vertigo answered.

"Rasheed." The Abomination spoke softly. A distant look invaded its eyes. A trickle of drool rolled out of the beast's foul mouth. The thought of fresh flesh and warm souls was too much for it to handle. The drool hit the stone floor with a sizzle. "So be it, Father Vertigo, Rasheed will fall."

The Abomination looked around the room; its yellow eyes

darted back and forth. More drool dripped from the creature's open mouth. The thought of feeding had driven the Abomination into a frenzy. It hungered. It craved. It needed.

"I hunger…" it hissed, staring at Vertigo.

"As you will, Abomination. I will fetch a slave from the breeding pits. Feed as you will," Vertigo said in an emotionless tone.

The Abomination smiled as more drool rolled down its chin.

Chapter 25
Rasheed

Like a white pinnacle of light, the city of Rasheed rose from the battered earth. The mighty walls of the city were white-washed with a mixture of clay and white marble dust. The effect made the city walls glimmer in the sunlight. Rising more than a hundred feet in the air, the walls of the city surrounded the entire perimeter of Rasheed save the harbor front. Pits and chunks of the walls had been blasted away in past conflicts when artillery fire had slammed into the glimmering walls. Never had an army breached the defenses of the mighty city.

Circular towers were set at regular intervals along the wall. Purple flags whipped in the wind rushing in from the harbor. White sea gulls rode the thermals and wind currents around the tops of the towers.

The walls of the mighty city-state were manned with the Rasheed Militia, clad in white and silver uniforms. Dozens of guards patrolled along the walls, brandishing automatic weapons.

Rasheed was the powerhouse of the south, the focal point for civilization and order in the southern reaches of the Darken Realm. The mighty city had stood for over thirty generations, serving as the hub for all trade and commerce in the southern lands. Fisherman and naval merchants frequented the port on the southwest portion of the city. Miners hailing from the northeast brought coal and steel from the nearby Coal Wastes. East of the city was a fertile stretch of land that skirted the coastline and brought farmers and ranchers. From the north came the nomadic tribesman of the open wastelands and trade caravans hailing from the frigid northlands. All of this activity came together in the city of Rasheed. It was a melting pot for all the races of the Darken Realm, a place to find almost any culture imaginable.

The five companions neared the great road that led into the east gate of the mighty city. Many travelers and merchants packed the road in both directions. As they pressed onward, the great city walls loomed into view. Washed in white clay, the walls extended many stories into the air. Both Jared and Tani gasped as they caught sight of the city ahead of them. Neither had seen such enormous architecture.

To Globulus, it was home; to Banion – a place of fortune in his mercenary days; and to Mineera, it was another place where she was considered an outcast. As merchants passed by in droves, they stared in disbelief and hatred at the five companions. They all recoiled at the sight of Mineera walking along the great east road of Rasheed. Many uttered gasps of astonishment, others backed away in fear. None were happy to see a filthy Reaper Kai in their presence. Though all despised her, not a single peasant had the courage to curse her.

Mineera kept her head low and stared at the ground straight ahead of her. She dared not make eye contact with anyone she encountered. Jared eyed Tani with a look of urgency as he watched the reactions of the peasants. Tani shot back an equal look of alarm. Both were thinking the same thing: it was almost time to part company with Banion, the witch, and the mutant.

The east gate of the city was nearly five stories tall at the apex of the large archway. Wooden doors, reinforced with steel and thicker than a man's girth, stood open in the noonday sun. Tani squinted and looked high above his head. It almost made him dizzy to stare at the top of the archway. Jared patted Tani's shoulder and urged him to move on. Slowly, the young scholar did, but he did so with a look of wonder on his face.

Globulus led the way, for he was the Master of Arms in Rasheed, the King's trusted aid and bodyguard. As the beastly hippo approached the interior of the tall gate, a complement of Rasheed soldiers moved to greet him.

"What devilry is this, Master Globulus?" the lead guard sneered as he raised his weapon. The crosshairs of his gun rested on Mineera's chest.

"We have captured this Reaper Kai witch. King Toil himself has asked to interrogate her." Globulus was stern, and his gaze did not waver.

"So be it." The guards saluted the mighty hippo, but kept their gaze on the woman garbed in red.

"Fetch us a carriage. I do not want to alarm the populace by taking this witch through the city," the mighty hippo ordered the soldiers.

"Of course, sir." The guard snapped his fingers, and a carriage was dispatched from the nearby stables.

The royal carriage came into view, led by two jet-black stallions. They came to a halt before the band, and the four humans got into the carriage. Globulus, unable to fit, simply walked along side the trotting horses.

Jared and Tani both ran their hands along the interior of the coach, which was covered in fine, soft fabrics. They had never felt anything softer in all their days.

"Silk," mouthed Banion as he smiled at the youths. With a sigh, the rancher leaned back and tipped his cowboy hat over his face. He propped his legs up between the tribals, and relaxed, not saying another word.

With that, an uneasy silence came over the coach. Jared and Tani stared at Mineera apprehensively. Mineera could feel their eyes on her, and looked up at the two with quick glances. She was stunning when her eyes fell upon them. Brilliant blue eyes and tan skin with delicate features were the highlights of her face. Black wavy hair cascaded out her red hood. The witch was truly beautiful, but still made the tribals uncomfortable.

Unable to stare back at her, both Tani and Jared stared out the windows of the carriage and watched the sights passing by.

The inhabitants of Rasheed were simple people with a colorful culture. Most of them wore white or tan robes with headdresses of the same color. Their language was noisy, filled with chirps and clicks, but was overall a derivation of the ancient tongue with heavy accents. If one was unable to see, one might think that the noise was produced by a host of birds, and not humans.

The carriage passed through the merchant district of the city. Dozens upon dozens of merchants flooded the narrow street. Many people milled about, including a mutant here and there. One such mutant, a camel, was haggling over a curved sword, and the human he haggled with obviously couldn't stand mutants one bit. An argument broke out between the two, and ended up with them shoving each other.

Exotic fruit and foods from all over the realm were being

sold at various stands. Jared stared in awe at the strange sights before him. Weapon merchants sold a variety of guns and swords. As he viewed the swords, his hand moved to the hilt of the mighty Scar Blade. He smiled to himself, for there was nothing better in the bazaar.

An alchemist was selling a variety of potions and salves. Tani smiled to himself, lost in thought. He imagined a whole host of potions he himself could make and sell in such a market. The youth pressed his glasses up his nose as he poked his head out the window of the carriage. One of the merchants was selling gunpowder, and Tani made a mental note of the location. The young scholar's supply of dynamite was almost spent.

Finally, the carriage passed out of the busy street and pressed northwards through the city, passing through the residential district. Small wooden and clay houses lined the streets. The sight made both the tribals smile, reminding them of the houses in Scarskin. Children were playing in the street, kicking a ball back and forth while laughing and yelling excitedly.

The royal carriage pressed deeper into the city, and the houses became larger and more intricate. Two story houses with splendid lawns came into view. Trees and bushes lined the street, and it was readily apparent that the carriage had passed into the wealthy district of Rasheed.

Jared squinted in the sunlight, focusing his gaze on another set of walls coming into view, with an enormous palace of white marble tucked away beyond them. He gasped and examined the mighty palace in astonishment. Dozens of towers and gardens dotted its side. Gold covered steeples soared majestically, their vibrant purple flags blowing in the salty sea breeze coming of the harbor. With a tug, Jared pulled on Tani's arm, and the young scholar stared wide-eyed as they approached the palace. The coach was stopped at the gates, and the tribals could hear the mighty Globulus speaking to the guards.

"Hail Lord Globulus." The palace guard, clad in royal purple garb, bowed before the mighty hippo. "It has been many weeks since last we met."

"It has been many weeks filled with strife," Globulus said in a dark tone.

"Where is the rest of your team? They must be tired from

such a journey into the northlands," the guard said with a look of confusion on his face.

"I am the only one who left the north alive." The mutant spoke in a solemn tone.

The guard did not respond, and his expression turned fearful. Motioning to the top of the gate, the guard ordered the doors to be opened for the carriage.

The thick steel doors of the palace were pushed open, and the carriage moved inside. Finally, the door of the carriage opened and the four emerged.

They found themselves in the courtyard of the palace. A lush green garden came into view surrounding the courtyard. Bright colored birds fluttered through the air. Sweet fragrant smells greeted their noses. Moist, cool air brushed across their faces. This was no mere garden, it was a paradise hidden in the middle of the city. The tribals were in awe of the sight.

"I have never seen anything more green," Jared said in a dazzled tone.

Banion chuckled and shook his head. "Damn kids."

A host of palace guards garbed in purple came before the company of five. The leader was known as Reimal, a stout warrior who was missing his left eye.

"So your mission was a success," Reimal sneered, searing Globulus with a wicked glance. Globulus and Reimal had never liked each other. Reimal was always jealous that he was not one of the King's advisors and the mighty hippo was.

"Success?" Globulus grunted. "You see any of my men? You call this a success?"

"It's a shame your leadership was not up to the task. If it was, some of your men would still be standing beside you," Reimal said in a hateful tone.

Globulus did not respond to the taunt; he simply issued an order. "Take the Reaper Kai to the north wing of the palace, set guards outside the door, and do not let anyone enter but me. Is that clear?"

"Yes, sir." Reimal spoke while staring at Globulus with malice.

"Take Banion and the tribals to the west suites, and make sure they are well tended to," the hippo dispatched another set of orders.

"Yes, sir," the head guard shot back.

The guards led Mineera away, weapons ready. Another set of guards led Banion, Jared, and Tani through another entrance.

With that, only Globulus remained in the courtyard with Reimal.

"The princess wished to speak with you upon your return. She is in the south garden by the pool," Reimal said while turning his back to Globulus.

The hippo took a moment alone in the courtyard. He stared around the walls of the palace and smiled to himself. "It's good to be home," he uttered to himself. With that, he made his way towards the south gardens of the palace. Tall trees lined the walkway as it curved through the fragrant garden. Bright flowers were planted in clumps near the base of the trees. Short bushes lined the perimeter of large, open patches of perfectly tended grasses.

Finally, the hippo came to the edge of a clearing. Ahead of him stood a delicate woman garbed in light blue and white. As the hippo pressed into the clearing, it appeared that the woman was talking to someone concealed near an oak tree. She turned abruptly towards Globulus as he entered the clearing, and a shadow melted into the undergrowth of the garden. The shadowy figure near the oak tree made the hippo feel uneasy, but he made his way towards the princess anyway. Maybe Globulus had *imagined* the shadowy figure.

"It has been long since you were in my presence," Marion Toil, princess of Rasheed, addressed the travel worn mutant hippo.

"Indeed it has, my lady." Globulus dropped to one knee and bowed before the princess.

"I trust your mission is complete?" Marion asked. Her face was ashen white, and her blond hair was revealed under her transparent purple veil. The princess had blue eyes, but it was a dark shade of blue. Though she was delicate and beautiful in appearance, she was formidable, extremely formidable. An air of confidence surrounded Marion Toil, and her mere presence was intimidating and imposing to many.

"Complete is a good term, my lady. All our troops were slain before we reached our borders," Globulus said mournfully, shaking his head as he spoke.

"The cost of war is never easy," Marion said in a heartless tone. "The traitor is here in the palace?"

"Yes, my lady, in the north wing under guard at this very moment."

"Good." Marion Toil moved forward and urged the mighty hippo to sit with her on a stone bench. The mutant did so, and Marion continued to quiz him. "The guards told me that you did not enter the city alone."

"That is true, my lady. A Reaper Kai squad ambushed us in the Coal Wastes. Banion O'Neil and his two companions came to our aid. If it were not for his help, I fear we would have never made it back alive."

"Banion O'Neil?" Marion said with a jolt of hatred.

"Yes, my lady..." Globulus viewed her reaction cautiously. Many in Rasheed knew of the dangerous gun fighter, but none more than Marion...

"You serve me and this family, master mutant," she said in a harsh tone. "I know my father finds favor in Banion O'Neil, but I do not."

"Yes, my lady, I am sorry. The journey has been long and I am weary." The hippo retreated, taken aback by her flash of anger at the mention of Banion.

"My father seeks your council this evening. You will dine at his table as you are accustomed to," Marion ordered the mutant. "You may take your leave."

"Yes, my lady." Globulus rose and headed north to the edge of the garden.

As the hippo disappeared from view, Marion made her way towards the foliage of the garden. The shadows moved, and a form stepped from behind a tree. A mutant stepped forward and stood near the princess.

"Did you hear that? Banion O'Neil is in the city," Marion said in a wicked tone. "It seems fitting that the darkness has given me this prize right before the fall of this city."

"Ah, yes, yes indeed! Banion O'Neil, the mighty gunfighter! Ah yes, yes indeed!" The mutant hissed. Bearing metallic implants and a host of weaponry, the mutant opossum licked his yellow teeth as he spoke.

"I will make the one that killed my mother pay." Marion's dark blue eyes became darker.

"What would you have me do, mistress?" the opossum hissed while he stroked a dagger on his belt.

"I want him killed before he leaves the boundary of the palace. I will have Reimal contact you with the location of his room," the sinister princess said malevolently.

"Ah, yes, my mistress, he will die indeed!" The mutant giggled and licked his lips in anticipation. "Once he was the best mercenary in the Darken Realm. With his passing at my hand, I will be the most feared mercenary in all the land."

"Now go, Guillotine! I do not want to be seen with the likes of you until after the fall!" Marion said in a harsh tone, and the mutant disappeared into the foliage.

Globulus, still slightly uneasy, had concealed himself at the other side of the clearing. His enormous form was barely hidden by a stand of tall cattails rising from a pristine pool in the garden. Although he could not hear what was being spoken, he was close enough to catch sight of the mutant assassin known as Guillotine. Next to the legendary Banion O'Neil, Guillotine was the most feared mercenary in the Darken Realm, and had become a force to be reckoned with in the past few years.

Sensing a presence in the garden, Marion whirled around. The hippo crouched and concealed himself further. She could feel someone hidden, but didn't know where. Scowling at the foliage, she stormed off towards the palace. When she was out of view, Globulus rose and made his way back via the courtyard. As he walked, suspicion clouded his mind. The mutant had sworn an oath to protect the royal family, but he couldn't help but wonder why the princess of Rasheed would be consorting in secret with an assassin.

Chapter 26
The Great Library

The tribals were escorted to the west wing of the palace. Under an escort of palace guards, they slowly trudged under the vaulted marble ceilings and through interior gardens that led to halls and an endless maze of passages and rooms. They passed room after room, until they were both confused.

Finally, Jared and Tani were brought to a splendid room overlooking a series of hanging gardens. Banion had long since disappeared into his own room, and the guards left the tribals in their spacious room, which could easily accommodate a dozen people.

White marble columns rose into the air and eventually came together in vaulted arches which comprised the ceiling. Black and white marble covered the floors. At irregular intervals, large openings in the floor gave rise to a thick rush of plant life. Open balconies circulated moist ocean air into the room. All in all, the room was the most spectacular place the tribals had ever seen.

"I don't know what to say." Jared shook his head in disbelief as he stared about the room. His ponytail bobbed back and forth as his head swayed from side to side.

"What are we doing here?" Tani said in amazement. "How did we ever get here?"

"I am not sure. It seems like a lifetime ago when we left the village. Not even three moons have passed since we took our leave." Jared shook his head.

"After everything we have seen, after everything we have survived, to end up here..." Tani spoke hesitantly, his voice dropping to a whisper. "We are just tribals, desert trash to these people. Why are we here? Huh, Jared? Why are we here? Look at this place." Tani pointed around him, holding out his hands in disbelief. "This is a room for a king, not for us."

"I don't get it either. Banion appears to have connections here. Banion seems to be more important than we thought." Jared nodded to his friend.

"What have we gotten ourselves into? A war is brewing, and we are caught in the middle of it. Should we even be here?" Tani inquired while rubbing the sweat from his brow. He took a brief moment to remove his wire-rim glasses in order to clean them.

"No, we shouldn't be here," Jared said, his voice quiet yet confident.

"I agree. Banion is crazy and doesn't care about his own safety. He is going to get us killed. And that witch is the enemy, as far as I can tell. Throw in that talking hippo and I say we're in a really bad place. Not to mention this war." Tani was frustrated, and felt relief finally letting it all out.

"We need to leave soon," Jared said. Tani nodded in agreement. "But I am afraid we can't just leave the palace without permission. I almost feel like a prisoner and Banion is the warden."

Tani chuckled. "Yeah, a crazy warden."

Jared laughed himself.

"I haven't had rest in weeks, but I'm too anxious to sleep. Let's explore the palace, if the guards will let us," Jared suggested.

Tani threw his pack down, as did Jared. Jared removed the Scar Blade from his waist and hid it under a stand of foliage near the balcony.

With that, the tribals pushed the ten-foot tall wooden door open. They pressed into the hall and found it to be empty. No one stirred, and the palace was washed in an eerie silence. The interior halls had no windows, and were lined with black marble. An icy darkness clung to the halls, and a chill hovered in the air.

"Weird," Jared said as he peered down the silent corridors. Tani agreed with a nod, and they pressed on down the main hall.

Their footsteps echoed with each movement. As they walked, they felt oddly alone. A creepy feeling washed over both of them. With fear and hesitation lingering at the edge of their minds, they moved more quickly down the dark and gloomy hall of black marble. Finally, the hall came to an end, and a white staircase descended down into the darkness.

Like a black pit with a shard of silver spiraling downward, the staircase seemed to be swallowed by the dark passage below. With a look of reservation, Jared took the first step down. Tani followed, and they descended into the darkness. As they pressed onward, oil lamps came into view along the wall of the stairwell.

Orange flames stood tall in the still air, flickering only with the tribals' passing. Finally, the two came to the end of the stairway. They looked ahead, and found an archway leading into a dark room filled with parchments and ancient books.

Tani gasped as they moved into the room. From wall to wall, from floor to ceiling were books and parchments, many from before the fall of Man. More oil lamps were situated near the center of the room, adjacent to finely crafted marble tables. Plush leather chairs surrounded the tables. Upon closer inspection, the tribals noticed three more archways leading out of the central room. Each archway led into a catacomb of books and scrolls.

"This is amazing," Tani gasped.

"It sure is," Jared agreed.

As they spoke, they heard something shuffle in the darkness, just beyond a dark archway.

Abruptly on guard, both tribals backed away from the archway. Slowly, a figure moved in the darkness. Step by agonizing step it hunched. Finally, it pushed its way out of the darkness and squinted at the tribals. A man of extreme age and hideous appearance moved into the dull light of the ancient library.

The man was hunched, and a great lump of flesh rose from his shoulders. The hair had long since fallen away from his pasty white head. It was apparent that this man had not been in sunlight for many years. Long, yellow fingernails grew from his withered hands. Slowly, he staggered closer to the youths from Scarskin. With much labor, he spoke softly to Jared and Tani alike.

"Eh... what do we have here? Outsiders, I reckon by the looks of you. I don't get many visitors down here, and when I do, they are usually part of the royal family. Who are you and what brings you here?" the derelict librarian spoke in a weary, haggard tone.

Still not knowing what to make of the old man, Jared took a step forward and spoke to him first. "I am Jared and this Tani. We are guests of Globulus."

"What brings you down here?" the librarian pressed, taking a step forward. As he did, light from a nearby lamp illuminated his face. Jared and Tani took a step back, for the old man's face was covered in warts.

"Chance brought us here. We were exploring the palace, and

came here by chance," Tani said while staring through his glasses at the old man.

"Chance, eh?" the librarian chuckled. "Well, come in and make yourselves comfortable. As I said, it's not often I get company."

Not knowing what to think, the tribals moved to a marble table, and each took a seat in one of the old, worn leather chairs.

"Now, what can I dredge up from these halls for you two?" the wizened librarian quizzed the youths.

Jared shook his head; he didn't know what to request. Tani, being more enlightened and always thirsty for knowledge, responded immediately. "History," the scholar said in a confident tone.

"History, eh?" the librarian chuckled. "History of what, young master?"

"History of the Reaper Kai," Tani replied.

A dull silence filled the room. The librarian shot Tani an uneasy look. Even Jared felt a chill run down his spine when Tani requested such a dark topic.

"Reaper Kai, eh?" This time, the librarian did not chuckle. He moved off slowly into the darkness and returned with a book bound in leather. There was no need to wipe dust from the book; it was frequently used by King Toil and his war advisors.

"I can outline some of the more prominent points for you lads. I am well versed in the history of the rise of darkness." The elderly librarian smiled, and Tani shivered in reaction to the look in his eyes.

The librarian passed the book to the tribals, who drew close. They opened the book and thumbed through it. Horrid pictures of demons, human sacrifice, and black rituals lined the pages. With horrid fascination, they looked at the book in the dim light of the library while the old man told the story and history of the Reaper Kai.

"Our texts and records go back nearly eight hundred years. We had thought for a long time that out history was the oldest in the Darken Realm, until we came in contact with a great empire far to the north. That empire is known as the Iron Kai Empire. Their records go back much further, and it is speculated that the Iron Kai Empire emerged from the ashes of the old world." The librarian spoke softly, and the tribals were enthralled by the story. They had each wondered about the Reaper Kai, and Jared was happy that Tani had the courage and the forethought to ask about such a subject.

"It is said that the Iron Kai were born from the death and chaos of the apocalypse. From very early on, they hoarded ancient machinery and technology. They embraced the artifacts that destroyed the old world, and continued to build complex machinery even after other parts of the world had ceased to understand the mysteries of the ancients. So the Iron Kai grew, and slowly gained a large territory in the northern forests of the world. Deep in their past, an event occurred that shook the foundations of their mighty empire." The librarian paused a moment for effect. Jared and Tani were on the edge of their seats.

"Other northern tribes possessed technology, and there arose feuds and wars that used technology of old. It was said that the Iron Kai were on the verge of victory over all the tribes in the north when a black plague erupted in their empire. The populace was decimated. Thousands and thousands died, and nothing could stop the spread of the disease. The Iron Kai retreated and tended to the plague in the Empire. In those dark times arose ones who could see the future, speak to the dead, and summon nightmares. These people were feared, and were ultimately blamed for the spread of the plague. A decree was sent out across the Iron Kai Empire calling for the death of these witches and seers." Jared and Tani were enthralled by the story, and dared not interrupt.

"These witches and psychics were thus driven underground in the Empire. They formed secret guilds and societies to practice their newfound powers. As the years passed, their presence in the empire grew. Great witch-hunts formed and thousands were slain in the chaos. Finally, after hundreds of years of fear and witch-hunts, a faction of the Iron Kai emerged from the darkness, calling themselves the Reaper Kai. While the Iron Kai were children of technology and ancient lore, the Reaper Kai were children of the shadow, born of darkness and followers of evil. And once they emerged from the Empire, they defied the Iron Kai and vowed to crush them, pervert all the lands, and twist them into darkness. With nearly one in ten of the populace in the clutches of the Reaper Kai's will, a bloody civil war erupted, thrusting the north into darkness for three hundred years."

"Three hundred years? Our records barely go back that far," Tani said in astonishment.

The librarian chuckled. "The strength of the Reaper Kai was strongly underestimated. While the Iron Kai could crush any army with the might of their technology, the Reaper Kai fought a war based on darkness and fear. Very few could withstand the might of a Reaper Kai priest. The war was long and bitter, but slowly, the Iron Kai pushed the Reaper Kai out of the Empire. The Reaper Kai fled and disappeared from all human knowledge for a great length of time. All had forgotten the ancient terror, thinking that they had been destroyed or driven apart by corruption."

"The Reaper Kai were not defeated, nor were they driven apart," Jared said.

The librarian nodded and continued his story. "Quite the contrary. In the time they 'disappeared', they banded together and created an entire society. An archpriest known as Father Vertigo appeared and unified the Reaper Kai factions into a focused entity. All thought the Reaper Kai were lost to the darkness until an army appeared at the edge of the Iron Kai territory. After a massive assault, the army pushed deep into the Iron Kai empire before it was driven back. The mysterious attackers were called 'Biogtechs', for they were an ancient technology that merged artificial life with organic life designs."

"Biogtechs. It's all beginning to make sense. I wager that during the 'disappearance' of the Reaper Kai, they managed to unlock ancient secrets of their own," Tani theorized.

"Indeed, young scholar. The Biogtechs were a construct of the Reaper Kai army. They used them to test the defenses of their ancient Iron Kai enemies. Not only did the Iron Kai feel the sting of the Biogtech armies, but other northern empires were assaulted as well. And then, one day, the attacks stopped. Diplomats were dispatched from the newly formed Reaper Kai Empire with a message of peace. Since then, there has not been a full-scale attack made by the Reaper Kai. We have lived an uneasy truce for the last twenty years or so," the librarian concluded.

A silence filled the room. The tribals' minds were spinning. Each thought suddenly about Mineera. She was a diplomat for the Reaper Kai. She was the key to this invasion. Suddenly, Jared's face wrinkled in dismay.

"No large scale attack? What do you mean?" he said in disgust. "A truce? You have to be joking."

The librarian was confused.

"We witnessed several thousand Biogtechs lay waste to a town in the Frontier," Tani added, equally disgusted.

"That's impossible..." the librarian stammered.

"Not impossible. We were both there," Jared confirmed.

"The Reaper Kai would not dare attack us!" the librarian said with a look of fear. "King Toil wed a Reaper Kai priestess to seal a truce between our two empires!"

"What?" Tani said astonished. "After everything you have told us, and after everything we have seen, why would anyone want to make a truce with them?"

"I cannot speak any more of this!" the librarian was fearful he had said too much. He snatched the book from the tribals and retreated into the darkness of the library. "You need to go now!" he hissed.

The tribals were shocked and angered by what they had just heard, and retreated from the library back to their room.

"This is getting worse and worse," Jared said after he shut the door to their room.

"I agree," Tani said. "But at least we know a little more about what is going on."

"We do?" Jared protested. "How so? We know that the King of Rasheed wed a Reaper Kai. If that is so, why did they try to kill Mineera? Why would the Reaper Kai try to kill Mineera if they have a truce with Rasheed? I heard Globulus say she was a diplomat. If Rasheed and the Reaper Kai are allies, why kill a diplomat? Why would the Reaper Kai kill one of their own? If she is a diplomat, then why is she a threat?"

"I don't know." Tani shook his head. "But I don't think they are allies. I think a war is about to erupt, and we are caught in the middle of it. We need to get out of here soon."

"Yeah, we need to get out of here." Jared shook nodded his head. "You think Banion will tell us more about what's going on?"

"Not likely," Tani said, pushing his glasses up his nose. He narrowed his green eyes and looked around the room, deep in thought. "But maybe someone else would..."

"What? Who?" Jared asked, confused.

"Mineera," Tani said in a calm voice. "I bet she can tell us more."

"Mineera? What are you, crazy? You wanna figure out what is going on from a Reaper Kai?" Jared was stunned.

"Why not? the enemy wants her dead. She can't be all that bad," the young scholar said.

"She is the enemy!" Jared countered.

"Good point," Tani sighed.

"That leads us back to our first plan. We need to leave, and get far away from this place. Who cares what's going on?" the young warrior declared, and his friend nodded in agreement.

"Yeah, you're right. We need to leave Rasheed and get as far away as possible," Tani said. "But still... I am so curious."

Jared shook his head in disgust, but finally agreed. "I am, too... I guess... a little..."

"Wanna take another walk?" Tani smiled.

Jared knew exactly what he was thinking.

"Ugh!" he said, scrunching up his face. "Yeah, okay... I am curious also."

With that, the tribals left their room and headed off towards the north wing of the palace in search of Mineera's room.

Chapter 27
Deal with the Devil

There was a knock at the thick wooden door. Banion approached it cautiously, his right hand dropping to his hip, just a few inches above his gun belt. He moved to the side of the door and answered.

"Yes?" he asked loudly, as his hand hovered above his silver revolver.

"It's me, King Toil sent me to fetch you," Globulus boomed at the closed door.

The door creaked open, and Banion stepped into the hall. Globulus considered him oddly, and Banion stared back with a dispassionate look on his face.

"So, King Toil wants to see me?" Banion said while walking off with the mighty mutant hippo.

"Yes," replied King Toil's master of arms succinctly. Globulus was not letting anything out, and Banion was well aware of this fact.

With that, they stopped talking and pressed on through the palace. As they moved, palace guards regarded the two with blank looks.

Finally, they reached the royal dining hall. The room was filled with purple clad palace guards. A great wooden table ran the length of the hall; with nearly fifty chairs surrounding it, it was an impressive sight. The table was empty save for an aged man sitting at the head of the table.

King Toil was nearing sixty years, but his features were much more worn, much more haggard. He showed nearly a hundred years of worry trenched into his face. Long white hair drooped down from around the rim of his bald head. A full white beard covered his jaw.

Banion approached cautiously, and with good reason. He had done work for the kingdom of Rasheed in the past, ever since the incursion and revolt in Dune Station. King Toil and Banion had a quiet truce between them. Though Banion had destroyed a pact laid out between the Reaper Kai and Rasheed, he was still highly valued and trusted by the king. The crazed rancher had completed many dangerous missions in his mercenary days, and the king found Banion more useful than most of his 'trusted' palace guards.

"It's been a long time, Banion O'Neil. Is it by chance that you end up once again in my palace? I think not. Your appearance was a portent of doom for this kingdom." King Toil spoke softly while staring into Banion's empty, hate-filled eyes. "Leave us alone!" the king shouted to the palace guards, ordering them all to exit the room; only Globulus was allowed to remain. The purple clad palace guards shuffled out, leaving the three alone.

"My appearance often means dread," Banion nodded, not breaking his eye contact with the king.

"I am afraid to wonder why the legendary gunfighter is now in my dining hall." Toil spoke in a quizzing tone. "I thought you had retired, and were herding sheep or other loathsome beasts in the north land."

"I would still be doing so if my home still existed." Banion's expression was dull and lifeless as he spoke of his home.

"Please sit and eat with me, Banion O'Neil." The king waved his hand for Banion to sit at a place at the table fully set with a plate of warm food. Banion sat but did not eat.

"I came to warn you." Banion's tone was blunt.

"Of course, I know already what has happened in the north. Many refugees have already sought asylum within the walls of this city."

"If you knew what I have to say, why have I been brought here?" the crazed rancher quizzed.

"I thought we could haggle." The king took a brief moment to eat a bite of ostrich meat.

"Haggle? I have nothing. What do you want to haggle over?"

"Your skills. I find it very interesting that you arrived when you did. I have need for the best skilled mercenaries in the land. I have assembled six teams of mercenaries already, and I could use your help." The king spoke without taking his gaze off Banion.

"For what mission?"

"A mission that you will find most interesting." The king

drank his fine wine, pausing to inhale its aroma. "What do you want most of all?"

"I don't know what you're talking about," Banion responded, eyes narrowing.

"Come on, what is the secret dream that you whisper to the darkness in the hatred of your twisted thoughts? What drives you beyond what most men would retreat from? You know of what I speak. What drives you? Hate, I think. And hatred of what, Banion?"

"You know me well. I want them all dead. Every last one of them," Banion said with rage in his voice. "I pray to the darkness to have the strength to kill all of the Reaper Kai."

"That's why you came here, isn't it? Not to warn us, but to join us. You know war is at hand, and you want a part of it. But not just a part of it, you want to be the solution to all the misery. I will give you that opportunity." King Toil had reeled Banion in, and his gaze never wavered.

"What do you have in mind?" Banion asked, clearly intrigued.

"I have offered a generous reward to six of the best mercenary teams in the whole realm. I will let you form a seventh team. But I am willing to bet you will do this mission for me without any reward."

"Go on."

"The mission is a race that most will not finish. I will offer the governorship of one of my provinces in return for a fully functional nuclear weapon."

"What?" Banion stared at the king, shocked and amazed.

"It's time to send the Reaper Kai a message. I am going to eradicate them. We are going to launch a nuclear weapon at their capital city." Toil had a heartless look in his eyes as he spoke to Banion.

A chill rolled down Banion's spine. His mind was swimming. A vision of his mother's burning body flashed through his mind, followed by a vision of his 'uncle' being beaten to death. Finally, Lily flooded his thoughts. His eyes darkened and anger flashed through his being. Banion struggled to fight the feeling of evil coursing through him. Suddenly, he was calm, giving in to the feeling. It was madness, but it was what his heart truly wanted.

Yielding to the perverse joy of mentally incinerating the Reaper Kai in a blinding flash, he smiled dully and focused on King Toil.

"You're right; I don't need any reward to do this. I want this more than anything." He was grim when he spoke, and this response was exactly what the king was looking for: a man so driven by hate that he would do anything in his power to stop the Reaper Kai.

"I thought you would, for I never met anyone as consumed by sickness as you. I know I can trust you to the end. But there is one small detail." The king's face had lightened, and was more relaxed after he realized that the insane, aggressive Banion was on his side.

"What detail?" Banion quizzed, still ecstatic from the thought of the mass genocide of the Reaper Kai.

"You need a mercenary team, and there is one person I insist you take with you."

"Who?"

"The traitor, this Mineera. She was one of the best and most powerful of the Reaper Kai. Your best chance is to use her help." As Toil spoke, a look of disgust covered Banion's face.

"The witch? I would have killed her myself if it weren't for Globulus. We can't trust her." Banion's eyes shined in rage as he spoke.

"You're right, we can't trust her. That's why I want her to go with you. If she betrays us, you are the best person I know to deal with her. I can't leave her in the city."

"Then let's just kill her!" Banion stirred and growled.

"That is the crux of our dilemma. She has intimate knowledge of the Reaper Kai. It would be folly to lose such knowledge, but also folly to let her undermine this war and this operation." The king spoke slowly, and Banion was none too happy with his words.

"You know what you're asking me to do? Travel with the enemy?" the crazed rancher argued, his face quivering.

"Yes, I do. But she is your best asset. According to our intelligence, there were few that could stand against her in the Reaper Kai Empire. That is how she rose so high in the empire. She is powerful and gifted in the arts of combat. Her psychic abilities are potent. She can help you more than any soldier or mercenary in my service." Toil was trying to work his charisma on a madman.

"If it were not for her prowess, we would have never escaped the prison, Banion. She is gifted but tormented. Her obsession with you is strange. She claims to have known you all her life. This twisted fascination could be a benefit." The mighty hippo joined the conversation, taking a seat at the enormous banquet table.

"All my life, they have taken and pillaged! You cannot ask me to take her with me!" Banion yelled in anger.

"That is what I am asking. If you want this, you must compromise and take her."

The room grew silent. The king tipped back his glass and emptied the wine from it. It stung his throat as it went down. He smiled as he felt its warmth in his body. With a smile, the king closed his eyes and sniffed the last drop of wine.

"So be it. I will take the witch with me, but I will not vouch for her safety. If I suspect her of anything, she will die immediately," Banion growled.

"Fair enough, Banion O'Neil." The king smiled. "Now, how about the rest of your team?"

"I have no others. The witch and I will go alone." The rancher spoke softly, with a distant look in his eye.

"What about the tribals?" Globulus asked.

Banion laughed out loud, rolling his eyes. "The tribals? Jared and Tani?"

"The one with the spectacles is skilled in explosives, and the warrior boy seems skilled enough," Globulus added.

"I will go but they will not! I will not take two kids with me to look for a nuclear bomb!" He growled again at the hippo and the king.

"The choice is yours, but I hope you would take more warriors with you on this journey." The king was pleading with Banion to reconsider.

Banion ceased to speak. He grabbed his fork and poked at the strange meat on his plate. "You and those damn ostriches!" Banion said, pushing the ostrich meat around his plate. The king poured him a glass of wine and pushed it towards his plate. Banion grabbed the glass and drank it down without taking a breath between gulps.

"So, we have a deal, then?" Toil pressed the crazed rancher.

"Yes, you have a deal. I will get your nuclear weapon," Banion replied.

The king smiled, and the trio had a fine meal. As they sat, Banion could not help but think that he had crossed some terrible line. He pushed the thought from his mind as he fantasized about the Reaper Kai incinerated by a blinding flash of nuclear energy.

Chapter 28
The Prophet Mineera

Mineera was running through a dark palace with high vaulted ceilings. White columns rose and met the heights of the roof above. As she ran, a vague feeling of familiarity coursed through her.

Up a circular staircase Mineera ran, round and round until she reached a stone landing atop the twisting stairwell. Her surroundings were a rush of images: torches hung along the dark marble hallways; the palace was strangely silent; no guards stirred; there was a faint smell of incense.

Making haste, she finally came to a wooden door. Her heart pounding both out of fear and fatigue, Mineera pushed the door open quickly.

With an explosion of panic, a man sleeping near the door sat straight up and turned his head towards the open doorway. The man's face was scarred, and his dark eyes were like an icy black pit filled with surprise and immense anger. His hand moved and grabbed a silver revolver from under his pillow.

A gunshot rang out. The man turned just in time to see a shadowy figure on the balcony. A burst of blood erupted from a wound in the center of his chest. Clenching his teeth, the scar on his face contorted in a twisted mass of pain. The man in bed clutched the wound and his eyes rolled back. The gun fell from his hand. The assassin on the balcony jumped into the palace garden below, hidden by the shadows of the night.

"Mineera..." he gasped as the woman stood stunned in the doorway.

She ran to his side and pressed her hand into the warm bloody wound on his chest, tears running down her face. She was panic-stricken, and try as she might, she could not stop the flow of blood erupting from his chest.

"Don't leave..." she whimpered, and his hand clutched hers. "Damn it, don't die."

Her love was strong, but death was stronger. The man's eyes grew dark, and his hand fell from hers. He ceased to stir, and sadness welled up in her fragile soul. Mineera's grief was overwhelming as the deranged rancher died in her arms.

"Banion..." Mineera whispered in terror, cradling the lifeless body.

Mineera startled upright from the clutches of the dream. She looked around, fear rushing through her. The walls and surroundings of her dream were all around her. It was as if she had woken up and jumped straight into another dream. The palace of Rasheed was where Banion would die, and Mineera was now in that very location.

She staggered to her feet and looked around the dark palace room. Shadows covered the palace, and a cool, moist sea breeze rolled in through the open window near the balcony. Green foliage and flowers danced in the breeze. The adrenaline from her dream was dissipating as she stared about the darkness of her room. She closed her eyes and felt the cool air brush across her face. A smile graced her lips as she soaked in the solitude and safety of the palace. When she opened her eyes, she jumped back with fright.

An entity made of light was standing before her in the dark palace room. The entity was all too familiar to the traitor of the Reaper Kai.

"Mineera..." the angel uttered with a whisper.

Mineera moved forward cautiously. For a moment, the psychic maiden felt frightened, and wondered if she was hallucinating. She bowed her head before the spectral form now standing in her room.

"Your reverence is blessed, but there is no need to bow before me. Save your prayers for my master, my lord and savior." The angel moved forward and placed its ethereal hand upon her forehead. As it did, Mineera felt a peace wash over her. There was no strife, no agony, only a serene, pleasant solitude. Mineera closed her eyes and began to converse with the glowing entity.

"Time is short," the angel whispered. "The death of the one from your dreams is close at hand. As we speak, evil schemes his demise."

"What is your will?" Mineera replied.

"All your life, you have never been able to change what you see in your dreams. This is a consequence of your emergence in evil. But now, the shroud of darkness has lifted. Your soul is free, and you are bound only by the freedom of choice. You must have faith in yourself and in me. If you do this, then you can save the tormented soul of Banion. If your faith wavers, he will die, and the devil will claim the land as his paradise for an eternity of darkness." The angel spoke softly while caressing Mineera's head.

"How can I save him?" she questioned.

"That is not for me to answer. The answer is inside you. It has been bound inside you like a prison. Let it escape and you will have your answer." With that, the angel began to dissipate. "Remember the key to ending all of this suffering is to save Banion. If you save Banion, you will save the Darken Realm..." Like a whisper, the presence faded until nothing more could be heard.

Mineera was filled with peace as the angel left the room. She looked around her, staring about the darkness of her palace room. Fighting off the strange feeling coursing through her, Mineera wondered if madness was taking her. Were the visions of the heavenly specter real? Or were her visions simply conjurations of her fragile mind, created by a lifetime of guilt and regret?

Suddenly, there was a knock at the door. She spun around as the door creaked open. Globulus pushed the door open and looked oddly at Mineera.

"Who were you talking to?" Globulus looked around the room suspiciously, half expecting to see an imp or demonic servant hiding in a corner.

Mineera did not respond.

"You have guests," the hippo said, still trying to figure out who Mineera had been talking to just a few moments prior.

"Guests?" Mineera quizzed.

Jared and Tani moved into the doorway, staring at her curiously.

"Come in." Mineera motioned the tribals into the room. She was confused by their presence at first, but her powers of perception were beginning to take over. The intent of the tribals' thoughts was becoming apparent to the psychic maiden.

The door closed, and the two tribals stared at Mineera hesitantly. She looked back at them with quiet expectation. "What can I do for the children of Scarskin?"

"We just wanted to say hello," Jared said sheepishly. Even in the darkness, Mineera could tell that Jared's face was turning red.

"Indeed," she replied, motioning the tribals to join her on the balcony of her room. The trio stood quietly on the balcony. For the first time in their lives, the tribals caught sight of the ocean. It glistened in the darkness as the moon hovered just above the horizon. A cool salt sea breeze rushed past them. For a brief moment, the tribals stood in awe, gazing at the dark sea beyond the palace walls.

"I've always loved the sea," Mineera said in a matter-of-fact tone. She smiled and rested her arms on the railing of the balcony. "I would often stare out into the sea on my trips to Rasheed. I miss the sea. It's good to be back here."

"Yeah, it's rather extraordinary," Tani responded. The thought of such a large body of water seemed awe-inspiring, especially to the tribals, who were from the edge of the wastelands, a land devoid of moisture.

"I came from the northlands; endless forests that glisten with new fallen snow in the winter. The peace of the wild lands is astounding, but the cities... the cities are filled with my kin, my countrymen. Their savagery and disregard for all others is beyond comprehension. You know why I love the sea so much? I find solitude in the waves crashing ashore, and I know my brethren are far away, very far away. It's in those moments that I found real peace. I was able to abandon their sinister lifestyle and find a part of myself that felt lost. My diplomatic trips to Rasheed were always my favorite." Mineera spoke softly, but with a sincerity in her eyes that was heart-warming.

A quiet moment went by. The trio stood upon the balcony and watched the rising moon, feeling the moist breeze wash over them. At that moment, the trio felt at peace. As the moon rose higher, the waves crashed against the shore, and white sea-foam splashed in the air, glittering in the moonlight.

Mineera smiled at the tribals. "You want to know about Rasheed and the Reaper Kai, don't you?"

"Yeah," Jared stammered, unable to figure out how Mineera knew.

"Tensions between Rasheed and the Reaper Kai were most

intense many years past, roughly thirty years ago. To solidify a bond between the two empires, King Toil wed a Reaper Kai priestess. Her name was Asagara," Mineera began, and then grew silent. She stared out at the ocean.

"That's all?" Jared asked.

"No, but I made you feel uncomfortable by 'guessing' why you were here. I thought a normal question and answer would make you both feel better," she added.

Both Jared and Tani nodded uncomfortably.

"So what happened?" Tani interjected.

Mineera smiled, and then continued. "They wed, and an alliance was formed between the two empires. Unfortunately, Asagara had other plans. She used her influence to weaken several neighboring provinces. These provinces joined the Reaper Kai. 'Joined' is a misleading word, I guess. They were urged to join, or face annihilation. Asagara Toil was out of control, and King Toil refused to acknowledge her actions. He was fearful to countermand his mate and ruin the alliance."

"So King Toil ignored the plight of the provinces in order to maintain a truce between Rasheed and the Reaper Kai?" Tani asked.

Mineera smiled at Tani. "Well spoken, tribal. Indeed, that is what King Toil did. He ignored the suffering and murder. Finally, fate intervened, and there was a great rebellion in one of the provinces. Dune Station was one of the provinces taken over by the Reaper Kai. A local uprising led to the demise of Asagara. The revolt was bloody, but it severed the connection between Rasheed and the Reaper Kai. With Asagara dead, King Toil no longer let the Reaper Kai pillage the land. He sent diplomats to the Reaper Kai, warning them to stop intervening in the southern reaches of the Darken Realm. The Reaper Kai returned the diplomats' severed heads back to the gates of Rasheed. Since then, there has been an uneasy truce between the two empires. Neither empire has openly acknowledged its hatred of the other, and a drawn-out game of chess has been waged quietly over the years, with neither empire willing to make the first offensive move."

"Dune Station?" Jared picked out the name of the town from Mineera's explanation of the truce. "That sounds familiar."

"Yeah, I've heard Banion speak of Dune Station," Tani added.

Mineera fell silent. The traitor of the Reaper Kai also knew of Dune Station, as well as vague details involving Banion and the revolt. Not willing to confront the topic of Banion and the great revolt, Mineera simply stared at the sea, ignoring the tribals' confused looks.

Her silence made Tani and Jared uncomfortable.

"What does Banion have to do with the death of Asagara Toil?" Tani asked in a confused tone, acknowledging that the psychic was purposely hiding information from them. The scholar was astute and had put pieces of a sinister puzzle together by using logic.

Mineera ignored the question and simply stared out at the ocean waves. Feeling her scorn, the tribals became restless, no longer feeling welcome.

"Ah..." Jared stammered. "It's getting late; we better get back to our room."

"Have a good night, tribals of Scarskin." Mineera spoke softly, without turning to watch them leave.

Hastily, they left her room and moved through the dark halls of the palace. Finally, they made it back to their room with a few more questions then they had when they left.

"Dune Station, eh?" Jared said to Tani.

"I wish I could remember what Banion said about Dune Station," Tani replied with an inquisitive look on his face.

"Yeah..." Jared said, yawning. "There is tension around that topic and Mineera was hiding *something* about Banion, Dune Station, and the Toil family."

"Agreed, what she is hiding is a mystery." Yawning also, Tani looked over towards the balcony and the cool air blowing in from the ocean. Rubbing his eyes with drowsy motions, he spoke once more. "Let's get some sleep."

With that, the tribals rolled out their sleeping mats on the balcony, and fell asleep in the cool air of the nearby sea.

Chapter 29
Nova 7

"The choices we make can reforge the world, or bring it to ruin…" Banion whispered with a distant look on his face. With much apprehension, he opened the door to the room and went in.

The tribals looked at Banion with surprise as he entered their room. He moved slowly toward them, his expression distant. Guilt and dishonesty wore heavily on his heart, but he didn't care. It was a means to an end. The tribals would serve their purpose well enough.

"Let's go," Banion ordered the tribals.

"Huh? Where are we going?" Jared asked, puzzled.

"Leave your gear, we'll be back soon," Banion fired in response.

"Sure, Banion," Tani agreed, weariness in his eyes.

"I need to introduce you to someone…" Banion was more mysterious with each passing minute.

The two tribals followed without question. They pressed on into the halls of the palace. Each step filled the tribals with dread. It was as if they were taking their last steps, as if they had already been condemned to die, and each passing step brought them closer to oblivion. The anxiety and tension were thick.

Jared breathed heavily, wondering what was going on. Tani's mind was racing; his green eyes darted back and forth while thoughts filled the scholar's mind. They pressed on, rounding a corner.

The hall they entered was vaulted, and lined with bronze statues of all the past kings who had ruled Rasheed. Slowly, the trio moved amongst the silent statues as the youths' anxiety mounted. They passed from the hall of kings into a circular dome which rose many stories high. Wooden edging was laid upon the fine marble, climbing to the top of the dome. The tribals gasped upon entering the dome, and then gasped again. Instantly, they were set on edge. The anxiety turned to panic. For standing alone in the center of the domed room was a person garbed in blood red robes. A hood covered the person's face. Jared stopped dead in his tracks, as did Tani. Banion halted before the lone figure standing before them.

There was a brief moment of silence in the hall. Not a single person stirred.

The red robed figure turned towards the trio and advanced one step forward. With face still hidden, the figure approached. Tani took a step back, and Jared whispered, "Reaper Kai."

Banion held his ground as the figure moved forward. The tribals cowered before the presence of the stranger. Finally, the red robed figure halted in front of Banion and pulled her crimson hood back.

The fear was gone. Mineera looked at them with bright blue eyes contrasted by her dark skin. She neither frowned nor smiled. Totally indifferent and regal she stood, as if unmoved by any emotion, whether good or evil. She stared at Banion with a look of dispassion.

Banion gave her an uneasy look. Finally, he spoke. "Are you ready?"

"One can never be ready to go to war. One can never be ready to hurl themselves into the fray against an unmovable enemy bent on hate and destruction." She looked at each of the tribals in turn. "So let it be. We now stride forth as soldiers without a home. The real question is if you two are ready?" Mineera focused her gaze on each of the tribals once again.

Not knowing what was about to happen, both tribals stepped back with a scowl of confusion on their faces. "Ready for what?" Jared inquired.

"They are ready," Banion answered for them.

Banion moved off down the hall, and Mineera followed. Tani shot Jared a look of alarm, and then hesitantly moved off after the deranged rancher and the red robed witch.

The man without home or reason stopped before a great door. Globulus greeted the four and nodded in approval to each in turn. With that, the mighty hippo pushed open the enormous steel doors.

The four moved on into a great room littered with purple clad palace guards and a horde of mercenaries surrounding a large black stone table. An elderly man with a crown of gold and silver stood at one end of the table, regarding the four as they entered.

"And finally, this is the seventh team. I trust you all have heard of Banion O'Neil." King Toil stared at the crazed rancher. As his name was spoken, a gasp rose from the mercenaries seated at the table. While each was dangerous in his own right, each mercenary had heard the insane tales of bloodshed that went hand-in-hand with Banion's name.

The entire room stared at Banion and his motley assortment of companions. Some snorted and giggled at the sight of Jared and Tani. Others whispered oaths to their ancestors as they watched the red robed Reaper Kai traitor move towards the table. Many averted their eyes, not wanting to lock gazes with the insane Banion. All in all, the arrival of the four sent a tremor through the room.

"Be seated," Globulus commanded. The four took seats at the great stone table. Jared and Tani were bright red, and glanced nervously around the room. With their hearts in their throats, the tribals barely breathed or stirred; they simply stared about in awe. A fear had risen in their minds and spun down to the pit of their stomachs.

King Toil, still standing before the mighty table, looked around the room with eyes harshly set. He commanded great respect, and each person in the room gave him such respect. He spoke a series of words which sent a chill down everyone's spine. "All of you in this room are as good as dead."

Panic rose around the room. All the mercenaries stared about uneasily. A deathly silence overcame them. No one stirred or breathed. The king looked at each person seated at the table in turn. The lump in Jared's throat grew as old King Toil eyed him. Tani felt as if he was going to be sick.

"The enemy has known about this meeting for quite some time. Agents of the enemy are in this room as we speak, though I know not who they are. Every one of you will be an enemy of the Reaper Kai and will be marked for death. But I urge you to hold your ground and not to flee this chamber. Hear my words, for they ring true. I have a mission to end all missions. And for this service, I will make you a prince or duke if you will. For your service and success, you will be crowned as royalty in my kingdom for as long as it stands."

Wide-eyed looks of fear moved about the room. Only

Banion smiled.

"The Reaper Kai have long been feared, and it is time to put an end to them." Toil spoke harshly, and several mercenaries stood up in fright.

One such mercenary spoke to the aged King in disgust. "You are insane! I want no part of this! It is suicide to openly challenge the Reaper Kai!"

"Yes, it is insane. That is why we will win," Toil boasted, staring the mercenary down. With some constraint, the mercenary finally sat back down, his arms folded defiantly across his chest.

"As I said, it's time to send a message. It is time to send a message that will resound through all of history. We have lived and survived the menace of darkness. We have hid and have slowly been worn away by evil. This will end. For when your mission is complete, we will drive a stake into the heart of evil itself. For when our resolve is fulfilled, not a single Reaper Kai will walk this earth. I am calling for the complete eradication of the entire race of them!" Toil boomed, his cheeks quivering in anger.

More fear rolled through the room. Another mercenary jumped to his feet to challenge the king. "What do you have planned, you old fool? What is this madness you speak of?"

The King locked gazes with the mercenary. The room fell quiet, each of its occupants rigid with tension. They all eyed the old king with a frustrated fascination. Finally, after many moments had passed, the king spoke.

"Your mission is to recover a fully operational nuclear weapon," Toil said in a calm tone.

A silence filled the room. The converged mercenaries were unable to comprehend what they had just been asked to do. Even the tribals from Scarskin had enough knowledge of the past to cringe in terror.

The eerie silence continued for some time.

"For this weapon, I will grant governorship of one of my provinces until death takes you," Toil finished, and the crowd reacted with an overwhelming sense of betrayal. It was no secret that the enemy had spies everywhere. Each mercenary now had a target on their chest simply by being in the room. The King had manipulated the entire lot of them. Whether they accepted the task or not, the Reaper Kai would find and kill them all. Many shook their heads in disgust, and many stared at Mineera in horror. Most of them viewed the traitor of the Reaper Kai as the enemy.

"Damn you!" a tall mercenary stood up and shook his fist at the king. King Toil only smiled. "You have given us all a death sentence! It matters not if we agree! The enemy will make sure we all die!"

King Toil smiled again. "I suggest you don't fail." His tone was uncaring. With that, King Toil summoned his Master of Arms.

Globulus appeared before the crowd with seven fat envelopes. He unceremoniously threw the packets at each mercenary team leader. "This mission is project Nova. Each of you has a call sign. There are seven Nova teams. Each packet contains information on enemy strength and structure. This information will give you an advantage in fighting and eluding the enemy. This information will give you an edge, and was provided by a high-ranking enemy diplomat who defected from the Reaper Kai Empire." Globulus took a brief moment to consider the crowd. "The packet also contains enough money to fully outfit each of your teams."

The crowd was stunned as they opened the packets of information and found wads of money pouring from the envelopes.

"Time is not on our side. The enemy is already moving in on our position. The north is being razed and sacked as we speak. We have dispatched emissaries to elicit the help of the Iron Kai, Mord Techs, and the Steel Crag Mining Guild, as well as dozens of other smaller provinces and kingdoms. Our riders have been dispatched to anyone we could imagine might help fight the Reaper Kai. We cannot withstand the enemy forever. You must complete this mission with all due speed. We fear the enemy is marching upon us, and it will be a difficult fight."

"This is impossible. No nuclear weapons still exist!" a mercenary argued with the mighty hippo. "It matters not how much money you give us!"

Globulus did not respond to the mercenary's challenge. "The king's birthday is in three days time. You are welcome to the safety of the palace until the day after his birth celebration. I suggest you make use of this time to come up with a plan of action. You are all welcome to celebrate with the king. I wager this will be your last night of peace. I fear many of you will perish before leaving the walls of this city. The enemy's assassins and agents are already swarming the streets." With that, both the king and his Master of Arms left the room under the escort of the purple clad palace guards.

The room turned into a shouting match of cussing and threats. The king had betrayed the mercenaries, and they were none too happy about it. The gathering dispersed within moments.

Only Banion, Mineera, Jared, and Tani remained.

"So, we got lucky number seven." Banion smiled and looked at his team.

"What have you done to us?!" Jared said harshly.

"I gave you a chance to leave in Pontiac City. You wanted to come along, so here you are!" Banion said, rising from his seat.

"I never wanted this!" Tani spoke bitterly.

"Ok, fine, kids. Leave," Banion ordered with an angry look in his eyes.

"What?" Jared was annoyed. "You heard them! We are all targets now! Tani and I have no choice!"

"Yeah, kid, you're right." Banion smiled.

"Manipulation is an evil trait, but somehow, I feel this is a good thing." Mineera spoke cryptically. The trio simply looked at her in confusion.

"You heard Globulus, we have three days time. I suggest we use it to our advantage." Banion looked at each of them. "Nova 7," he smiled. "Lucky number seven... Let's get going."

Banion moved out of the war room. Mineera followed without a word. Jared and Tani held their ground, staring at each other in horror. Fighting the feeling of betrayal, the tribals followed Banion and Mineera.

Chapter 30
Fighting Fate

"Banion…" A whisper rose from the darkness.

Mineera sat straight up in her bed, and a terror filled her soul. Her anxiety mounted as she stared around her. The surroundings were all too familiar. The fear rising in her stomach was taking shape. She stared around her dark chamber, a tear rolling down her face.

"No… please no!" she moaned. Verifying the reality of her perceptions, she pushed her fingernails into the palms of her hand. Pain rose as blood trickled from the wounds. "It's no dream…"

Rocked by panic and a sense of urgency, Mineera jumped to her feet and pushed the door of her room open. Two purple clad guards stood before her room, eyeing her suspiciously.

Focusing quietly and bringing herself into a state of meditation, the witch formed thoughts of slumber. Concentrating on the guards, she directed her thoughts at them. They moved as if in a daze, staggering back and forth. Finally, they crashed to the floor, caught in an intense slumber, both of them snoring. Mineera had successfully put the guards to sleep using her psychic abilities.

Satisfied with her action, Mineera stepped over the sleeping guards and pressed on into the dark interior of the palace. Her goal and destination was Banion's room.

She made her silent way through hall after dark hall. Torches flickered in her passing. Images of her movements reflected dimly in the black marble walls of the interior passages. Finally, propelled by both duress and speed, Mineera made it to a junction in the palace. She found herself in a high vaulted dome with white marble pillars soaring over her head.

Mineera was running through a dark palace with high vaulted ceilings. White columns rose and met the heights of the roof above. As she ran, a vague feeling of familiarity coursed through her.

Up a circular staircase Mineera ran, round and round until

she reached a stone landing atop the twisting stairwell. Her surroundings were a rush of images: torches hung along the dark marble hallways; the palace was strangely silent; no guards stirred; there was a faint smell of incense.

Making haste, she finally came to a wooden door. Her heart pounding both out of fear and fatigue, Mineera pushed the door open quickly.

With an explosion of panic, a man sleeping near the door sat straight up and turned his head towards the open doorway. The man's face was scarred, and his dark eyes were like an icy black pit filled with surprise and immense anger. His hand moved and grabbed a silver revolver from under his pillow.

A gunshot rang out. Time stood still. The bright flash of the muzzle illuminated the bedchamber. Mineera heard a scream rising in the depth of her soul. Begging for mercy, she held her faith. She believed in something impossible. Mineera believed without a whisper of hesitation that she could save Banion from death. As an act of defense, she raised her hands and screamed. A barrier of blue energy formed instantly around Banion. The bullet screamed towards Banion's chest. The metal projectile rammed into the barrier of spiritual energy. The bullet halted as it struck the shield of energy, then fell harmlessly to the floor.

The assassin on the balcony cursed at the sight of Mineera. The attempt to slay Banion had failed. Hurried steps rang out on the marble. Banion trained his weapon on the shadowy figure on the balcony.   Firing two rounds, the deranged rancher steadied his weapon. To no avail, neither bullet bit flesh, and the shadowy assassin launched off the balcony into a garden below.

Mineera felt a rush of energy strike her. She staggered back and forth. Dizziness filled her. Bright blotches of light blocked her vision. Pain erupted in her head and body. Blood vessels tensed and broke in her body. Streams of blood flowed from her eyes, nose, and mouth. Unbeknownst to Mineera, she had broken a law of fate. She had done the impossible; Mineera had changed the course of the future. She had fought against the vision she had seen her entire life, and succeeded in changing it.

A tremble of energy coursed through her. Screams of anger filled her ears; demons and devils cursed her soul. She had made the ultimate betrayal. Mineera had saved Banion from death itself.

She had cheated fate, and betrayed the darkness that had ruled her soul.

The feeling of dizziness was overwhelming. Warm blood poured down her face. Her legs went limp and she crashed to the floor. Darkness took her. And then, all was silent.

Banion jumped from his bed and rushed to Mineera's side. Her body was convulsing on the floor. With fright in his eyes, Banion crouched near Mineera and clutched her in his arms. As he cradled Mineera, an odd sight made his hair stand on end. A faint wisp of smoke was rising from the unconscious Mineera.

Black smoke was rising from her arms. Confused by the smoke, Banion pulled back the sleeves on her robes. He recoiled in fear. The tattooed snakes on her arms were writhing and moving upon her flesh. The sinister snake tattoo was the mark of the Reaper Kai. All initiates were branded with the image of the serpent. With horrid fascination, Banion looked on. The smoke was rising from the tattoos. The snakes continued to reptate and gyrate upon her flesh. Finally, they ceased to move. The smoke continued, and slowly, the tattoos vanished. Stunned, Banion looked upon Mineera, for she no longer bore the mark of the enemy. No longer did the sign of the beast brand Mineera.

Concerned, Banion lifted Mineera's head and wiped the blood from her nose and mouth. He gently caressed her head, watching her breath slowly.

Banion's mind was swimming. An intense fear filled him. Clutching his chest with Mineera's head in his lap, the deranged rancher probed his chest for wounds. He found none. For some strange reason, Banion felt that he should be dead. Shrugging off the feeling, he focused on sounds in the palace hall. Guards, having heard the gunshots, were charging to Banion's room.

Banion comforted the unconscious Mineera while lost in his own thoughts. Time and time again, his hand moved to his chest. He could not shake the feeling that a bullet hole should be in his flesh. Banion could not shake off the feeling that he should be dead.

Chapter 31
The Mouse Roars

Banion, deep in thought, exited Mineera's chamber. Worry covered his face. With his brimmed hat hiding his eyes, he pushed past the guards and moved into the hall of the palace.

The tribals were waiting quietly near a tall stone pillar. Without a word, he approached and looked at each in turn. With a nod and a furtive look of concern, he urged the two from Scarskin to follow.

Obeying his silent order, the two proceeded behind him.

"We need to get ready for the journey," Banion said, muted.

"Is Mineera better?" Jared quizzed. The young warrior had heard about the bizarre events in the palace the previous night, and was concerned about Mineera.

"She still hasn't woken up. King Toil's royal surgeon is mystified why she is still unconscious." Banion spoke in a dull tone, rubbing his chest with a distant look.

"What's the plan, Banion?" Tani pressed with an uneasy look in his eyes.

"We will take a ship across the gulf to Dune Station," Banion said, noting that his words had clearly piqued the interest of his companions. "We will meet up with some old friends, then head out into the southern wastes. An arms dealer in the southern wastes, known as the Runner, is legendary for scouring old world military installations. Just south of Dune Station is a town known as Shape Home. Somewhere near that town is where the Runner has his 'market'. There is a good chance that he knows where we can find a nuclear weapon, or at least can lead us in the right direction."

"Dune Station, huh?" Tani added hoping Banion would add some information. The wily scholar was thinking about the conversation they had with Mineera. She had alluded to a dark tale about Dune Station and Banion was somehow connected.

"Yeah, I grew up there." With that, the deranged rancher stopped speaking and moved off.

They passed dark halls within the heart of the Rasheed palace. Black marble walls clung coldly to their surroundings. Silent halls greeted them with sweeping expanses of intricate stonework. Overall, the surroundings were an uncomfortable mixture of claustrophobic surfaces and excessive open spaces.

Finally, the trio reached the boundary of the palace and pressed on into the city of Rasheed.

The quiet solitude of the palace disappeared behind them. They were plunged into a world of crowded streets and marketplaces. Modest wooden buildings lined the streets. Colorful tarps and cloth hung over the alleys and byways. It was somewhat like walking through a cave of brightly dyed silks.

Patrons and citizens of all cultures were crowded together in the streets. The bazaar in Rasheed was well known, and merchants from all over the Darken Realm owned shops or haggled deals in the narrow streets. Many of the merchants were dark skinned and wore brightly colored robes and headdresses. Spices, rare cloth, weapons, and curiosities from all corners of the civilized southlands were being exchanged and bargained over in feverish intensity. The marketplace was wild with excitement. A loud auctioneer was selling an assortment of clay pots created by a local artist. Another man was spinning around with brightly colored scarves streaming through the air. A street jester was juggling while standing on a barrel, amusing the laughing children. Smells of roasted meat flooded the alleys, mingling with the scents of exotic flowers and spices wafting in the air in uneven bursts.

The people chattered in a host of languages and dialects. Birds and other beasts added their own unique language to the market. Gulls circled above the food stands, swooping down from time to time and trying to steal scraps of food. Wild cats and dogs also milled about the streets, searching for tidbits of discarded bread or fruit.

All in all, the bazaar was an assault upon all five senses. The sights, sounds, and smells were overwhelming.

"There is another shopping district beyond this one. It's rough, so be alert. With enemy agents so near, we need to be extra careful. Be on your guard, tribals. If something seems wrong, it probably is." Banion spoke in a low tone while placing a hand on each of their shoulders. The tribals nodded, and Banion pressed on through the crowd. Finally, the trio came to an alleyway near the back end of the Bazaar.

A dark aisle lay before them. The walls of the alley were narrow and descended into a tunnel. A smell of rancid rot filled the air. Smoke streamed from the tunnel, adding to the darkness of the foul hole before them.

"This is it, the passage to the Gutter Hollows, the mercenary district of Rasheed," Banion said.

"Wonderful," Tani shot back sarcastically.

With an uneasy step, the tribals followed Banion. The slope descended, seeming to grow more littered with filth with each step. As the tunnel opened, the trio found themselves in a dark underpass beneath the city of Rasheed. Shapes huddled near the walls of the dark passage. Homeless citizens and outcasts milled about in the dark hole. Metal barrels filled with garbage burned slowly, giving off light and smoke.

Laughter rolled from the darkness. A naked man, covered in dirt and reeking, staggered forward. His teeth were gone and he giggled as he moved toward them. A psychotic, manic look covered his face. He staggered on, reaching out to grab young Tani. Banion grabbed the bum and pushed him back. With uneven steps, the naked maniac crashed to the filth-covered floor of the tunnel, letting out a scream and then starting to giggle uncontrollably. Hardly able to breathe, the maniac laughed himself into a series of convulsions. Jared and Tani were horrified. Banion stepped over the bum, and the tribals moved on slowly after him.

The trio moved forward, and the shadows moved with them. Three figures, cloaked in black, took interest in Banion and his newly formed crew. With light steps, they slunk up behind the trio. Banion and Tani were unaware of their presence until they heard the metallic clang of Jared's sword clearing the scabbard.

Jared spun around and parried an attack, deflecting the metal knife intended for his back. Banion and Tani spun around, both startled and unprepared for the attack. The thugs were quick, but Jared was quicker. He engaged all three of them at the same time. A battle erupted in the dark under-pass. Banion drew his revolver.

Tani, seeing Jared engaged in battle, smiled and grabbed Banion's gun arm. With a look of confidence, Tani urged Banion to put his revolver away.

"Just watch, Banion," the young scholar grinned. "These three won't know what hit them."

Stunned, Banion looked on at young Jared. With absorbed fascination, Banion watched Jared fight the thugs. Slowly, his gun arm dropped.

Clumsy strike after clumsy strike was directed towards Jared. Each attack was harmlessly batted away. With each parry, the thugs grew more enraged. With heightened intensity, they assaulted the young teen wielding the mighty Scar Blade. Even though it was three against one, the thugs were outmatched. Jared was a superior warrior with a mighty weapon; he treated the thugs like children, slowly humiliating them. Banion was stunned; he never imagined Jared was such a force to be reckoned with. Mostly, Jared had shied away from conflict, but this battle was familiar to him. His attackers were human. There was no robotic death machine to be seen. There was no mutant terror in the shadows. These were human thugs, derelicts of society, and dregs of humanity. Jared had no problem focusing on the battle.

The sound of battle brought more thugs into the fray. Two more attacked, wielding clubs. Jared, now outnumbered five to one, had to step up the fight. Instead of toying with his foes, he was focusing on wounding them. With precise strikes, he gashed and sliced into them. The bite of the blade was too much, and the thugs retreated. With wounds on their arms and legs, they dared not continue the struggle.

"You damn idiots!" a voice boomed from the darkness. A huge man, well over six feet tall, strode forth wielding a sledgehammer. It was the chief of the rogues, and he was none too happy that a young boy had defeated his crew. "I will kill him myself!" The thug sounded a war cry and charged young Jared.

Jared held his ground, preparing to defend against the assault. Fear flooded him. The thugs could be repelled, but Jared knew the chief could not. The chief would fight to the death. Jared had never slain another man before, and he found himself freezing.

Suddenly, a shot rang out in the tunnel. The thug chief fell to the ground, a gaping gunshot wound blossoming on his chest with a spray of crimson gore. The chief ceased to stir. Jared turned around to see a silver revolver glittering in the dark passage. Banion held the weapon before him with a grim look on his face. At the sight of the dead chief, the thugs ran off into the dark passage.

"Thanks..." Jared said, his expression withdrawn. He knew he had frozen, and felt a rush of shame.

"I thought I would spare the loss of your humanity a little longer." Banion spoke with a look of compassion in his dark eyes. He moved over to Jared, resting his hand on the youth's shoulder. A smile covered his face, and a chuckle erupted from his mouth. "I have never seen someone hold their own like you just did."

Banion moved off, and Jared took a brief moment to recover. It was the first time that Banion had been proud of young Jared. Jared felt a sense of empowerment. No longer was he just following Banion. Jared felt like a full companion.

Shaken, but with an air of confidence, he moved off to follow Banion, shrugging off the image of the dead rogue in the passage. Tani pushed the thought out of his mind as well. Being around Banion had often brought death and destruction, and it was becoming commonplace to the tribals.

The trio emerged from the underpass and found themselves in the slums of Rasheed. Strange mutants milled about while mercenaries congregated in alleys and dark places. The buildings were dilapidated and falling apart. Many were boarded up or had collapsed. Banion took a brief moment to look around. Finally, his eye fell upon a structure at the south end of a line of buildings.

Urging the tribals onward, Banion entered the building. The shop was dimly lit, but covered wall to wall with weapons.

"Eh..." A squat man approached Banion inside the weapon shop. "Your money has been sorely missed, misfit of the wastes!" the rotund shopkeeper spoke with a hint of affection.

"Aye, I haven't had need for such weapons in many years," Banion stated while looking around.

"Well, what will ya have, Banion? Eh?" The shopkeeper licked his lips.

"Show me assault weapons. The bookworm here..." Banion pointed at Tani, "...needs a variety of explosives. I will choose the other one's weapons."

The squat shopkeeper showed Banion a variety of weaponry. Finally, Banion settled on an assault rifle with a massive one hundred round rotary ammunition drum. With much joy, the shopkeeper took Banion's money. His eyes were wide and he grinned as he counted the grubby money.

Tani was lost in his own thoughts. He stood before a wall of explosives. There were grenades, dynamite, plastic explosives, land mines, flash bang grenades, demolition charges, and various detonators. Mischief sparkled in Tani's eyes. The cogs of his mind were spinning, and he was enjoying every minute. He looked over at Banion and spoke.

"How much can I buy?" Tani grinned, and Banion grinned back.

"We have more than enough money. Buy all that you can carry!" Banion exclaimed, and the young scholar was set loose.

Tani grabbed a burlap sack from off the floor and began to fill the bag with explosives. After a flurry of grabbing, the burlap sack was filled to the brim. He placed the bag on the counter, and the merchant greedily punched away at an ancient adding machine. The machine clicked and whirred, and Banion threw down a wad of money on the counter.

"Grab me a submachine gun for the other kid, and two hundred rounds of ammo," Banion ordered the merchant, who bounced joyously through the shop. He came back with a sleek submachine gun with a collapsible stock. Banion tossed the weapon to Jared, who eyed it dubiously.

"You're good enough at close range. It's time I taught you how to fight with a gun," Banion said, looking at Jared soberly. Jared turned red and nodded back while clumsily handling the automatic weapon.

The trio finished their purchases and left the shop, heading back to the palace. Banion led the way. Jared followed close behind. Tani struggled and lagged behind them, trying desperately to carry the huge burlap sack filled with explosives.

Chapter 32
A Quiet Truce

The night had washed over the city. Cool breezes rolled through the open window near the bed. The moon had risen, its white light bathing the shadows in an eerie silence. The palace was dark and quiet.

Banion pushed into the chamber. In the darkness, he breathed softly. He trembled with every step. Guilt and sadness racked the deranged rancher. Slowly, he moved forward. His heart leapt in his chest. Gripping his own hands tightly, he moved closer to the bed.

A figure was sleeping in the bed near the window. Moonlight shone through the curtains. The figure did not stir. Bathed in light, Banion stared quietly at Mineera. Finally, he moved forward and crouched beside her.

With a trembling hand, he advanced to touch her hand with his own. Banion hesitated a moment, then finally touched the back of her hand. She did not stir at his touch. Banion's dark eyes were brimming with reservation as he clasped her hand and caressed it. Sadness filled him. He shook his head back and forth. A tear rolled down his cheek, running across the mighty scar on his face. Banion could not help but feel that he should be dead. There was something screaming inside of him that didn't feel right. He shook his head again, and wondered how and why Mineera had saved him from the assassin. While deep in thought, Banion continued to rub Mineera's hand.

Suddenly, Mineera's hand stirred and clasped Banion's. Her breathing became erratic. She stirred from her slumber. Her blue eyes opened in the moonlight. With much effort, Mineera sat up in bed, and stared at Banion with a look of madness in her eyes. A frantic look of recognition coursed through her. Initially thinking that Banion was dead, she finally comprehended that she had saved him. She had saved the man who had tormented her dreams. Elated by her success, happiness welled up inside her soul. Mineera had done the impossible; she had saved Banion from death and changed fate. Finally, a smile crossed her lips and she leaned forward.

With as much strength as she could muster, Mineera embraced Banion. Not believing her eyes, she pressed herself against him. He trembled under her touch. Confused, he pushed her back and stared at her with terror in his eyes. He gazed at Mineera like a frightened child.

Still weak, she clasped his hand with her own shaky hands. A frail smile still covered her face.

Tears welled up in her eyes and she began to weep. Mineera cried softly, and Banion moved forward and placed his hand on her shoulder. Consoling Mineera, Banion caressed her cheek with his rough hand. He wiped the tears from her face, and she stared at him without moving.

Edging forward, she stared into his eyes. He gazed back, his heart pumping quickly in his chest. Mineera grasped his hand and caressed it. Finally, she moved forward and pressed her lips against his. Softly, she kissed him. Banion felt his blood begin to simmer. He embraced her and kissed her back.

Suddenly, a fierce anger rose in him. A vision of Lily flashed through Banion's mind. Guilt flooded through him. His blood boiled and he shook with rage. With a madness growing in his dark eyes, he pushed Mineera back forcefully.

She recoiled in shock and stared back at Banion in terror. He shook his head in disgust. A look of sorrow filled her. Scared, she wept again. Slowly, she shook her head back and forth. She could feel his rage and fear. Trying to speak with her heart, she held up her hands in an act of submission.

He snorted at her and rose to his feet. Banion stood above Mineera, glowering at her with a dark look in his eyes. Blackness and an empty void were all Mineera could see in the darkness, for Banion's eyes were mastered by hate.

Stepping back, Banion pointed his finger at her, shaking his head in disgust. With that, he stormed out of the chamber and disappeared into the palace beyond.

Mineera stared at the moon and cried softly, alone in her thoughts. She could still feel his pain. She could still feel his fear. Mineera had never known a person more torn by hate and sorrow. He was a man hurt by his past. She cried softly, without thinking of herself. She thought of Banion, and wished secretly in her heart that she could save him. She wished secretly that she could save him from himself.

Finally, still weak from her ordeal, she drifted off into an uneasy sleep. Her slumber was tormented by visions of Banion lost in a haze of darkness. And in this darkness, a fear trembled forward to embrace her. She had saved Banion from death, but death was still coming for him. The black cloud swirled around Banion. Finally, the darkness engulfed him, leaving Mineera alone upon a hill above a mighty battlefield littered with the corpses of slain soldiers.

Her dreams lasted into the late hours, ripped with sorrow and filled with misery. For Mineera had betrayed the darkness and the darkness had responded, sending a host of wicked dreams into her soul as she slumbered, tempting her back home, tempting her towards a life of evil, tempting her towards madness.

Chapter 33
The Iron Kai

The great meeting came to order. A thick set, strong man with a fiery red beard stood before a large wooden table. His eyes shifted from side to side. With a look of disdain, the stout man tipped back an enormous beer stein, dumping the last drops of liquor into his mouth. Unceremoniously, he wiped the beer from his beard and slammed the stein onto the table.

"Report, Captain!" the red bearded man commanded loudly.

"Emperor Gunther." The captain nodded at the red bearded man standing at the head of the giant wooden table. "The Reaper Kai army is on the move. Ten thousand Biogtech soldiers with a full war complement left their capital city nearly a week ago. Our scouts have just returned with the news. The army is capable of a full siege, and I fear their target is Rasheed."

"Ah, Rasheed..." Gunther said softly, moving away from the table. He walked across the cold stone floor of the great citadel and approached a large window overlooking the Iron Kai fortress of Stonen. Looking down, he viewed the defenses of the great city.

Stonen was the capital of the Iron Kai, and the most fortified location in all the Darken Realm. The mighty citadel was built out of the very rock of the mountain. Fortifications and buildings dotted the side of the mighty mountain, but the rock face concealed the majority of the city. An elaborate network of passages, tunnels, and workshops had been carved into the very mountain itself. For generations, the Iron Kai had toiled to improve the mighty city. With over two hundred thousand inhabitants, most of whom never saw the light of day, Stonen was an eerie society of highly industrious cave dwellers with a technology base that rivaled that of the ancients.

Emperor Gunther gave a loud sigh as he viewed the mighty city. For an eternity, the city had withstood countless assaults. But the might of the Reaper Kai was seeking to engulf all the lands. He knew in his heart that in the end, Stonen would be the last haven of mankind against the darkness. He also knew that it would not hold forever, for the might and mischief of the darkness was more than any opposing force could ultimately match.

Looking out over the gun turrets and missile batteries dotting the hillside gave Gunther a quiet sense of calm. For the moment, the Iron Kai were at peace. The Reaper Kai had not made any advancement towards the Iron Kai borders. But this was a tense truce. For hundreds of years since the great civil war, the Iron Kai had held a vigil over the north, waiting and hoping that the cruel world had swallowed the remnants of the Reaper Kai. But this hope was in vain, for in the secrecy of years of seclusion, the Reaper Kai had grown strong and mastered technologies once thought lost to the entire world. And now, the Reaper Kai had set their sights on the mighty city state of Rasheed to the south.

"What other news have you, Captain?" Gunther boomed as he swung around. Gunther was tall and mighty. Breaking six feet in height, with over two hundred pounds of muscle covering his thick bones, he was large and intimidating, a truly mighty monarch.

"The Reaper Kai are bringing light armor with the formation, and something curious…" The Captain fell silent and turned red.

"Curious? How so?" Gunther questioned with a stern look on his face. He stroked his red beard as he quizzed his military advisor.

"I don't know how to explain it, sir… The Reaper Kai have some sort of wooden crate in the center of the army." The Captain stammered as he spoke.

"Spit it out, Captain!" the emperor roared.

"The crate is enormous, and it is being pulled by dozens of oxen. Our scouts have no idea what the crate holds, but they fear the worst." The Captain finished his assessment of the mysterious wooden crate, and Gunther was none too pleased.

"So, the Reaper Kai have a secret weapon?" Gunther was obviously irritated, and none in the room wanted to break the uneasy silence.

Gunther was silent, and the captain was worried and embarrassed to speak. Finally, the captain broke the silence. "That is not all, my lord."

Gunther stepped forward, shouting at the captain, "Out with it, man!"

"Our spies near Darkpine forest claim they caught sight of Vertigo riding in the formation near the wooden crate," the captain explained, now fully engaging Gunther's attention.

"Vertigo, you say?" a wicked grin covered the emperor's face. A fire danced in his eyes. After a moment of silence, the mighty monarch spoke. "Captain, ready a host of gun ships. Dispatch them and assault this formation. If our luck holds, we can slay their foul master." Gunther grew silent, his eyes darting around the room. "What fortune is this? Father Vertigo has never left the capital in all his years. Now we have a chance to end his legacy of darkness."

"Yes, my lord, the gun ships will be dispatched at once." With that, the captain turned to leave the Truce Hall, heading off toward the subterranean air fields within the mighty mountain.

"Captain!" Gunther boomed, and his advisor stopped dead in his tracks. He whirled around and regarded Gunther with a look of respect.

"Yes, sir?" the advisor awaited the emperor's decree.

"What is our status at sea, Captain? Do we have ships within striking distance of Rasheed?" Gunther inquired.

"No, sir, no military ships, only two freighters," the Captain said with a strange look on his face.

"Dispatch them at once to Rasheed. Perhaps we can lend aid if the battle goes ill," Gunther boomed.

"It will be done, my lord." The captain bowed and headed off towards the underground airstrip.

Gunther shook his fists and grabbed a full stein of beer. He lifted the stein into the air and drank a mouthful of the fine ale. Placing the stein back onto the table, Gunther stared around the Truce Hall, which was filled with diplomats and military personnel. He looked at each in turn, his face turning grave.

"I know we have a 'truce' with the Reaper Kai, and this attack on their master will bring about a stiff reprisal. But I fear we have left the Reaper Kai alone for far too long. They are growing strong and are seeking to engulf the entire Darken Realm in war. We know all too well that the Reaper Kai will attack us in the end. They hate us more than any other empire. Instead of waiting here for the end, we are going to attack!" Gunther spoke in a confident tone.

As Gunther's speech rang throughout the Truce Hall, a murmur of terror rolled through the room. Open war with the Reaper Kai would have dire consequences, and most did not relish the thought of such war. Although none in the room wanted a war, all knew in their hearts that it could not be avoided. The dark times when the empire was rocked by the great civil war were still commemorated in their legends. All knew in their hearts that the Reaper Kai would stop at nothing to wipe the Iron Kai off the face of the earth.

"Our people will fight and die for you, Lord Gunther!" A diplomat rose and voiced his support for the emperor. An unanimous outpouring of support followed. Soon, the entire hall was filled with loud battle cries, and recited battle hymns.

And then, abruptly, all came to silence. Several Iron Kai soldiers pushed into the Truce Hall with a strange visitor.

The soldiers carefully watched the visitor with immense distrust. They trained their automatic weapons on him, their trigger fingers ready.

The visitor was short and pale in complexion. His entire body was hairless but rippled with muscle. His eyes were solid white and eerie to look upon. He crouched and hunched when he walked.

"Mord Tech..." Gunther whispered in awe. It wasn't every day that a neighboring empire sent one of their own into the Truce Hall, especially an enemy nation.

"What brings a Mord Tech into the Truce Hall?" Gunther boomed, and the visitor hunched forward slowly towards Gunther.

"A gesture of war brings me here!" The Mord Tech spoke in a tone which was quiet but harsh.

"Indeed!" boomed Gunther. "It has been a great many years since we have warred!"

"And it will be a great many years longer before we shed blood in anger against one another again," Whispered the Mord Tech diplomat.

Gunther shook his head slowly and ushered the visitor onward, seating him at the mighty table in the Truce Hall.

"It has been many years since we have seen one of your kind in these lands. What brings you into this hall?" Gunther asked.

"For generations, we have skirmished and battled over land

and resources. Though we have fought small battles, we have never raged war against each other. It is for this reason that I think we can draw a treaty between our great empires."

"The tide of war will soon be against us, so a treaty might be to my liking." Gunther stroked his red beard as he spoke.

The pale skinned Mord Tech smiled and began to speak. "No longer should we fight over resources and land. I have a deal for you. I would like to annex the lands near the Darkpine forest and split them between our two mighty empires. All I ask for is military aid in this endeavor."

All in the room knew of the lands near the Darkpine, for they were the lands tainted by the foul Reaper Kai.

A smile appeared on Gunther's face. "The lands of the Darkpine, eh?" Gunther was trying to comprehend what was happening. Only a few minutes ago, he had issued an attack against the Reaper Kai. Now, an enemy diplomat was forging a truce to put an end to the dread Reaper Kai. It was almost too much to believe. "What fortune is this?" Gunther smiled at the thought. Open war was about to erupt, and the Iron Kai now had the support of a neighboring empire, a powerful neighboring empire. The smile turned to a wicked grin. Gunther spoke once more. "Military aid you will have, diplomat of the Mord Techs. From this day forth, there shall be a truce between our empires."

"Your terms are well stated, Lord Gunther. I shall return home with the news of our alliance. The Reaper Kai shall tremble and be turned to dust." The Mord Tech spoke while bowing before Gunther. "When will the attack begin?"

"It has already begun," Gunther stated. He ushered the diplomat to the great window.

Two enormous metal doors wheeled open in the side of the mountain. The rumble of machinery could be heard. Ten helicopter gun ships emerged from the underground airstrip. They were painted green, and adorned with the symbol of a hand clutching a hammer, the sign of the Iron Kai. The gun ships rose into the air in formation, heading off towards the south with great speed.

The Mord Tech diplomat smiled at the sight of the gun ships. "Our forces have already attacked and sacked two of the Reaper Kai's border towns."

"So it has begun. May our road be paved with victory taken

from spilled blood!" Gunther boomed. The Mord Tech diplomat smiled at his bravado. "Death to the Reaper Kai!"

An alliance was thus formed between old rivals from the old world. For even though they had bickered and squabbled, they were both determined to destroy the threat growing and festering under the stench of evil near their borders. And so it began; war erupted in the Darken Realm, a horrid war that engulfed all in death and destruction.

Chapter 34
The Great Banquet

And so it was that old King Toil aged yet another year. In his wisdom and charity, he had founded a celebration in honor of his birth where, each year, an enormous banquet was held for five hundred of his closest friends.

The palace of Rasheed was filled with diplomats, dukes, wealthy businessmen, and soldiers of renown. The Great Hall was filled to the brim. Jesters and entertainers of every type milled about the crowd in an effort to keep the party festive and light. Whispers were already going through the hall that the Reaper Kai and Rasheed were now at war. No one knew for sure save the mercenary teams and King Toil's trusted soldiers. Even though the shadow of war was looming over the kingdom, the party was vibrant and full of life.

Festive music rolled through the hall. Fine meals were being served at the edges of the great hall. The center of the room was reserved for the royal ball.

Nova 7 was seated at the edge of the dance floor. Jared was content to rip large chunks of meat off a turkey leg. Tani was engrossed in some sort of gadget, his stumpy fingers fumbling with the device. Banion was angry and refused to look at the rest of them. Mineera had discarded her red robes and had donned an elegant evening gown. From time to time, she shot Banion uneasy glances.

The party had hundreds of guests milling about the Great Hall. Most were dressed in fine evening-wear. The women wore soft, full-length dresses, while the men wore a variety of uniforms or clothing fit for the wealthy.

King Toil sat near the center of the room on an elevated stage with his daughter, Marion, and a host of bodyguards. Globulus was only a step away from old King Toil. The tone of the party was joyous, but King Toil was worried beyond endurance. He had officially put his head on the chopping block. To defy the

Reaper Kai openly was a certain death.

With a broad gesture, the king rose from his throne on the podium and waved his hands above his head to gain the attention of his party attendants. It took but a brief moment for the crowd to come to silence. The king stood before them, nodding in approval at the whole room.

"It takes a wise man to have as many friends as you all! I am grateful for your presence here on my fifty eighth birthday!" as old King Toil spoke, the crowd cheered him. "I hope you all have a good time here tonight! And with this toast to you all, the dancing shall begin." King Toil raised a goblet of wine and smiled at the crowd. "To you!" he yelled. The crowd responded with loud cheers.

With that, the band began to play. Couples, from the wealthy to lucky peasants, lined the dance floor. Slowly, they danced with wide, sweeping movements. The music was formal, as was the dancing.

As more and more guests took to the dance floor, Mineera eyed Banion at length. He could feel her eyes upon him, but refused to look at her. She gave a loud sigh and rose to her feet. Graceful and beautiful, she moved forward in her elegant white ball gown, pressing on until she stood before Banion.

"I just want to apologize," Mineera said earnestly. Banion, still feeling guilty, continued to evade her eyes.

Finally, she leaned forward, taking hold of his hands and pulling. Though graceful, she was quite strong, and managed to pull Banion to his feet. Finally, his eyes met hers and there was a moment of silence between the two. Banion tried to avoid her gaze, but she wouldn't let him. Banion's eyes grew softer, and he stared uncomfortably at Mineera.

She pulled him forward, toward the dance floor. Banion felt odd and followed reluctantly. At last, they found themselves in a sea of dancing people. As they moved closer to each other, Mineera's expression was stern. She began to speak to him softly as they danced.

"I never meant to cause you pain." Mineera's voice was honest. Banion looked into her eyes and found comfort there.

"It's hard…" Banion said, anger rising in his voice. He held his rage in check and continued to dance with Mineera.

Jared poked Tani, and the two stared at Banion and Mineera dancing. Jared spoke suddenly while shaking his head. "As if we didn't have enough problems already."

Tani scrunched up his nose in disgust, and then quickly went back to fidgeting with the device in his hands.

As Mineera continued to dance with Banion, he loosened up a bit. He was less rigid, but still out of sorts. He drew her close and stared at her intently.

"Don't deceive me," Banion said, his eyes hostile and suspicious.

"I won't," she said in a confident tone.

Though she was full of conviction, Banion still did not trust her. Even after everything that had transpired, he still couldn't bring himself to believe in her.

"You up for all this?" Banion asked. "This trip isn't going to be pleasant."

"It couldn't be any worse than being thrown in a Reaper Kai prison and sentenced to death," Mineera said dryly.

"Good point." Banion chuckled.

Dark brown eyes filled with an icy blackness met the soft, caring eyes of Mineera. They stared at one another for a moment, ceasing to dance as they considered each other. Banion nodded his head in approval, as did Mineera. They locked eyes for a brief moment longer.

Suddenly, a gunshot rang out.

All hell broke loose.

The crowd on the dance floor scattered, and a host of guests began to scream. Banion whirled around and caught sight of King Toil clutching his chest. He was staggering back and forth on the podium. Blood dripped through his fingers as his face went ash white.

The bodyguards had grabbed Toil and were shielding him. His strength gave out, and the king crashed to floor. The crowd in the hall ran about and cowered in fear. Banion looked in horror and groped at his belt. All of his weapons were back in the palace room. None of the guests were allowed to bring weapons to the banquet. Cursing under his breath, Banion ran forward, drawing an imaginary line in his head from the dying king to a place upon a raised balcony above the dance floor. Pointing, Banion shouted like a madman.

"Up there, damn it!" Banion screamed, and the palace guards responded by training their weapons upon the balcony.

Seeing a shadowy figure crouched near the edge of the balcony, the guards opened fire. Bursts of gunfire hit the balcony's walls. Coming under fire, the assassin rose and bolted away. Due to the distance and the shadows on the balcony, none could determine his identity.

"There he goes! Kill him!" Banion yelled as he watched the situation unfold with a feeling of helplessness.

Jared and Tani were on their feet. Jared's hand rested uneasily on his belt, for the Scar Blade was in the tribal's room. Tani also felt helpless, for he was unarmed as well.

Mineera retreated as the palace guards sprung into action. The purple clad guards took aim at the balcony once more and fired another volley. Their shots were too late, for the assassin had already departed.

The crowd was in chaos. Many fled the room and ended up streaming out of the banquet hall like a pack of crazed animals. Screams of fear and panic rolled through the hall. People rushed about, falling over one another in their fancy costumes.

King Toil struggled upon the podium. Globulus clutched the king's chest and tried to stop the bleeding. The wound was terrible. The king convulsed a few times as his eyes rolled back and forth.

"Marion…" the king gasped.

The princess moved forward with a blank look on her face. She stared in a daze at her father dying before her. Some inner turmoil rocked her soul as she stared at her father breathing his last breath.

"Marion…" Toil gasped again. With a weak gesture, he held out his quivering hand for his daughter.

Marion knelt down before her father. She took his hand and clutched it. With that, his grip loosened and his breath stopped. King Toil ceased to stir for there was no life left in him.

The room was still. No one dared speak. Globulus averted his gaze, motionless. Marion Toil looked on dully at her dead father before her. She did not stir, nor did she shudder. The princess was lost in an internal conflict of some sort. Racked by the battle within, the princess stared on at her dead father without blinking.

Banion bowed his head and paid his respects to old King

Toil. As he raised his head from the silent prayer, a strange sense of familiarity filled Banion. Though he had known King Toil for years, Banion had never seen his daughter before, and for good reason. With an unwavering gaze, the deranged rancher stared dully at the princess. There was something familiar about her. Something he couldn't put his finger on. It was as if Banion was staring at a ghost, and it was a disturbing feeling. Jared finally spoke and snapped Banion out of his daydream.

"We're in deep trouble, aren't we?" Jared said to Banion, his voice hushed.

Banion turned to face Jared. "Trouble? You have no idea, kid." He shook his head in disgust, then fell silent. With a nod of respect, he removed his hat and bowed before the dead king one last time.

Jared, Tani and Mineera stared on as well. It was the end of an era. King Toil was the most beloved ruler in the history of Rasheed. Now he was only a memory, growing colder and more distant by the second. This chill was fueled by the rumor of war just beyond the horizon. It was an omen of ill intent, a whisper in the darkness, a fleeting glance at fading hope.

Chapter 35
Marion Toil, the Great Betrayer

A great tower of marble rose high into the air. It pierced the icy darkness of the night. From this vantage point, Marion Toil looked down below at the kingdom of Rasheed, her new kingdom.

It was only a mere hour after the death of King Toil. Marion had secluded herself within one of the mighty towers of the palace. Already, shock and panic had reached the streets. Thousands upon thousands of citizens had poured from their homes and hit the streets of Rasheed. Most carried candles and held vigil around the perimeter of the palace. The sea of people milled about, each with a tiny point of light, a small burning candle lit in reverence of their beloved king.

Marion was silent as she stared at the crowd surrounding the walls of the palace. Many wept and many stood silent. She stared at the mass of candles with disgust, sneering at the horde of lost souls. The new Queen of Rasheed hated every one of them. A dry smile crossed her lips as a thought coursed through her twisted brain. Each light down below would soon be extinguished. Every ray of hope would be quashed.

She trembled with anxiety. At last, a calm came over her. The new Queen crossed the tower room, kneeling to open a chest on the floor. Unceremoniously, she stripped off her dress and grabbed a blood red robe. With a flicker of hesitation, she gazed at the garment. Finally, a wicked look twisted her features, and she donned the blood red robes of the Reaper Kai. The betrayal was complete; Marion Toil was now one with the enemy.

"Reimal!" Marion shouted.

A squat, thin and wasted palace guard entered the tower. He bowed in reverence to the queen.

"Yes, my lady." Reimal's tone was submissive.

"Are your teams ready?" Marion quizzed the head of the palace guards.

"Yes, my lady. All the teams are ready. They await your

command, highness," the weasely head guard said, a wicked smile on his face.

Marion stood silently for a brief moment, as if paralyzed by some form of inner turmoil. At last, she shook her head in disgust, feeling the red robes about her body. There was no going back. Marion was a traitor, and she had betrayed the kingdom of Rasheed. She was about to sell out her own people in order to gain status in the Reaper Kai Empire. Her father had already fallen to a hired assassin, an assassin hired by Marion Toil herself. Now the entire kingdom was ripe with fear and ready to fall as well. After ordering the death of her own father, selling out the rest of her kingdom would be easy.

Marion grabbed a radio handset and brought it to her mouth.

"This is Marion Toil, all teams report." Marion spoke confidently into the radio.

"Alpha teams reporting. All seven teams in position for entry. I repeat, all seven entry teams are ready and awaiting orders," a voice responded from the radio.

"Beta team ready and awaiting commands, my lady," another voice crackled from the headset.

"Delta team in position and ready," a final voice responded.

Marion was pleased that all of the teams were in position. "Alpha team, entry team seven report."

A moment of silence stretched on following Marion's command.

"Entry team seven leader reporting." The voice on the other end was grim.

"I have a change in your orders," Marion said softly.

There was a moment of silence. Reimal was staring at Marion with a quizzical expression.

"Your will be done, my lady," the leader of entry team seven responded.

"Kill all of Nova 7…" Marion paused. "Except Banion, I want him taken alive. I will make him suffer long and hard for what he has taken from me!"

The radio remained silent.

"Lord Vertigo gave strict orders to have all of the Nova teams killed. Is it wise to go against his orders?" Reimal quizzed the Queen, his face concerned.

"Is it wise to go against my orders?" Marion questioned him, a look of hatred in her eyes. "I am queen. Obey me, or spend the rest of your life rotting in my dungeons!"

"My lady..." A response issued from the radio. "Banion O'Neil?"

"Yes, I want him taken alive. Is there a problem?" Marion yelled into the instrument.

"No... no... I just..." the entry team leader stammered. "It's just... Banion is so... well, my lady... Banion O'Neil is dangerous."

"And I will be too, if you fail me!" Queen Marion was irate, and beginning to lose control. "You have your orders, carry them out!"

"Yes, my lady. We will take Banion alive and slaughter the rest. Not a single Nova team will make it out of the palace alive," the entry team leader promised.

"They had better not, for your sake!" Marion warned.

The radio fell silent. Reimal's eyes were wary and fearful. Marion sized him up with a sneer.

"The time to strike is now. The populace is in chaos after the death of my father. None of them suspect a full army of Biogtechs is ready to assault the city. This is the perfect time to lay waste to Rasheed. With all the palace guards under my control, we will not fail. The gates will be in ruin in under an hour, and nothing will stop the Reaper Kai from taking control of this city!" Marion was triumphant, smiling in glee as wicked thoughts mastered her heart and soul.

"There is only one guard I fear may ruin our plans," Reimal warned, and Marion knew of whom he spoke.

"Leave Globulus to me. I will deal with him myself. He would not dare to assault or oppose us. He is loyal to our family." Marion spoke with conviction, but Reimal was not so sure.

He shook his head, looking at the clock. "The hour grows near, my lady."

"Indeed, Reimal. Prepare your troops to defend the palace against the Rasheed Militia," Marion commanded. "We will be a target of the army when they discover our betrayal."

The time had finally come. The well laid plans to destroy the kingdom of Rasheed would soon be realized. Brushing her hands across the blood red robes, Marion felt a rush of evil fill her soul.   Shaking with an evil fury filling her, she ordered the destruction of her own kingdom.

"Team Alpha."   Marion spoke into the radio.   "Execute attack plans."

"Team Alpha responding. All seven entry teams are en route to targets," the leader of team Alpha responded.

"Team Beta. Execute demolitions attack," Marion ordered.

"Demolitions team ready and assault team moving on the target," the leader of team Beta replied.

"Delta team. Execute demolitions," the evil queen ordered her palace minions.

"Delta assault team engaging.   Demolitions team on standby," the Delta team leader responded.

The palace guards were loyal to one cause: the royal family. Many of the guards suspected that Marion was responsible for the assassination of King Toil, but the lure of Marion's wealth and her promises of power subverted many from gallant thoughts. They knew that what they were doing was wrong, and didn't care. They maintained their loyalty to the queen no matter how twisted she seemed.

Marion fell silent. The sound of gunfire echoed through the palace. The slaughter of the Nova teams had begun. In the distance, more gunfire could be heard in the streets. The treacherous palace guards were killing the Rasheed Militia manning the two mighty gates in the city. A loud explosion was heard as the east gate was blasted to ruin.

In the darkness to the east, a mighty army stirred. Ten thousand Biogtech assault drones moved towards the city. In the center of the formation was a giant wooden crate drawn by forty oxen. With dread and doom, the army marched.

The city was in chaos due to the death of the king. This death would be a mere shadow compared to the horror about to be unleashed upon the unsuspecting citizens of Rasheed.   With demonic trumpets sounding, the Reaper Kai priests offered prayers to dark powers. The siege of Rasheed had begun.

Chapter 36
When Darkness Falls

There was a field filled with bright yellow and purple wild flowers. The valley was secluded in the mountains, far from harm and far from chaos. The sky was blue and the sun was warm. Butterflies bobbed from flower to flower. Lush green grass grew tall and strong.

Mineera was deep in meditation, and she smiled as the calm imagery filled her mind. A peaceful essence enveloped her as she prayed serenely. The rest of Nova 7 eyed her suspiciously. As she prayed, Mineera whispered softly, as if having a conversation. Banion shook his head in disgust. Jared and Tani shot each other odd glances.

Mineera imagined herself walking in the bright and lush mountain field. As she walked, a wind rose from the tops of the snowcapped peaks. A dark, ominous cloud began to form around the top of the white mountains. Gradually, the storm grew and the sun itself was lost. A darkness rose across the field. The lush land began to wither. The sound of flies and carrion birds could be heard. As Mineera stood in the center of the field, a wretched feeling began to flow through her. Something was wrong.

"Get away from the door!" Mineera jumped to her feet and screamed at the top of her lungs. Instinctively, she raised her hands in defense towards the door of the palace room. Banion jumped to his feet and raised his mighty assault rifle in alarm. Jared and Tani stared at Mineera with shock.

An explosion rocked the room. A demolition charge had reduced the door to a smoking ruin in a devastating blast. The shockwave from the explosion was powerful, but Mineera was ready. A barrier of white light surrounded her as she stood near the blasted door. Shrapnel and debris from the explosion ricocheted harmlessly off the barrier of psychic energy.

"Son of a bitch!" Banion yelled, leveling his mighty weapon at the open doorway. Without warning, he opened fire. The crazed cowboy fired several bursts through the doorway.

Banion's spray of fire had caught the entry team off guard. One of the traitorous palace guards was felled by the gunfire. The entry team immediately counterattacked by lobbing a series of stun grenades into the room. The grenades detonated in front of Mineera, but her spiritual barrier protected her and the other members of Nova 7.

The bright flashes from the grenades, however, blinded Mineera and she staggered backwards. Her concentration was broken, and the white barrier dropped. Tani rushed forward and pulled the stunned psychic maiden out of the doorway. Instantly, gunfire erupted from the hallway. The palace guards opened fire, and dozens of bullets ripped through the room.

With a flurry of movement, three palace guards rushed the door. Banion took solid aim and sprayed the troops moving into the room. Round after round struck flesh and the guards were torn to a bloody mess. Their bodies crashed to the floor in a chaotic dance of misery.

"Fall back!" Banion yelled while walking backwards with the assault rifle pressed to his chest.

Jared and Tani, still stunned, hastily grabbed their gear and shouldered it. The tribals ran with Mineera in tow towards the balcony.

Banion laid down covering fire and continued to fall back. The enemy was strong in number and with another push, they rushed inside with weapons blazing. Dozens of enemy bullets raced through the room. Marble shattered as the sound of gunfire hummed. A shower of debris was formed by the attack, raining down with a clatter as Banion made every effort to kill anything that moved in his field of vision.

Without a hint of fear, Banion controlled the assault rifle like a professional. He fired short bursts at anything that he saw move. The crazed rancher had a wicked aim, and left two more guards dead on the floor. The rest of the entry team took up defensive positions behind the marble columns in the room and returned fire. Banion pushed off onto the balcony, quick as a cat. Bullets zinged by him as he ran.

Tani was trembling as he pulled the pin on a grenade. He released the clip and rolled the weapon across the floor into the chamber. A boom erupted from the grenade, leaving a palace guard torn in two.

"Nice shot, kid!" Banion screamed while firing another quick burst into the room. "Do something quick, bookworm, or we're all dead!"

Jared was filled with fright as he held his new submachine gun in his shaky hands. Mineera had recovered somewhat, but was still having a hard time seeing. Tani dropped to his knee and pulled a demolitions charge from his pack. Skillfully, his stumpy hand rigged the detonator. Within seconds, a structural support column on the balcony was rigged with the explosive.

"Good to go!" Tripwire yelled as he pushed his wire-rim glasses up his sweaty nose.

"Get the hell out of here!" Banion yelled.

Jared and Mineera moved to the edge of the balcony, which overlooked the palace gardens below. With only a ten-foot drop to another roof beneath, and another ten-foot drop to the garden, the escape route looked promising.

"Ten seconds!" Tani yelled as he set off a timer on the detonator. Jared and Mineera had already dropped off the balcony onto the roof, and the young scholar ran and launched over the edge. Banion fired another burst and followed the rest of his team over the balcony's edge.

The entry team, unaware of Tani's surprise, rushed onto the balcony just as the demolition charge blew. With a deafening boom and an immense shockwave of energy, the charge exploded, tearing the support column apart. Several guards were caught in the blast, and their mangled burning bodies were thrown into the air. The rest of the entry team met the crushing force of more than a ton of marble collapsing on top of them.

The battle ended just as abruptly as it had started. Tani had successfully killed all of the remaining members of the palace guard extermination squad.

Nova 7, still pumped with adrenaline, made their way quickly across the rooftop. Banion held the rear position, training his gun back onto the balcony from time to time. No more enemies could be seen.

The team halted as Jared crouched in the darkness of the palace rooftop. He quietly pointed to the east, and a sense of wonder and fear washed over Nova 7. Fires were burning in the city. Near the great wall, the fires leapt high into the dark night. More flames were ablaze inside the wall as well, consuming homes and shops in their path. An eerie silence washed over Nova 7 as they watched the flames of war eat the eastern part of the city.

The palace grounds were silent. Suddenly, gunfire erupted in the distance and screams could be heard. More gunfire echoed all around the palace. Screams rolled throughout the palace grounds from all directions. The other Nova teams were under attack.

The solemn group members looked at each other in the darkness. None of them spoke, but the gravity of their situation was apparent. Booms sounded in the eastern part of the city. Alarm bells were ringing in the distance. Rasheed was being invaded.

"This is a setup," Banion whispered in the darkness as he crouched on the rooftop. "All the other Nova teams are under attack as well. Hear the gunfire in the palace? We barely survived, and I doubt many of them will survive. The east city gate is down, by the looks of things. That leaves the city wide open to attack." Banion pulled his night vision binoculars free from his long coat and peered east through them.

He shook his head in dismay, putting the binoculars back in his coat. "I could see several thousand Biogtechs near the main gate. I fear this city is lost. Rasheed cannot withstand such an attack without the walls for protection."

"What do we do?" Jared asked, wide-eyed with fear.

"Escape is our only option. The east gate has fallen and the north gate is the only other way out of the city." Just then, another loud explosion lit up the night. The blast rose from the north wall of the city. "Scratch that, the north gate just went down."

The team crouched in the darkness, keeping silent for a long moment.

"Hey, bookworm?" Banion whispered.

"Yeah?" Tani responded in a hushed tone.

"Could you drive a boat?" Banion quizzed.

"Yeah, I could figure it out, Banion," Tani replied.

"Good. Here's the plan: Mineera and Tani, get to the harbor and commandeer a boat. Jared and I will meet you there," Banion ordered.

"What?" Jared was confused. "Where are we going?"

"Back into the palace," Banion said, his voice a sinister whisper.

"Back into the palace!" Jared said in alarm. "What on earth for!?"

"We need to get to Globulus. Unless we find him and get him to rally the city troops, no one will escape this attack. We need to give the city time to evacuate, and without leadership, the city will fall within hours. Now that King Toil is gone, Globulus is the only leader who can rally the troops." Banion spoke wisely, but Jared was still filled with fear. "Look Jared, all the people of Rasheed will die unless we raise the Rasheed army."

"Don't take too long. I sense Reaper Kai drawing near, and I can feel the presence of Vertigo himself." Mineera spoke in a whisper.

Jared looked at Tani in horror, and Tani looked back with an equal look of shock. The thought of being separated was down-right terrifying. Jared wondered if the two tribals would ever see each other again; being killed in the invasion seemed like a distinct possibility. Tani nodded and said goodbye, looking uneasily at Mineera.

With that, Mineera and Tani dropped off the roof into the palace garden below. Banion eyed Jared with a flash of madness in his eyes and then slapped him on the shoulder.

"Come on, kid, we have a kingdom to save!"

Chapter 37
Flight to the Harbor

The garden was cool and dark. Gunfire echoed every now and again from within the palace. Concealed by the darkness, the two crept forward. Mineera led the way, while Tani tried to keep up with his fully loaded bag of explosives strapped to his back.

They made their way behind the trees to keep hidden. As they moved, shadows moved about the open areas. The traitorous palace guards had learned of the escape of Nova 7, and had stepped up their efforts to locate and kill the missing mercenary team.

Mineera was adept at concealing them, and they managed to elude multiple patrols. Finally, they came to the palace gate. The courtyard loomed before them, brightly lit with torchlight. A garrison of purple clad troops was manning the gatehouse.

"I see only six of them, and can feel two more close by," Mineera whispered.

Tani pulled out a grenade and pointed at it.

Mineera shook her head in disagreement. "Perhaps a more subtle approach would be advised. I do not want to draw the rest of the palace to the gate."

Tani looked confused, but Mineera was already submerging into a state of meditation. A calm came over her, and she concentrated on the guards at the gate. She projected an intense mental image of calming sleep. Suddenly, all of the guards fell to the ground, caught in an unnatural slumber. Mineera rose to her feet and staggered back and forth; the use of spiritual energy was taxing to her body and soul. Tani stared in amazement, and suddenly felt lucky to be on Mineera's side and not her enemy.

With the gatehouse crew neutralized, Mineera and Tani rushed forward across the open courtyard. Tani fidgeted with the gate controls for a few seconds, and the gates swung open. Hastily, the two exited the palace.

The streets of Rasheed were in chaos. Screaming civilians and soldiers were running about in seemingly random directions.

With the death of King Toil, the city was in a state of panic without leadership. The Rasheed army was unorganized, and was making critical mistakes while trying to defend the north and east gates of the city.

Mineera pressed on into a mob of crazed citizens who had filled the street. They were filled with panic, and Mineera could feel each and every one of them. Tani eyed her with concern as she fought to remain in control. She seemed to be losing the battle, and he placed his hand on her shoulder. She forced the mob's thoughts out of her mind and they pushed on through the crowd.

Finally, Tani and Mineera found themselves in a large open square. Rasheed troops had hastily erected two machine gun nests and were preparing to engage the enemy. Mineera was suspicious, and didn't understand how the enemy could have pushed so deep into the city already. Her suspicions were about to be answered.

A sick feeling coursed through the psychic maiden. An overwhelming demonic presence was approaching. She braced herself and moved off between the machine gun nests. Rasheed troops numbering at least fifty had filled the square.

Screams of anguish could be heard a few streets down. Gunfire and blasts were drawing near. A ragged and terrified squad of Rasheed troops suddenly flooded the square, fleeing in panic. The stunned troops defending the square looked at each other in shock. More screams could be heard from the next street over.

Something roared in the darkness. A terrified voice filled the air. "No!" the voice whined. The screaming became more intense, and then there was silence.

Mineera gripped her hands tightly. Something wicked was drawing very near. She could feel its presence, and it had almost reached the square.

A tremor rocked the earth. Boom, boom, boom, a hushed silence then another boom. Something huge was moving through the dark street near the east end of the square.

The troops braced themselves and readied their weapons.

A dark monstrosity pushed itself into the square, and chaos flooded through the Rasheed troops. The visage of the beast was so horrid that no one save Mineera could look upon it.

Tani fell to the ground, cowering in fear. He hid his face and moaned in terror. The rest of the soldiers in the square also fell to the ground, gripped with panic, none able to look upon the demonic beast.

Mineera crouched near Tani and placed her hands on him, trying desperately to console him. But there was nothing that could avert the power of this creature. For the creature was born of darkness, and had grown strong for hundreds of years, feeding off the flesh of the living.

The Abomination moved into the square and roared with glee. "So much warm flesh!" it screamed. The troops cowered while Mineera remained concealed at the west edge of the square.

Only those whose essence was extreme evil or those of pure righteous conviction could look upon the Abomination without fear. Mineera was such a person. She looked upon the beast as it strode forth to kill the troops.

The demon was taller than a two-story building and thicker than a bus. Sick green bloated flesh covered its body. At uneven intervals were human faces, screaming and moaning in terror, rising from the beast's sickly skin. For each victim who had been eaten became part of the demon's flesh. The faces of hundreds dotted the belly of the monster. Each was twisted and contorted, and had seen hundreds of years of torment being trapped within the body of the monster. In its right hand, the Abomination carried a mighty black steel cudgel drenched in gore. Its head was grotesque and distorted. A set of yellow, demonic eyes scanned the helpless soldiers. Black teeth smeared with blood and a tongue coated in human flesh topped off its grisly appearance.

The monster strode forth and brought its weapon to bear on the soldiers. None were able to see the monster, but all could feel its presence. Many of the soldiers crawled across the ground in random directions in a desperate attempt to escape. The demon smiled and smashed the helpless soldiers with its mighty weapon. The blade was dull, but smashed the troops into piles of pulp. The beast slowly worked his way across the square, squashing and crushing all he saw.

The soldiers could not look upon the beast, and the sounds of the dying were too much to handle. Many of them fled, while others fired randomly about like blind men, hoping to kill the beast.

With glee it moved. Every once in a while, the demon would grip a soldier and eat him alive. Within seconds after the remnants of the soldier slid down its throat, another new tormented face appeared on the belly of the beast. With each meal it consumed, the Abomination grew slightly larger and hungrier.

Mineera knew she could not face such a creature alone.

"Flee, Mineera. This is not your day to slay this beast," a voice spoke softly in her mind.

Shaking off the horrid bloodshed she was witnessing, she pulled Tani to his feet and pushed him down an alley. The further they moved from the beast, the more Tani's fear diminished. Finally, they had escaped the scene of the carnage, and Tani was able to control himself once again.

"What was that, Mineera?" Tani asked with anguish on his face. "Nothing in my darkest dreams compares to the fear I felt. Nothing can stand against such a foe." Tani shook his head in despair.

"You're wrong…" Mineera was distant as she spoke. Gradually, she came back to reality, and pushed on through the alleyway.

Pockets of fighting had erupted all over the city. The Biogtech soldiers had been pouring in through both gates, and all ten thousand enemy troops were now within the city walls.

Evading the combat, they moved from street to street, battle to battle. Finally, Tani and Mineera made it to the harbor.

Thousands of refugees had already begun to swarm every boat that they could find. Since the enemy held the city gates, the only escape route was by ship. Mineera and Tani looked on at the mass of thousands trying to escape.

"There is no way…" Tani shook his head as he viewed the refugees fighting over anything that could float.

"God will save us," Mineera said triumphantly.

"What?" Tani quizzed.

Mineera did not respond. Tani turned away from her in despair. A feeling of helplessness washed over him. He shook his head in dismay. It wouldn't be long before the Biogtech army secured the harbor.

Chapter 38
The Lord of Darkness Falls

Jared crouched just a few feet behind Banion. The sound of gunfire echoed about the grounds of the palace. The night air was cool and crisp. Jared shuddered, holding his hand on the hilt of the mighty Scar Blade.

Just ahead of the two, a heated firefight had erupted in an open courtyard. The Rasheed troops were engaged in a bloody battle with the treacherous palace guards.

With a calm movement, Banion rose to his feet. He pressed the stock of the assault rifle against his shoulder. Breathing evenly, he trained the gun's sights upon the chest of a purple clad palace guard. Gently, he squeezed the trigger. Two rounds flew forth.

With a spray of blood and a scream of pain, the guard fell to his knees, clutching the horrible wounds on his chest.

Without hesitation, Banion continued his assault. Clad in his brown long coat, the deranged rancher took aim and began to slay any palace guard that he saw. Shot after shot hit their mark. Jared shivered in awe as he watched half a dozen guards die swiftly, in the blink of an eye. Sickly fascinated, the young tribal continued to look on.

Finally, the palace guards retreated back into the interior of the building. The Rasheed troops looked around in awe; none of them could discern who had brutally slaughtered the palace guards.

The wraith of death strode forth from the shadows with mighty weapon in hand. His eyes were dark and heartless. A mighty scar crossed his cheek, and his cowboy hat concealed his face with a deeper darkness than that created by the already dim light.

Following carefully behind him was a youth dressed in animal hides and simple cloth. His shaky hand rested on the hilt of an ancient sword. Hesitation and fear swirled in the tribal's eyes.

The Rasheed soldiers were filled with hope and relief at the sight of the legendary gunfighter Banion. The leader of the troops moved forward to speak with the mythical soldier.

"Deceit runs high, Banion O'Neil. We were ambushed near the north gate by these guards. Soon after, the north gate fell, and we were forced to retreat." The leader was shaken, but managed to maintain his composure fairly well.

"Aye, we were attacked as well. We must find Master Globulus to rally the defenses, or this city will surely fall," Banion said while scanning the darkness around the courtyard. His eyes were constantly searching for enemies.

"Globulus?" the militia leader quizzed with a concerned look. "If the palace guards have betrayed the city, what chance is there that Globulus is behind this scheme?"

"I doubt Globulus would be part of this treachery. He is noble and courageous, not vile and deceptive. Let's move," Banion ordered.

With that, the troops fell behind Banion and Jared.

With confident moves, Banion strode forth, and all the soldiers followed. The soldiers had heard legends of the mighty gunfighter, and all knew he had fought for Rasheed in the past. Without official leadership, the soldiers looked to Banion.

"Leave none of the traitors alive!" Banion yelled, rallying the troops. They let out a war cry and rushed the entrance to the palace.

With a quick push they breached the palace doors. Their assault was met with a hail of lead. The palace guards had already fortified the entrance. Gunfire and explosions rocked the room. Several soldiers on both sides fell in the opening exchange.

Banion led the charge, managing to take up a defensive position behind a marble bench. Jared followed and hid. Several other Rasheed soldiers took up positions around Banion. The other forces held the entrance.

The hall was large and tall. A balcony and stairway rose up and up into the heart of the palace. The palace guards were holding all of the balconies and the staircase as well.

The battle was furious. Already, the white marble floors were stained with the blood of the dead. Horrid displays of death were all around. Corpses were piling up, but there were many, many more soldiers still fighting for their lives.

"Covering fire!" Banion yelled, gaining the attention of the

Rasheed soldiers battling with the legendary hero.

The Rasheed soldiers stood and fired a barrage of bullets at the staircase landing. The gunfire was so thick, the soldiers guarding the landing dove for cover to void getting shot. Banion took the advantage and ran full force with Jared following meekly behind. His motions were skilled and controlled; Banion fired bursts of weapon fire at his enemies on the balcony. The attack was fierce, and the palace guards were stunned.

The cover fire was more than enough to enable Banion to reach the main landing of the great staircase. Several palace guards were caught unaware as Banion moved in for the kill. Stationed only a few feet away from the guards, Banion opened fire and sprayed three traitors of Rasheed. They all were felled by the gunfire.

The main landing was taken, and Banion pushed upwards as Jared followed hesitantly, with wild-eyed fear on his face.

"For Rasheed!" The Rasheed Militia yelled. They ran full force after Banion.

The palace guards retreated deeper into the palace, setting up positions in a long hall lined with large marble columns.

Banion hit the top of the stairs and dove for cover. Several palace guards opened fire, barely missing the deranged rancher. The Rasheed soldiers topped the stairs, and another intense gunfight broke out. Back and forth they volleyed. Several more died on each side of the battle.

Banion was getting discouraged. It was unwise to charge a secured position, and even more unwise to linger. His brain worked feverishly to come up with a plan.

Just then, the tide of battle turned. At the far end of the hall was a mighty figure. Many wounds covered his thick skin and mighty body. Master Globulus strode forth, carrying his fully automatic rotary machine gun. His eyes were fierce as he scanned the battle ahead of him. The Rasheed soldiers looked on uneasily. All knew that Globulus was head of the palace guards but his allegiance was in question. Would the mighty hippo side with the traitorous palace guards or the noble Rasheed Militia.

"Hold your fire!" Banion yelled as the mighty hippo continued his way down the hall.

"Fools! Retreat now! Victory is ours!" the palace guards

yelled.   They watched Globulus move down the hall with his weapon in tow. All the palace guards knew that Globulus protected the royal family.

"We have to drop him! All is lost if he reaches us!" the Rasheed soldiers yelled to Banion.

"Hold your fire!" Banion yelled again. He looked at the visage of the mighty mutant bearing down on them. Banion had known Globulus far too long to believe that he would be part of this uprising. The palace guards, on the other hand, had been under Globulus' command for years, and would never believe that he would side with the Rasheed soldiers. "There is no way Globulus would side with these traitors!"

And so the mighty mutant moved into the center of the palace guards. With every step he took, the palace guards became more joyous. They were anticipating watching the mighty Globulus thrash the Rasheed Militia.

When he finally reached the center of the palace guards protecting the hall, he gave a deafening cry and leveled his mighty machine gun at the palace guards. To say they were surprised was a massive understatement. Globulus swung back and forth, firing the weapon full auto at the shocked palace guards. Within seconds, almost all were left in shreds of gore. Whirling and yelling he went, his weapon hummed away, tearing flesh and splintering bone. The power of Globulus was unmatched. Screams of agony filled the hall as the treacherous guards died in a hot flurry of lead. Finally, the last of the palace guards fell. The walls were drenched in gore and the floors were littered with pools of blood.

All who had witnessed the sight were shocked and horrified. Many had seen war, but few had seen such carnage and death wrought with such speed.

The angered hippo looked around him. Banion rounded the corner and regarded him with an enigmatic expression.

"Nice work," Banion smiled.

Globulus looked on at Banion without a smile or hint of emotion. "Dark powers are at work. All of the Nova teams are slain or missing save for you, Banion."

"Indeed. Darkness is at work. The city gates have fallen, and a host of Biogtechs are razing the city as we speak. You must get Princess Toil out of the palace and prepare the city's defenses.

Without leadership, this city will surely fall." Banion spoke quickly, and the mighty mutant listened intently.

Finally, he nodded. "Agreed, Banion. I was in search of the Princess before I encountered this battle. Lieutenant!" Globulus boomed, and a Rasheed Militia officer moved forward from the troops. "Send word to the Rasheed Militia to fall back to Majab street and Reiser street. We can blow the bridges and hold the river front."

"Yes, sir." The soldier saluted Globulus and made his way with a few other soldiers into the heart of Rasheed.

"Banion, Jared, and the rest of you, come with me. The princess needs our protection!" Globulus roared, and all followed. Little did they know that Princess Marion Toil was the last person that needed protection, all of them still unaware of her betrayal.

With that, the war band progressed deeper into the palace. The halls were dark and the candles flickered. There was a chill in the air. Quickly, they pressed on, meeting no resistance. The further they pushed, the darker and more chilled the air became.

"Something unnatural draws near." Banion spoke under his breath. Only Jared heard him, and was dismayed by such talk.

Finally, Globulus held his hand in the air. The group fell silent and crept forward. They could hear the sounds of chattering. It chilled them all, for the sound that filled the air was the sound of beasts calling out. It sounded like a pack of wild animals gibbering around a fresh kill.

Banion crouched and peered around a corner. Several hunched figures in red robes were moving slowly down the hall. Their faces were twisted and hideous, for they were no longer men. Hate and anger had filled their souls. Such torment had reduced them to horrid avatars of evil. Where as once they had been men, no semblance of humanity now remained. Their faces had twisted and their snouts grown in length. Red eyes scanned the darkness ahead. Fur covered their faces, and they looked more goat than human. A host of Goat Minions was inside the mighty palace of Rasheed and were completely unaware of Banion and the soldiers with him.

A door was ahead beyond the corner. Light was moving within.

Banion knew the stories from the north all too well. He had heard horrid tales of the Goat Minions, and knew they were Father

Vertigo's bodyguards. They were no normal Reaper Kai; the Goat Minions were the most vicious and inhumane of all the Reaper Kai. Their cruelty was profound. Fighting them would be a losing battle as their savagery was legendary.

Eight red figures walked down the hall towards the hidden companions. Banion knew the band could not stand against such foes. He eyed the candlelit doorway ahead of him for some time. Finally, he acted, rushing toward the door. All his crew followed hastily.

As Banion crossed the hallway, a scream of alarm arose from the Goat Minions. They bayed and bleated at him. Banion breached the candle–lit room, as did his companions. As the last of them entered, he slammed the door shut and jammed a wooden beam across the door, barring the passage of the hideous Goat Minions.

Banion turned around, and a chill of terror shot down his spine. Standing at the far end of the chamber were two more figures, one clad in red and the other in black and blue robes. As the sound of the door slamming rolled through the room, the two figures whirled around.

The first was none other than the Princess of Rasheed, young Marion Toil, clad in the blood red robes of the enemy. A sense of shock crested through Banion, Jared, Globulus, and the Rasheed soldiers. The robes she wore branded her as a traitor, a servant of the enemy.

The other figure was an old man. His beard was white and was forked at its end. Dark black eyes filled his rotted-out eye sockets. Pale white and ashen was his face, and the stench of death wafted from him to fill the room.

"Vertigo…" Banion mumbled.

Just then, a heavy thud hit the door. The Goat Minions were trying to enter the room. Vertigo looked at the wood barring the door with distaste. His guards were unable to help the Lord of Evil in this encounter.

"Globulus," Marion said softly to the hippo.

The mighty hippo stood his ground, stunned, as his mind swam. Suddenly, things were beginning to make sense, but he dared not believe in such things. How else could the assassin have gotten into the palace? How else could the gates of the city have fallen with such ease? How else could King Toil have died? A fever

flooded him. Anger rose in him. Excruciating tension filled him.
He stared at the Princess with extreme hatred.

"Globulus, come to my side. Protect me from this rabble.
You are sworn to serve this family. Protect me." Marion caught the
hippo's eyes with a strong, persuasive gaze.

Anger coursed through him. He was losing control.

"Such delicious suffering, such wanted hate and despair!"
Vertigo proclaimed, smiling at the hippo.

"Protect me..." Marion spoke softly, and Globulus became
sleepy. He felt a foreign presence slipping into his mind. With as
much strength as he could muster, the mutant hippo fought to
remain in control. Some perverse force was begging him to protect
the princess, calling him to join the sinister princess.

Thud. The Goat Minions were attempting to break down the
door.

"Ah, Banion, such fortune. I spent a lifetime looking for
you. What twist of fate brings you to my door? My very home... I
am blessed indeed," Marion crooned, smiling at Banion. "I have
begged the darkness to deliver you to me..."

A faint sense of familiarity filled Banion. As the Princess
smiled, Banion felt a fear creep into him. It was as if he was
reliving a dream. Her face was familiar. A memory erupted in him.
He had seen her before...

"...Dune Station." Banion whispered. His face turned white
as his gaze grew dark. Old memories, horrid visions of the past
ripped through his brain like an ice pick. A flare of hatred exploded
through his as he watched the demonic princess scowl with a wicked
look. He had seen her sickly face before... "Like mother like
daughter!" the deranged rancher yelled. "I'll do to you what I did
to her!"

With that, Banion raised his weapon and opened fire, but
Vertigo was too quick. A blue barrier of spiritual energy surrounded
both Marion and the Lord of Evil. The bullets ricocheted harmlessly
off the barrier. The psychic shield had protected them from harm.
The other troops scattered and took up positions around the room as
the sound of gunfire rang out.

Thud. Bang. The Goat Minions moaned and roared outside
the door, hinges groaning as they battered the door.

Globulus fought to remain in control. A presence was trying to undermine his soul, and he struggled to keep from losing his grip. Tears rolled down his cheeks. Memories of King Toil moved through his fragile mind. Sorrow filled him. A sense of betrayal rolled through him. How could Marion betray her own people? How could she do such a twisted thing? He didn't want to believe it, but it was the only explanation.

A clattering filled the room. Marion sat motionless behind the barrier of blue energy. She was deep in meditation. Fear and evil festered in her heart, and she prayed to the darkness for power. The darkness answered. The clattering grew stronger. A dark smoke rolled across the floor. A set of legs emerged from the smoke, then another, and yet another. The smoke spread, and more clattering arose. Forms emerged from the dark smoke. A host of spiders grew upon the floor. Soon, hundreds clattered and skittered. A mass of arachnids formed and took shape. The swarm attacked.

Several of the Rasheed soldiers were caught off guard. The horde of spiders burst forth. Like a wave, they crashed over a nearby soldier. Enveloped in soft furry legs, the soldier screamed, but his screams were in vain. He felt stings and pricks on his skin, as venom filled his blood. Within seconds, the poison overwhelmed him. He ceased to struggle and spiders enveloped his entire body. With a crash, he fell to the floor, and the host of spiders moved forth to claim another victim.

Banion aimed at Vertigo and fired several bursts. The Lord of Evil simply smiled and raised his hand in defiance. Not a single bullet bit his flesh; the barrier of energy repelled every attack. With a bitter smile, Vertigo motioned, and suddenly, Banion gagged. Blood lurched from his stomach. He retched bile and blood on the floor. The gunfighter's belly stung in pain. Vertigo smiled and squeezed his fist. An immense pain struck Banion's flesh. He retched again, falling to the floor. The dark father squeezed his fist again, and more pain filled Banion. Blood ran from his ears. Gore dripped from his mouth. Father Vertigo was killing Banion with an unseen force.

A flash of movement caught Vertigo by surprise. Something quick and agile had charged him. The barrier could not stop an attack at close range. A flash of blue metal sliced the air. The Scar Blade breached Vertigo's shield.

The attack missed its mark, and Vertigo retreated a step.

Drawing a twisted dagger, the dark lord cursed the youth who had attacked him. Unable to focus on Banion, Vertigo lost his hold over him. The pain subsided in Banion and he brought himself to his knees, dazed and shaken by Vertigo's psychic attack.

The fear was gone from Jared. Something had snapped. The pain and suffering that Banion was experiencing drove Jared into a battle frenzy. He strode forth, and his expert combat skills kicked in. He moved in on Vertigo quickly. Without hesitation, the young tribal from Scarskin assaulted the age-old Lord of Evil.

With a yell, the youth dove forward and plunged the blue blade into Father Vertigo. The blade bit flesh and shattered the old man's ribcage, pushing onward, emerging from Vertigo's back. The smell of death filled the air as Jared's blade impaled Father Vertigo. A spray of black filth erupted from the horrid wound. Jared pulled back, freeing the mighty Scar Blade from the Lord of Evil.

As Jared moved back, a look of hatred covered Vertigo's face. He pointed his twisted hand at the youth. "How dare you!" he screamed, as a wail of demonic voices screamed in unison from Vertigo's open mouth. "You think that a puny tribal boy can bring about my ruin? How foolish you are!"

His words were cut off. Banion had recovered from his wounds. With blood still dripping from his mouth, he steadied his assault rifle and took aim. With great pleasure, he pulled the trigger and kept it down. The weapon fired full auto. Round after round struck Vertigo. No barrier saved him, nothing protected him. Banion held the weapon under control and kept firing. Vertigo rocked back and forth as his body was torn. Dozens of bullets pierced his body. Black gore spewed forth, spraying from open wounds. Banion was content with the carnage and kept firing. Nearly another dozen bullets tore into Father Vertigo. Finally, he collapsed on the floor in a shower of misery.

Banion jumped to his feet quickly and ran forward, stopping only a foot away from Vertigo. With hate in his eyes, he trained the weapon on Vertigo's forehead and fired three times. All three bullets hit their mark. He nodded his head in approval, grabbing Jared's shoulder. Jared nodded back, with a dazed look on his face.

As the Lord of Darkness fell in battle, Marion was shaken, and she jumped up and ran towards the balcony. Several of the guards took aim and fired. None hit, and Marion Toil, the Great

Betrayer, escaped the battle. The host of spiders disappeared in a puff of black smoke with Marion Toil's passing.

Globulus recovered from the confusion and stared around blankly.

Banion took a step back as Vertigo's body began to glow with an eerie blue hue. Shapes and forms rose from his body and spun around it like a swarm of bees. Jared took a step back as well, staring in horror at the black ooze covering the Scar Blade and the sinister spirits erupting from the slain archpriest. More blue ghosts and evil spirits emerged from Vertigo's body and began to whisper. All who beheld the sight felt frightened but triumphant as well. Father Vertigo, Lord of the Reaper Kai, had been slain.

Thud. Bang. The Goat Minions screamed, still trying to break down the door.

"The back of the chamber leads down into the gardens. We must make haste. With such devilry at work, the city is surely lost!" Globulus called, rushing to the back of the chamber. The rest followed, hurrying to escape the room. The mighty mutant hippo stopped and pulled one of the Rasheed soldiers aside. "Head out into the city and order a full retreat. Order any soldiers you find to fall back to the docks!" The soldier saluted and headed off into the city to recover any broken troops he could find.

"Mineera and Tani are at the docks. Escape by boat is the only option," Banion added.

"So be it! To the docks! Let nothing stop us but death itself!" Globulus roared.

As the companions made their way toward the docks, the door shattered and the Goat Minions invaded the room. With much noise and anger they moved, with much strife and hatred they came. The minions fell about their fallen master and uttered dark prayers. In the still of the chamber they chanted, while the blue spirits moaned and screamed as they circled above his body...

Chapter 39
The Fall of Rasheed

An explosion tore into the side of the palace. A deafening boom followed. With a great crash, the mighty marble wall fell into a splintered mass of shards and rubble. Banion ducked and pulled Jared back. Just as he did, several chunks of stone crashed around them. Unscathed, but startled, Banion led Jared, Globulus, and several Rasheed soldiers deeper into the palace. Several additional blasts sounded as Reaper Kai artillery pounded the city.

In the dim light, they moved quickly and stealthily. Down many a dark halls did the group pass. At each junction, the torn bodies of the slain littered their path.

Banion rounded a corner just in time to see all hell break loose. A complement of palace guards was under fire.

A host of Biogtech death machines was pouring into the front of the palace. Over twenty could be seen in the main hall, and many more were pouring in through the open battered doors.

"Stop, we're on your side!" a guard yelled. His voice and life were cut short by Biogtech gunfire. Two Biogtech soldiers laughed with glee as their red eyes fell upon the palace guard. Without warning, they opened fire. The slain guard fell to the floor after being struck by over a dozen bullets.

Confused, the palace guards made a hasty retreat. The Biogtechs were supposed to be on their side. But this was of no consequence to them; the Biogtechs were only in league with the demonic Reaper Kai. So much for the deal. So much for glory in the new Reaper Kai Empire. These were all just lies; the Reaper Kai and Biogtechs were on their own side and no one else's. Many more purple clad guards were cut to shreds by Biogtech gunfire.

Banion brought his team into the main hall. Their entrance was so quick and deadly, that the Biogtech never knew what hit them. Following the massive Globulus, the Rasheed soldiers laid down a withering barrage of weapon fire directed against the Biogtechs. Splashes of hydraulic fluid and a shower of sparks filled the end of the hall. The Biogtech soldiers were annihilated.

The remaining robotic death machines returned fire. Globulus planted himself firmly like a tree in a rainstorm, standing tall as bullets streaked past him. Jared and Banion crouched behind the mighty mutant hippo, using him a living shield. The Biogtech counter attack left three Rasheed soldiers dead on the floor and two more wounded.

"Taste my wrath, you sons of bitches!" Globulus yelled, bringing his rotary machine gun to bear upon them. Dozens and dozens of rounds tore forth in a wide spray. Banion raised his assault rifle and mowed down more Biogtechs. Jared crouched and stared about, wide eyed with terror, loosely holding a submachine gun in his hand.

The firefight was intense.

"Shoot them, you idiot!" Banion yelled at Jared as he reloaded his mighty assault rifle.

Jared did just that. He brought the weapon around Globulus's side and pulled the trigger. Hot gunfire spewed forth in a chaotic whirlwind. Frightened and unaccustomed to such a powerful weapon, Jared fought to control the submachine gun. In merely a few seconds, the gun was empty, and Jared dropped it to the floor with a look of terror on his face.

Banion saw Jared's plight, and tossed him his long barreled revolver. "Just point and shoot, kid! Don't lose it, either, it was my uncle's!"

With a look of concentration on his face, Jared picked up the heavy revolver and aimed with both hands. The gun sights came to rest on the chest of a Biogtech coming through the door. He pulled the trigger. The mighty weapon boomed and recoiled in his hands. The high caliber bullet tore forward and rammed into the chest of the Biogtech, tearing clean through and causing a wicked spray of oil to erupt from the wounded robotic soldier. The Biogtech crashed to the floor.

Banion sprayed several Biogtechs as well, and three of them fell to his prowess. Meanwhile, the enraged mutant hippo was mowing down damn near everything else in the room. A pile of a hundred shell casings or more littered the floor at the feet of the mighty Globulus.

Finally, the room was empty of enemies. The Rasheed

soldiers moved in and followed Banion out the front of the palace.

The team moved on, finding themselves in the courtyard in front of the palace. The courtyard was empty, but the sounds of battle were all around them. Booms and artillery could be heard just to the north. A massive gunfight was raging just to the east. Screams sounded to the south. To the west, helicopters could be heard strafing the city.

"Helicopters?" Banion quizzed Globulus. "The Iron Kai are here as well?"

"Must be!" Boomed Globulus. "Perhaps there's hope for us after all!"

"Let's not count on hope. This city is taken. We must make it to the harbor," Banion said while moving towards the palace gate. Beyond the gate, the city burned...

*   *   *

"Mineera!" Tani yelled. Mineera did not respond. She was standing in the middle of a crowd of people, motionless, as if caught in a daze. "Mineera!" Tani charged into the crowd, pushing frightened citizens aside as he moved.

"Mineera!" He yelled, shaking her violently.

Finally, her eyes opened. "To the south," she said in a drowsy tone.

"What!?" Tani yelled.

"We have got to get to the south of the harbor. There are ships on their way in from the gulf. We can evacuate some of the civilians to the boats," Mineera said dreamily, still in a daze.

"How do you know that? How could you possibly know that?" Tani quizzed.

"I just do. Trust me," Mineera said in a confident tone. Her daydream was over, and she was firmly back in reality.

A green assault helicopter came in fast and low over the waterfront. Tani looked up in awe as the mighty gunship flew overhead. Suddenly, the attack copter stopped midair and hovered. Several rotary machine gun turrets came to life. The helicopter opened fire on a target at the north end of the harbor.

Panic flew through the crowd. Mineera could feel the pure terror of the people around her. It washed over her, leaving her drowning in a sea of misery. In a daze, she rocked back and forth, trying to fight off all the voices in her head. Tani stared at Mineera in dismay. Frustration filled the tribal and he grabbed the psychic maiden, pulling her through the crowd. He moved south, with Mineera in tow.

Two more gunships arrived and took up positions over the north part of the harbor. They also attacked the northern square, just beyond the storefronts.

Finally, Tani freed himself and the dazed Mineera from the crowd. He paused to stare oddly at two undefined shapes emerging from the darkness of the sea. Large metal forms pierced the darkness and lumbered forward. Tani took a brief moment to halt his frantic mind. At last, the steel juggernauts punched through the dark veil.

The tribal was relieved to see two enormous cargo freighters lumber into view.

How did she know? Tani said to himself as he stared at Mineera.

The two mighty ships halted, and several metal gangplanks dropped onto the dock. A complement of soldiers garbed in black military camouflage secured the deck side with a host of weapons at the ready.

Tani moved forward and waved to the soldiers. They motioned him onward.

"Who are you guys?" Tani asked, looking wide eyed through his wire rimmed glassed.

"Iron Kai Merchant Marines," a soldier said in a tough tone. "We are here to evacuate as many people as possible. Get on the ship," he ordered.

Tani simply nodded and pulled Mineera up the gangplank onto the deck of the cargo freighter.

"Citizens of Rasheed!" a loud voice boomed over a loud speaker. "Evacuation of this city has begun! Make haste to the south docks!"

The rabble of people moved like a pack of wild animals toward the two cargo freighters. Panic swept through the crowd. Many pushed and pulled. Screams could be heard. Many people were pushed off the dock altogether, ending up in the cold dark waters of the harbor. Tani shook his head in dismay as he surveyed the chaotic evacuation on the dockside.

The young tribal then looked northward, and his heart sank. At least one hundred Biogtechs had taken the north side of the harbor. They were attacking the crowd as they fled. Automatic weapon fire tore into the fleeing citizens with hideous results. The crowd was so dense that not a single bullet missed; every bullet fired bit flesh. Tani watched in horror as dozens of civilians died every second.

The green helicopters hovered and attacked the mass of robotic soldiers. The guns whirred, and many Biogtech were cut to shreds. The robotic death machines retaliated, forcing the helicopters to retreat.

Without the helicopters to stop the Biogtech onslaught, the north part of the harbor crawled with Biogtechs.

The helpless citizens piled onto the cargo freighters in frightening numbers and with frightening speed. Looking north, the tribal watched as nearly fifty civilians died in another frenzy of gunfire. Tani shook his head, and tears began to roll down his face. Never before had he witnessed nor imagined such horrible carnage.

Dismayed and demoralized, he looked down at Mineera. She had curled up in a ball on the deck and was moaning in terror. Every person in the harbor was racked with fear, and Mineera could hear each and every panicked soul around her. The combined pleas and terror of the crowd were maddening. The psychic woman was going insane hearing all the voices cry in terror.

Tani had almost given up hope when something in the crowd caught his eye. The mighty mutant Globulus was wading through the crowd of people. On each of his shoulders rode a familiar face. Banion was on one shoulder and young Jared was on his other. A host of Rasheed soldiers had taken up a perimeter around the docks, defending them to the death against the ravenous horde of Biogtechs.

"Banion!" Tani screamed toward the crowd on the docks.

Banion looked up and a smile graced his lips. "You are a sight for sore eyes, bookworm!"

Jared looked up, and hope filled him. It was good to see that his friend had survived the horrible night.

As the Biogtech horde pressed forward, the battle grew even more intense. But the Rasheed soldiers held their ground and maintained the harbor perimeter.

Finally, Globulus, Banion, and Jared made it up the gangplank and pushed their way to the bow of the boat. Nova 7 was reunited, and Globulus gave young Tani a nod of approval.

The fighting continued, but the freighters were full and could carry no more. The black-garbed Iron Kai soldiers retreated back to the ship and pulled in the gangplanks. Thousands and thousands more civilians were still stranded, and they cried in terror as they watched the gangplanks rise back onto the boats.

Hope was shattered. A whole host of Rasheed citizens were now trapped. With growing numbers of enemy forces cutting off escape into the city and the last of the ships leaving the harbor, over five thousand terrified souls knew their death was near.

The host screamed at the freighter. Tani could not look, and he covered his eyes and turned away. Mineera rocked back and forth in terror, the voices of thousands boggling her mind and sending her toward madness. Globulus, too, could not look at the crowd; he felt suddenly that he should be down there with his people. Jared was dazed, looking around in wide-eyed fear. Banion's revolver was still in his hand and he looked at the crowd with sadness in his eyes.

With a sense of empowerment flooding over him, Banion the deranged rancher looked at the crowd and made a silent vow: 'I will kill them all, I promise. These deeds will not go unpunished.' A tear rolled down Banion's cheek as he bid the helpless souls of Rasheed goodbye.

The engines roared to life. The freighters pushed backwards and lumbered into the darkness. Globulus was overcome with grief, and pushed his way silently into the crowd of the lucky residents of Rasheed who had made it out alive. Within a moment, he could no longer be seen.

Minute after minute passed. The harbor of Rasheed grew more distant. In the darkness of the night, four companions stared toward the ruined city. Each in turn stared in horror at the orange glow of fire that grew more distant by the second. The screams slowly faded away in the cool night breeze.

At last, the fires of Rasheed could no longer be seen. Banion turned to Nova 7 and looked at each member. Jared the warrior. Tani the scholar. Mineera the traitor. He smiled as he thought of himself. Banion the madman.

Each of them looked back, and a sense of commitment and responsibility filled them. They would make sure nothing like this ever happened again. Each would do everything in their power to stop the Reaper Kai.

A silent oath was pledged that night. Nova 7 would not stop. Nova 7 would never surrender. Nova 7 would embark upon a crusade to find a nuclear bomb to eradicate the entire Reaper Kai empire. Silent oaths were made in the darkness by each of them, oaths not easily taken, oaths not easily forgotten.

More information about the Darken Realm can be found at
www.darkenrealm.com.

The saga continues in book 2 of the Darken Realm series
entitled *Ruins of America*, available the summer of 2006.

www.ingramcontent.com/pod-product-compliance
Lightning Source LLC
Chambersburg PA
CBHW032039240626
47154CB00003B/984